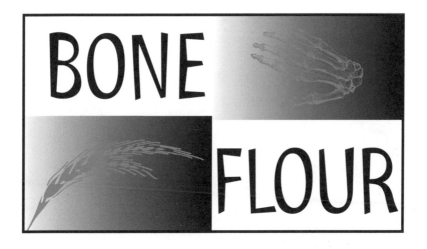

Susan K. Funk

Beaver's Pond Press, Inc.
Edina, Minnesota

ISBN 1-931646-31-7

Library of Congress Catalog Number: 2001099628

Book design and typesetting: Folio Bookworks
Cover design: Mori Studio

Printed in the United States of America

First Printing: February 2002

06 05 04 03 02   6 5 4 3 2 1

Beaver's Pond Press, Inc.

5125 Danen's Drive
Edina, MN 55439-1465
(952) 829-8818
www.beaverspondpress.com

to order, visit midwestbookhouse.com or call
1-877-430-0044. Quantity discounts available.

To WOOD
for sharing our life with all my "friends" in *Bone Flour*
while I was writing this book.

SATURDAY

Spring was late coming to Minnesota this year. The ice on the northern lakes had broken up just a week ago, and the morning sun reflecting off the surface of Lake Salish barely warmed the chilly May air. Emma Randolph hiked up the steep wooded path that ran from the northwest shore of the lake to a stone outcropping high above the water. The blue sky and bright sunlight shone through the barely-budded branches of the aspen trees lining the trail, and Emma could smell the red pines deeper in the forest.

She had arrived at the lake late the night before, after driving most of the two hundred miles from the Twin Cities in bumper-to-bumper traffic. It was the Opener—the first weekend of the walleye fishing season and a rite of spring for thousands of Minnesotans who made their way north to favorite lakes and secret fishing holes.

Emma's visit, however, was actually a business trip. Athena Bergen, a Minneapolis philanthropist, owned land thirty miles west of Lake Salish on a small bay in Lake Vermilion, and Emma was currently the favorite among three architects being considered for the design of a vacation home on the property. She planned to drive over to the site on Monday, armed with her camera and sketchpad, to familiarize herself with its topography, sun angles, and tree locations. Until Monday, she would enjoy a couple of relaxing days paddling her canoe around Lake Salish and listening to her father and his buddies swap fishing tales.

Emma had slept in, and it was mid-morning before she started out on her run. Her workout at the lake usually finished with a sprint up the quarter-mile from the shore. But this morning, the call of a rose-breasted grosbeak somewhere in the overhead branches slowed her pace to a walk halfway up the ascent. When Emma reached the path's end, she untied her purple fleece jacket from around her waist and pulled it on over her long sleeved T-shirt and black running tights before crawling out onto a large, flat boulder for a view of the lake.

Emma sat on the rock soaking up the gentle warmth of the sun. A bald eagle flew up from a treetop just below her, caught a thermal updraft, and soared out over the lake. The wind carried the big bird, with its white head and tail, over the far end of the lake and then back towards her over her father's rambling house nestled in the woods along the shore.

Far cry from my deadlines, computer eyestrain, and screaming clients, thought Emma, as she contrasted the scene in front of her with her hectic life down in Minneapolis. The memories and attraction of the simpler life at Lake Salish tugged at her.

Emma's great-grandparents, Katheryne and Henry Randolph, had bought the two hundred acres of pine and aspen forest on Lake Salish back in the early 1900s, even before the designation of the now-surrounding Superior National Forest. The family built a two-room, cedar-log cabin on the small lake, but spent only summer vacations on the property until the late 1930s when Katheryne, or Kate, as she preferred to be called, and her ten-year-old grandson, Sam, moved north from Minneapolis to make the cabin their permanent home; and Ely, the small town several miles to the southeast, their home town.

After Sam's discharge from the Army in 1946, he attended college in Madison at the University of Wisconsin, where he majored in history and met his artist wife, Ellen. When they were in their mid-twenties, Sam and Ellen moved back to Lake Salish to live with Kate Randolph. Sam taught high school history in Ely, and Ellen earned a modest income painting abstract watercolors inspired by the lake country. Although almost thirty-five years separated Kate and Ellen, the two women became fast friends and easily shared the Lake Salish household right up until Kate's death in 1974.

Emma and her older sister, Ginny, were raised in the house, and the thousands of acres of wilderness in the national forest and nearby Boundary Waters Canoe Area Wilderness became their backyard. Sam's summers were free; and the family spent them canoeing, fishing, and hiking, even when Ginny and Emma were just toddlers. By junior high school, the girls were able paddlers and campers and began taking long weekend excursions on their own. During college, both Ginny and Emma worked summers as guides for one of the large canoe outfitters in Ely.

In winter, the frozen lakes and snow-filled woods also brought the opportunity for countless outdoor activities. As children, they learned to cross country ski near the house on old wooden skis with leather straps and pine-tarred bottoms. By the time she was in high school, Ginny was racing competitively on the school ski team, but Emma continued to prefer the trackless beauty of the winter wilderness. In the mornings before school, she helped out a local trapper—snowshoeing or skiing to check out the parts of his trap line that he ran near Lake Salish. Her weekends often included winter camping with several of her hardier friends.

The original rustic cabin had been expanded over the years and now had three bedrooms, a large space that served as kitchen, living room, and dining room, and a screened porch. The home had also been modernized—first with indoor plumbing, electricity, gas heat, and telephone; and more recently, with satellite television and Internet access. But it never got any bigger or fancier than it needed to be. It was comfortable and solid, much like the four generations of the Randolph family who had lived in it throughout the century.

Emma looked across the water to the east bay of the lake and remembered her first campout without one of her parents or her great-grandmother. She and Ginny had been only eight and nine and had taken a whole canoe full of supplies for their one-night stay on the sandy shore of the bay. She smiled to herself as she recalled that years later, as teenagers, they would go for days in the wilderness with a lighter load than they had transported for that first solo adventure.

We had all the time in the world back then, Emma thought to herself. *How did things get so crazy?*

Suddenly, a chattering chipmunk interrupted her thoughts. Feeling scolded for squandering the glorious day mired in her conflicting priorities, she worked her way back across the rock to the trail and started down towards the lake. Ten minutes later, she emerged from the forest near the woodshed that had been her mother's studio and strolled across a small clearing to the back of the house.

As she walked in the back door, Emma saw her father standing over the stove skillfully tending two frying pans—one with scrambled eggs and the other with fried potatoes. Judy Garland sang from the stereo across the room, and Sam hummed and swayed along with the music. Sam Randolph was nearly seventy. But his full head of gray hair and his almost wrinkle-free face, together with his agile movements and lively smile, suggested a man in his mid-fifties.

"Smells great, Dad," Emma said, stripping off her jacket and hanging it on the large coat tree in the corner behind the door. "And thanks for waiting breakfast until I finished my run. I needed it after that crazy drive last night."

"No problem." He added a pinch of dill to the potatoes, gave one last turn with the spatula, and pulled down two plates from the shelf over the stove. "We'll call it brunch. Just like you people down in Minneapolis."

Emma rolled her eyes at Sam's friendly chiding of her urban lifestyle, while she took a familiar brown pottery mug out of the cupboard. She reached around Sam to grab the percolator on the back of the stove, poured herself a cup of coffee, and eased around the peninsula counter that partially separated the kitchen from the spacious living and dining area at the front of the house.

She sat down at the round, oak dining table over in the corner of windows looking out onto Lake Salish. Her eyes wandered to the fire blazing in the fireplace at the far end of the room and then to the painting of autumn birch trees hanging over the mantle. She stared at the canvas for a moment and then said, "God, sometimes I still expect Mom to come through that door."

Ellen Randolph had died suddenly of a brain aneurysm two years ago. Both Emma and Ginny had worried about how their father would fare without Ellen—his best friend and partner for almost forty-five years—and Emma spent many long weekends up at Lake Salish in the several months immediately after her mother's death.

Eventually, though, fishing pals and neighbors began to repopulate Sam's days; and old hobbies, like woodworking, and even some new hobbies, such as cooking, filled his spare time. During her visits in recent months, Emma joked about having to make an appointment just to get some time alone with her father.

Emma continued her reminiscence. "Remember how she'd get up early on Saturday to paint in the morning light and always came in just as you put the breakfast on the table? Her timing was uncanny. Like the two of you were in perfect sync."

Sam took off the apron covering his navy and green-plaid flannel shirt and his denim work pants. He hung it on the knob of the kitchen cupboard to the right of the stove. Then he carried the two plates heaped with eggs and potatoes into the dining area, placed them down on the table in front of Emma, and made his way across the room to turn down the stereo and put another log on the fire. "We were in 'perfect sync'," he said, as he returned to the table and sat down. "At least, most of the time. I miss her every minute of every day, but it's actually easier not having any regrets about our life together. Kind of strange, isn't it?"

"Not really. Just your usual good sense," she teased, digging into her breakfast.

"Well, if I make so much sense, why haven't you listened to me and moved back up here?"

Emma frowned at her father. "Come on, Dad! As I've explained to you the other nine thousand times you've brought up my living in Minneapolis, right now it's the best thing for my career. The only people building architecturally designed homes up here are rich people from the Twin Cities and I need to 'live among them,' as they say. At least until I get better established."

"You've been down there fifteen years. Over twenty if you count college and graduate school. How established do you have to be?"

"I don't know for sure, but certainly more than I am now. Besides, I have my historic-preservation work down in Minneapolis."

Sam ate several forkfuls of potatoes and finally answered after the long moment of silence. "I know you have your life down in the Cities, but you just seem so unsettled."

Emma knew her father was comparing her to her older sister, Ginny, who lived with her family just two miles from Sam. Ginny and her husband, Jack, were both physical education teachers and coaches at the Ely High School, and they were extremely active in the community. Their children, Annie and Ben, were self-confident teenagers, excelling at basketball and soccer, as well as academics; they were also very close to their grandfather.

Both Emma and Ginny physically resembled Sam with their dark features and wiry athletic builds, but only Emma had inherited his stubborn and excitable nature. Ginny's nature more resembled Ellen's thoughtful and consistent demeanor. This explained the sainthood conferred on Ginny by her father.

Emma had also loved this deliberate nature in her mother, but she was often angered by it in her older sister. Just fifteen months apart, they were too close in age, Emma thought, for her to consider Ginny's unsolicited advice as wisdom. So, while Emma greatly admired her sister's energy and even envied some of her accomplishments, long ago she had decided to escape Ginny's shadow and live her own life.

Sam looked over at his younger daughter. The night's rest and morning's exercise had removed some of the weariness he had noticed the night before. "Funny," he said between mouthfuls of egg, "when you were a kid, we could never get you to come indoors. Winter or summer. Always claimed you wanted to build a teepee up near that flat rock above the cabin and live off the land. Now you cancel vacations to sit in endless meetings defending old buildings. Maybe if you were at least getting rich—"

Emma put down her fork, pushed up the sleeves of her T-shirt, and faced her father. "Dad, you know I'm not a kid anymore. And you know I didn't become an architect to get rich. Just like you didn't teach high school history to get rich."

"Fair enough," Sam conceded. "But I worry about you. You're only forty years old and you always look so tired—"

"Hey," Emma again interrupted, but this time in a much lighter tone. "Don't rush things. I won't be forty until November."

Sam smiled. "Okay, I stand corrected. You're only thirty-nine and a half years old. And you always look so tired."

Emma took a deep breath and picked up her fork again. She knew Sam meant well. "I know you just want me to be happy, Dad.

And I am." Emma ate a few more bites of egg and potatoes. "But who knows? Once I've saved enough old buildings and gotten my name out there, I might still come back up here. God knows this 'middle of nowhere' could probably use a good architect. I think I've outgrown the teepee though. But a small cabin would suit me just fine."

Sam recognized Emma's efforts to calm their breakfast conversation and moved on to what he thought would be a less confrontational subject. "So how's Joe?"

"Okay, I guess. I haven't seen him for a few weeks. We decided to cool it for a while."

So much for safe questions, thought Sam. "Anything you want to discuss?"

"Not much to say. Joe's a politician, and it's hard to carry on any kind of healthy relationship with a politician in the middle of a statewide run. He needs time to campaign, and the only role I seemed to be playing was the resentful partner. Being apart is best for both of us right now."

"Sounds more 'best' for him, if you ask me."

A trace of Emma's earlier exasperation returned. "Well, I'm not asking you. And besides, I thought you would be pleased. You've never been his biggest fan."

Sam leaned back in his chair and raised both arms in protest. "Hey, I like Joe. He'll probably be a great senator. Hell, I may even vote for him." He chuckled at that notion. "It just seems to me that he has never appreciated you the way he should."

"On that point, you get no argument from me." Emma got up and cleared the dishes from the table. She returned with the coffeepot just as the stereo music ended. "Want me to put something else on?"

"No, don't bother," Sam answered.

She refilled both their cups while she shifted the conversation

11

away from Joe Buchanan. "You haven't asked about the riverfront mill?"

"I knew you'd eventually bring it up," Sam said. "And public radio does a piece on it from time to time anyway. Sounds like you're getting the best of Cousin Charlie."

"Dad, don't make this into some sort of grudge thing between Charlie and me. The Randolphs' ancient family squabbles have nothing to do with it." Then she added, "Look at Gretch, his own sister. She and Taylor are two of my closest friends—and important clients. That farmhouse I just finished for them over in Wisconsin was a big project for me."

Sam took a sip of his fresh coffee. "Well, Gretchen is a whole different kind of Randolph. She resembles more our side of the family." Emma knew that Gretchen was the only Randolph relative outside his immediate family that Sam had seen since he left Minneapolis as a boy, and that was only in the last few years when she had brought Gretchen and her husband, Taylor, up to Lake Salish for a few visits.

She returned the coffeepot to the stove and glanced up at the kitchen wall clock. "Oh, it's later than I thought. I told Annie and Ben I'd stop over around two with their latest Uptown shopping requests."

"With what?"

Emma loved her image as the hip aunt from the big city. "Oh, you know, all the stuff of vital importance to teenagers that they can't buy in Ely. Like funky clothes and CD's released in the last ten years. I'll head over to Ginny's after I clean up these dishes and take a quick shower."

As the right half of the sink filled with hot soapy water, she stared out the kitchen window. Two goldfinches, one male and the other female, were eating at the sunlit feeder in the back clearing. *Maybe the kids will be up for a hike this afternoon,* she thought as she noticed the thermometer just outside the window creeping up towards sixty-five degrees.

She loaded the dirty dishes into the wash water and leaned over to switch on the radio sitting on the counter. Except for Minnesota Twins baseball games, the radio was always set on one of nearby Hibbing's two public radio stations. Emma switched from WIRN, the news station, to WIRR, the classical music station, and heard the last few bars of a Mozart piano concerto before a newsbreak at the top of the hour:

"On the metro front, a five-alarm fire at the historic Randolph Mill in downtown Minneapolis was finally brought under control late this morning. No injuries have been reported, but physical damage to the century old milling complex appears to be extensive. The cause of the blaze is still undetermined, but suspicions point to the heating and cooking fires used by the homeless community that periodically takes up residence in the abandoned buildings along the river. The mill and adjacent buildings on the site have recently been the subject of a political and architectural controversy . . ." The radio droned on.

Emma slammed the counter with her fist. "That bastard."

Sam walked over to his daughter and chided her. "Now don't jump to any conclusions. Remember, you said this wasn't personal."

Emma wasn't listening. "Athena won't be happy, but I have to postpone my site visit. I need to get back to the city right away."

Emma hurried back to the bedroom that she and Ginny had shared growing up and she now used when visiting her father. She stripped off her running clothes and threw on the worn khakis and work shirt hanging on the back of the door. She wiped her face with a wet towel, smeared on some deodorant, and ran a brush through her short dark hair. Then she stuffed all her things back into her weekend duffel.

She returned to the kitchen just a few minutes later and handed a bulging shopping bag to Sam. "I'm going to leave these things for Annie and Ben. Can you deliver them?"

"Sure."

"Tell them I'm sorry I didn't make it over there. I'll catch them next time I'm up."

She gave her father a hug and was on the road back to Minneapolis within fifteen minutes of hearing the news of the fire on the radio.

3

Peter Randolph mixed himself a Bloody Mary and carried it over to the library windows. He had dressed this morning, with his customary care, in a gray cardigan sweater and expensive wool trousers. He sipped his first drink of the day and watched the gardener turn the last of the winter mulch down into the rose beds. The lawn beyond the formal garden sloped downhill to the shore of Hidden Lake sparkling in the distance.

The dark gray stucco house was one of only five on the small, exclusive lake in northwest Minneapolis. It had been designed and built by Peter's father, Marcus Randolph, more than seventy years earlier. Its ostentatious facade featured a four-story turret, a steeply sloped and multi-gabled roof, and a double-arched wood portico leading from the circular driveway to the front door.

Most of its gloomy twenty-eight rooms had been updated since Peter and his wife, Berta, moved into the house in the early 1970s. Only the library, in which Peter now stood, remained unchanged and still reflected the opulence of the 1920s. Its ornately carved double doors opened on the left, at the far end of the long marble-tiled central hallway that ran from the front entry to the rear, or lake side, of the house.

A stone fireplace with a wide walnut mantle dominated the wall opposite the doorway. Two oversized green-leather club chairs, a matching couch, and a low Queen Anne table with cabriole legs were all grouped on a worn oriental carpet that covered the parquet flooring in front of the fireplace.

Floor-to-ceiling matching walnut bookshelves, filled with books, mostly unread, lined the wall on both sides of the fireplace. Along the wall, running perpendicular to the fireplace and on the left as one entered the room, was an eight-foot-long bar, also made of walnut. Above the bar hung seven framed photographs—two, in black and white, of the old riverfront mill and the remaining five, in full color, of the current Randolph facility out in Bloomington.

The fourth wall of the room, where Peter was standing, held casement windows with diamond-shaped panes of leaded glass. Heavy gold-brocade draperies, now opened, hung at either end of these windows. A broad, antique desk of inlaid wood stood in front of the windows beside Peter.

It was early afternoon, and the house was quiet except for the ticking of the grandfather clock out in the hall. Berta was at the club lunching with a friend, and Margaret, their maid and cook, was in the middle of a two-week vacation back in her native Norway. Peter thought both women talked too much, and he had relished the solitude of the past couple of hours.

Then Peter heard Berta calling from the kitchen. He downed his drink and returned to the bar across the room. He quickly wiped out the tumbler, dropped in some fresh ice cubes, and refilled it with seltzer water. After smoothing down his silver-gray hair and buttoning his cardigan, he carried the glass out through the hall.

Peter entered the kitchen and saw Berta draping the fur-collared jacket of her expensive tweed suit over the back of a stool standing at the center island. She was rail thin, with salon-darkened chin-length hair, a small pointy nose, and darting eyes. *She looks more and more like a vulture everyday,* Peter thought.

Peter sat down on another stool. "How was the club?" he asked, although he really wasn't interested. Not much concerning Berta had interested him in years.

"Noisy," she huffed. "I don't know why people insist on bringing their children into the main dining room if they're going to behave like wild animals. And the food was terrible." She walked over to the sink to wash her hands and launched into a tediously detailed description of obnoxious five-year-olds, cold soup, and wilted lettuce. Peter sat and listened, but heard very little of her account.

Ten minutes into her rant, she stopped. "Before I forget, Charlie called before I went out. While you were out walking. He was glad to hear you were finally taking Gretchen's advice and getting some exercise."

Peter sneered. "What's it to him? Unlike his sister, he's already got me in my grave."

"What are you talking about?"

"Just something I wasn't supposed to hear."

"And what was that?" asked Berta, still standing at the sink.

"Charlie accused Gretchen of abusing her staff position at the hospital to get me into that program at the Heart Institute. Said they were wasting scarce resources on an old drunk—"

"Charlie would never say something like that. When did you hear this?"

"I overheard them arguing when they were up here last month for my birthday. They thought I was out back—"

Berta cut him off again. "Well, you must have heard wrong."

Peter shook his head. "No, I heard right. Charlie was in one of his moods. Remember, he showed up with Vicki Stephens. And you know how she brings out the best in him."

Berta frowned. "Oh, please! How could I forget that Stephens woman showing up? And your refusing to let her in."

"It was my party, and I didn't want her helping me celebrate my eightieth birthday."

"But it was you who hired her at the Company in the first place."

"We all make mistakes," Peter acknowledged bitterly. "But that doesn't mean I have to welcome her into this house." He wanted to get off the subject of Vicki Stephens. "Let's drop Vicki. What did Charlie want? Or did he call just to check up on my exercise regimen?"

"No, no," she said walking over to the center island across from him. "He had big news. Actually, he was surprised we hadn't seen it in the morning paper. I told him we have all day to read the paper and—"

Now it was Peter's turn to interrupt. "Just give me the news."

"I was getting to that," Berta said defensively. "There was a big fire at the old riverfront mill last night. No one was hurt. But there was quite a bit of damage."

Peter stood up suddenly. "How much damage? Where exactly was this fire?" he demanded.

"Calm down. You know you're not supposed to get excited," Berta scolded. "I don't know where the fire was. You'll have to ask Charlie. All he said was that this would be a big setback for that preservation group."

Peter looked away from Berta. Saying nothing, he abruptly left the kitchen and hurried back to the library. His hands were trembling by the time he made his way over to the bar. He mixed a second Bloody Mary and took a big gulp. *A fire; how convenient. God, would Charlie stoop to arson to destroy that old mill?*

Peter carried the drink over to his desk and sat down. He nervously dialed Charlie's home and office numbers. After several unanswered rings at both, Peter hung up and tried his son's cellular number. That phone rolled over to an answering machine, and Peter left a message asking his son to call him immediately. Then he turned his chair away from the desk and resumed staring out the library windows. His mind wandered back over the years.

Peter's grandfather, Henry Randolph, had founded Randolph Milling in the late 1800s when Minneapolis was just emerging as a national milling center. When Henry died in 1930, he left the business to his two sons—Peter's father, Marcus; and Marcus's younger half-brother, Will. By that time, the Company had grown into a sizable grain and milling concern.

The brothers had jointly managed the Company through the economic depression of the early 1930s. All that changed in the late 1930s when Will Randolph went to prison for the killing of Matthew Kelly, a local labor leader. For the next thirty years, Marcus Randolph lorded over the Company while it experienced astounding growth and prosperity.

After he had a serious stroke in 1965 at the age of seventy-six, Marcus finally turned the Company reins over to Peter, his son, who was almost fifty by that time. Marcus had always been openly critical of Peter's drinking and his lack of business acumen, and he had never intended Peter to be anything more than an interim president. The old man spent all of his remaining energy on the grooming of his grandson and namesake, Peter's son, Marcus Charles, who was known as Charlie. However, when Marcus died in 1971, Charlie was still in school, and Peter's bumbling watch over the Company had to continue for several more years. By the end of the decade, Randolph Foods had lost most of its market predominance to more innovative companies.

Peter retired in 1980. He had initially hoped that his daughter, Gretchen, would be his successor. She was every bit as smart as her older brother, but far more personable and ethical. Peter also delighted in wonderful visions of Marcus rolling over in his grave as a woman ascended to the presidency of his beloved Company. But Peter had supported Gretchen's decision to become a doctor and Charlie's drive to run the Company. So, at the young age of thirty, Charlie had become the president of Randolph Foods.

Now, more than fifteen years later, it appeared that Charlie was certainly up to the job. He had immediately cleaned out the remnants of Peter's ineffective cronies and then slowly refocused the Company's product lines. Within ten years, Randolph Foods was again highly profitable and had become a market leader in healthy convenience meals, one of the most rapidly expanding grocery niches.

In the meantime, Gretchen had become a successful and well-respected general surgeon. However, she hadn't managed to totally distance herself from the family business—nine years ago she had married Taylor Alexander, the Company's chief financial officer.

Behind Charlie and Taylor, Vicki Stephens held the number-three spot in the Company. As Berta had reminded him earlier, it was Peter who'd insisted back in the mid-1980s that Charlie hire Vicki Stephens as an account manager. Peter hated to admit it, but Vicki, now director of both sales and development, was a brilliant businesswoman. Her innovative marketing ideas and strong management skills made her every bit as responsible as Charlie and Taylor for the Company's ongoing success.

Early last year, Charlie decided that the Company had outgrown its location of the past thirty years in suburban Bloomington. He and Vicki approached the city of Minneapolis about developing a new corporate campus back on the Company's original riverfront site. They promised new jobs, economic development, and riverfront revitalization, all of which helped to secure preliminary support for the project. But the proposed demolition of the old mill, adjacent warehouse, and large grain elevator on the site proved to be a stumbling block to final city approval.

Countless gangs of teenagers and homeless street people had ravaged and vandalized the abandoned buildings over the years.

The harsh Minnesota winters had also taken their toll. The structures were now badly deteriorated and thought to be beyond salvage. Nevertheless, their threatened demolition attracted the attention of the Riverfront Historic Coalition, a group of local preservationists now aggressively headed by Emma Randolph, Charlie's second cousin.

Over the past decade, Emma and the Coalition had worked with countless federal, state, and local agencies to restore the federally designated historic milling district just upriver from the Randolph site. When finished, the area was to include a milling museum, mill ruins, several walking tours, and the refurbishing of several of the larger intact mills and elevators into condominiums and apartments—all financed by many millions of public and private dollars. Shortly after the Company had announced its riverfront relocation plans, the Coalition initiated an effort to extend the historic district downriver to encompass the Randolph property.

The Company officers knew that future inclusion of the property within the historic district would probably require preservation of some or all of the buildings on the site and had quickly applied for a demolition permit before formal expansion of the district could be realized. But the Coalition responded quickly and immediately filed for a judicial restraining order, which was granted late last year and prevented any demolition of the property during the lengthy federal expansion process.

This hiatus gave the Coalition some much-needed extra time to lobby City Hall for support of the extended milling district, and the group had made real headway with planning officials over the past several months. The Company was suddenly getting a lot of pressure from the mayor's office and from certain city council members to resolve its difficulties with the Coalition. Charlie and Vicki were furious over the significant delay of the project and the inevitable additional expense that they believed the Coalition's desired development changes would impose on the Company.

The striking of the hall clock returned Peter to the present. He turned back to his desk knowing he should also try to reach Vicki Stephens. As he looked up her number in the Company directory, his breathing became fast and shallow. He pulled one of his pills out of his pocket and popped it into his mouth, washing it down with his drink. After a few minutes, his respirations calmed, and he was able to dial Vicki's cell phone.

She answered on the second ring. It sounded like she was at a crowded restaurant or party. Vicki just laughed when Peter asked the cause of the fire. So he pushed on to his real concern. "I was wondering about the grain elevator. Was there any damage to it?"

Vicki immediately guessed the reason for this particular inquiry. "Oh, so that's where our little secret is hiding. Tell me exactly where, and I'll make sure no one finds it."

Peter didn't doubt that Vicki would take care of the situation. That was her specialty. Nevertheless, he was shaking when he hung up the receiver. He got up from the desk and once again walked over to the bar. *Just one more to calm my nerves.*

SUNDAY

4

Charlie Randolph parked his Jaguar on Second Street, three blocks east of the Company's riverfront property. Yesterday afternoon, he had called the mayor's media advisor to arrange for a morning press conference at the old mill, and it was scheduled to start in ten minutes. Charlie knew the television crews would already be setting up on the site and thought it best not to pull up in front of the cameras in his luxury vehicle.

Charlie started out up the street. Before leaving his townhouse this morning, he had taken one last look in the full-length mirror mounted on the backside of the entry closet door. As always, he looked like an advertisement for GQ. His closely cropped hair accentuated his aristocratic cheekbones and piercing blue eyes. His tall, trim body was appropriately clad — in a canvas barn jacket, khakis, and Gore-Tex hiking boots — for the tour of the fire-ravaged mill.

A few moments later, he reached the corner across from the old Randolph milling complex. It covered an entire city block on the west bank of the Mississippi River, between First Street and the higher Second Street where Charlie now stood. A chain-link fence surrounded the old rail yard on the corner directly opposite him. The tracks had been removed years ago, and a section of the fence had been cut away Friday night for fire truck access. Police tape now hung loosely across the opening.

Just as Charlie stepped off the curb to cross the street, a light-green Range Rover broke through the police tape barrier and roared onto the former rail yard. *Ah, Ms. Stephens has arrived,* observed Charlie. *And nothing like a little four-wheeling to draw attention to yourself. Probably that Rover's first, and last, off-road excursion.*

The vehicle stopped in front of a red fire-department pickup, which was parked next to a brick warehouse on the far side of the rail yard. Three fire fighters stood at the back of the pickup using a hose to dry the ventilators worn by an early morning crew that had been sent into the mill to check the several hot spots noted the day before. Even from across the street, Charlie could hear the air compressor mounted in the back of the truck.

He saw Vicki Stephens glance in her rearview mirror and flick back her expensively cut shoulder-length blond hair. Then she opened the door of the Range Rover, emerged out onto the driver's side running board, and waved to the fire fighters. She wore dark glasses, a closely-fitted beige linen suit with a skirt ending several inches above the knee, and three-inch heels. She was tall, close to six feet in her shoes, and thin.

She hopped down from the running board and immediately sank ankle deep in the mud created by the countless gallons of water dumped on the property in the last thirty-six hours. Charlie couldn't help but smile. It wasn't very often that the beautiful, smart, and extremely self-assured Vicki Stephens looked so ridiculous.

Charlie followed her onto the rail yard through the broken police tape and jogged over to the vehicle. He nodded to the firefighters and then turned to Vicki. "I know I pay you to do the dirty work, but this is above and beyond."

"Fuck you."

Vicki's response was barely audible over the sound of the compressor, but Charlie got the gist of it. He wasn't shocked. "I hope this investigation goes more smoothly than your entrance."

A female firefighter came over and handed Vicki a pair of bright yellow boots. Vicki thanked her and leaned on Charlie while she pulled them on. Under her breath, she said, "Don't worry. I've taken care of everything. Just do your part; play the role of the bereft property owner, and leave the rest to me."

"Whatever you say. Now, let's go. The mayor should be here by now." They made their way back through the opening in the fence and spotted an official-looking group of people standing farther along up on Second Street at the main entrance of the old mill. Charlie put on his best public face and waved.

As they neared the group, he saw Joe Buchanan, the mayor of Minneapolis. He noted the mayor's tweed jacket, pressed denim shirt, and brown flannel slacks. Charlie wasn't sure whether the look was intended to be populist, intellectual, or liberal. All three were public personas that Joe regularly exchanged.

Joe Buchanan had grown up in Northeast Minneapolis, the only child of blue-collar parents. Scholarships took him east to Dartmouth and Columbia for college and law school, but he eventually returned to Minnesota to practice labor law. His successful pro-union practice had eventually led to politics and three terms in the state Senate, followed by his current position as mayor.

He was very popular within his own Democratic–Farmer–Labor Party and was likely to be endorsed as their senatorial candidate at the upcoming summer convention. The Republican incumbent was ineffectual, and Joe stood a good chance of going to Washington after next November.

Joe and Charlie didn't travel in the same social or political circles, but recently they had spent considerable time together because of the Company's ongoing negotiations with the city over its riverfront relocation. Charlie found Joe pleasant enough, but he didn't believe him deserving of the "dynamic and brilliant newcomer to national politics" image that his public relations team promoted. Charlie believed that Joe Buchanan, like most of the politicians that he had worked with over the years, was power hungry and quick to accommodate influential supporters.

As far as Charlie was concerned, Joe's most impressive attribute was his long-time relationship with Emma Randolph. Despite Charlie's differences with his second cousin over the mill buildings, Emma was one of the few people he actually respected. Her interest in Joe suggested that there might be something more to the guy than Charlie could see. Of course, Charlie knew it was also possible that Emma just had lousy taste in men.

The fire and police chiefs, Andy O'Meara and Ken Johnson, were waiting with the mayor on the sidewalk in front of the badly charred front doors of the mill. Both chiefs were no-nonsense administrators who ran their departments by the book. Slouching in a rumpled trench coat and standing slightly off from the group was Vince Shillings, long a police detective in the arson-and-bomb-squad division. Vince was the exception to the staff of usually honest and hard-working city employees; he was lazy and was rumored to be on the take.

Yesterday, Charlie had been surprised to learn that Vince had been assigned to the mill fire as chief investigator. Vince hadn't investigated high-profile fires like this one in many years; his mostly administrative work appeared to be the department's way of sidelining him until he either retired or finally got caught doing something illegal. Charlie wondered if Vicki had had some hand in Vince's resumption of investigative responsibilities.

Rounding out the group were two local television crews and several reporters. Charlie knew the television stations would be clamoring for footage of the damaged buildings to fill their late afternoon news shows, and he had already decided to end the press conference with a quick look inside the mill if Andy O'Meara would allow their entry.

As he joined the group, Charlie greeted everyone with his usual condescending charm. Vicki arrived just a moment later, and Charlie added, "I bring with me the queen of fashion." The group laughed as he then nodded towards Vicki standing in her knee-high yellow boots. He couldn't resist the opportunity to tease her, even though he knew there would be hell to pay later.

Assuming a more serious tone, Charlie turned to Andy. "Your men and women really gave it their best Friday night. They put their lives on the line to save this old place. I'm extremely relieved no one was hurt. Randolph Foods, the Randolph family, and the whole city thank you."

As soon as Charlie finished, the reporters peppered him with questions. "How extensive is the damage?"

"Can the mill be saved?"

"When can we take a look inside?"

"What started the fire?"

"Hold on. I'll get to all of your questions in a minute," promised Charlie. "But first, Mayor Buchanan would like to say a few words."

5

Emma hadn't wasted any time since hearing of the fire the previous afternoon. During her five-hour drive back from Ely to Minneapolis, she called in brief statements on behalf of the Coalition to both the *Star Tribune* in Minneapolis and the *Pioneer Press* in St. Paul. When she arrived back in downtown Minneapolis, she tried to get down to the site, but was turned back by an overly zealous, young policewoman. Saturday evening, back at her place, she organized a phone conference with several other Coalition members and learned that no one was allowed access to the site until the fire and police department investigators could assure safety and finish their initial surveys. So her first calls this morning were to Andy O'Meara and Ken Johnson asking them to clear the Coalition's engineers and personnel for immediate entry into the damaged buildings.

From Ken Johnson, she heard that Vince Shillings would be heading up the investigation. Emma was aware of Vince's sloppy management of several past fire investigations, so she was outraged by his assignment to the mill fire. She thought it best, however, to keep her opinions to herself for now and not run the risk of antagonizing the police chief.

She also made a call to her potential client, Athena Bergen. Athena wasn't pleased with Emma's canceled site visit to her northern property. Emma soothed her by promising she would try to get back up there later in the week, although she had no idea how she could afford either the time if she drove or the air fare if she flew. On a chance, she left a message for an old Ely friend, Marv Flood. He was a charter pilot and sometimes let her bum a ride up to Ely if he had a half-full flight. However, he would be busy this time of year with early-season canoeists wanting connections from the Minneapolis airport, because the regional airline didn't resume its summer-only flight service until June.

Emma parked her six-year-old Subaru wagon on First Street in front of the Whitney Hotel, a very upscale hotel opened several years ago in another of the old riverfront mills. Over the roof of the hotel, she could see the tops of the high-rise office buildings in the central business district several blocks away. She got out of the car and walked around to the back hatch. It was another clear, cool morning, and Emma was dressed in jeans and a red flannel shirt topped with her fleece jacket. She took off her running shoes, pulled on some old work boots she kept in the back of the car, loaded film into her camera, and struck out along the west bank of the Mississippi to approach the Randolph property from its river side.

She proceeded along a deteriorated roadway that had once been First Street. It was scheduled for widening and repaving in the next couple of years as a further extension of the Great River Road, which would eventually run along the entire length of the Mississippi River from its headwaters at Lake Itasca in Northern Minnesota to the Gulf of Mexico. Emma crossed Portland Avenue and passed by the partially destroyed Washburn A Mill, another victim of fire just a few years before and now the site for the proposed milling museum.

She continued along the broken pavement for another block. There the dilapidated buildings of the old Randolph milling complex loomed above her. Her hours of studying old plans and photographs of the riverfront made it was easy for her to strip away the years. She returned to the days when the site was still fully operational and a key part of the Minneapolis milling industry.

The original Randolph mill, built in the late 1890s, had been sited majestically overlooking the Mississippi River at the end of the long diversion canal that channeled a portion of the river around St. Anthony Falls to power the flour mills lining its banks. It was a narrow, seven-story, limestone-faced building covering the western quarter of the block. It was designed to accommodate the vertical milling process—starting on an upper floor and then down through a succession of rollers, conveyors, and sifters on the floors below. The building was crowned by beautiful arched windows on its top floor, which had been converted into a research facility in the mid-1920s, one of the most modern of its day.

The mill's official entrance was on Second Street through heavy oak doors. Along the front portion of its long eastern sidewall, the mill abutted up against a squat three-story brick warehouse, which also faced onto Second Street. The corner formed by the back of the warehouse and the middle portion of the sidewall of the mill was lined with loading docks opening out to a rail yard crisscrossed with tracks and switches.

A massive concrete grain elevator, standing as high as the mill and topped with a two-story headhouse, towered over the rail yard. It had replaced the original wood elevator destroyed in a grain explosion and fire in the early years of the century. The elevator's short side ran along the remainder of the sidewall of the mill beyond the loading docks. The outline of five cylindrical storage silos formed the imposing back of the elevator along First Street. This exposure, together with the rear of the mill building, formed the view of the property from the river.

Several spur tracks had once carried freight cars loaded with spring wheat, mostly from the Dakotas, from the main rail line into the rail shed. Here the grain was unloaded into hoppers and carried into the elevator through a heavy steel door opening into the rail shed. Once inside the elevator, it was weighed and moved by conveyor belt up to the headhouse where it was directed by a movable spout into one of the storage silos. Another conveyor, larger and covered in corrugated metal, stretched from the headhouse to the sixth floor of the mill and carried the stored grain into the mill for processing.

The only time that Emma heard her father reminisce about his early childhood in Minneapolis had been just a couple of years ago, when Emma first told him of her efforts to save the riverfront buildings. Sam recalled Saturday morning visits to the mill with his father, Will.

That was the middle 1930s, and the flour milling activity along the river had since been greatly consolidated into just a handful of several large companies. Many of the smaller mills along the diversion canal had been demolished; and their intricate network of underground tailraces, used to carry the spent river water back into the main channel of the Mississippi, had been abandoned. Even the tailraces from most of the still-operating mills were no longer used because steam power had, for the most part, replaced the direct waterpower from St. Anthony Falls.

While Sam's father, Will, had experimented in the research lab on the seventh floor of the mill, Sam had played and explored among the ruins down along the river. To a young boy, the jumble of rock and the dark tailrace tunnels had been far more interesting than the work of his scientist father.

The noise of a news helicopter flying low over the buildings interrupted Emma's historical musings. She focused on the buildings now in front of her. The fire's devastation was immediately apparent.

The mill was the most severely damaged. Most of its roof and the upper four stories at the back of the building were caved in, and the rest of the site was now visible beyond its crumbled east wall. The roof and exterior of the brick warehouse looked badly charred, and all the glass had been knocked out of the windows. The rusted, covered conveyor, formerly stretching from the elevator's head-house into the sixth floor of the mill, now ended in mid-air and hung down at a sharp angle. Below, at the back of the elevator and near the sidewall of the mill, the rail shed was partially collapsed. Only the graffiti-covered concrete grain elevator appeared to be unscathed.

Emma climbed slowly up the hill from First Street along the western sidewall of the mill. As she rounded the corner to the front of the building, she caught sight of a group of people convened at its entrance, and she immediately recognized Joe Buchanan. Surprised by his presence, she felt flustered and considered retreating back down the hill.

But then she noticed her cousin, Charlie Randolph, and Vicki Stephens. *Looks like a party I need to join,* she concluded and continued towards Joe and the camera lights.

Emma had met Joe Buchanan several years earlier midway through his third term in the state Senate, while she was lobbying a historic-preservation bill at the State Capitol. She was immediately attracted to his quick wit and charismatic style. His rugged good looks, highlighted by an unruly mane of curly brown hair and deep-set hazel eyes, had also helped.

Emma proceeded cautiously at first because Joe had been recently divorced, but after a couple of months they were seeing each other every day, and Emma moved some things into his South Minneapolis home. After the legislative session had ended that year, they spent two weeks canoeing in Ontario and planning their future around a succession of evening campfires. Joe was going to quit politics after his third term and accept a teaching position at the University law school. Emma talked about teaching as well. Summers would be spent up at Lake Salish.

Unfortunately, there weren't any campfires once they returned to Minneapolis. Joe's teaching position had been put on hold after he was convinced to run for mayor, and it was finally scrapped altogether after his landslide victory six months later. Bowing to political propriety, Emma had moved back to her apartment during the campaign and had fallen back into her own hectic routine. She bought her own place shortly after Joe's election.

Nevertheless, the relationship had muddled on until his recent decision to jump into the Senate race. They had separated four months ago but continued to bump into each other from time to time.

"Of course, if our experts tell us that some or all of the buildings are no longer feasible to preserve, we'll have to talk to the court about lifting its order and allowing us to proceed with demolition," Emma heard Charlie saying as she neared. She smiled nervously at Joe and joined the group.

"Nice boots," whispered Emma, standing next to Vicki. She knew that Vicki was too smart to be provoked in front of the media, but it was always worth a try.

A reporter noticed Emma's arrival and asked, "Ms. Randolph, do you have anything to add?"

Emma had plenty to say, but tried to keep her comments brief. "Only that the Riverfront Historic Coalition will hire its own experts to do a structural assessment of the mill and other buildings. And those experts may very well not agree with Mr. Randolph's experts. This fire was a great tragedy, but the unnecessary demolition of these buildings would be an even greater tragedy and a huge loss to the city."

Joe jumped in before either of them could say anything more, apparently trying to head off what could become an awkward on-air dispute between Charlie and Emma. "Well, I understand that Chief O'Meara has given us the okay for a peek inside. Let's do it."

Charlie looked relieved. Emma seethed.

Emma decided to tag along for the trip inside and followed the cameras through what remained of the front doors of the mill. The group reassembled in the former lobby just inside the entrance.

Charlie nodded to Vince Shillings, who at once began to expound on his theories of the fire's origins. "Our best guess at this early stage of the investigation is that the fire started near the back of the mill . . . the exposed wood beams here, and next door in the warehouse, helped spread the fire pretty quickly . . . the limestone and brick exteriors, and the brave efforts of the firefighters, finally curtailed the blaze."

The group ventured no farther into the devastation, but the bright sunlight shining through the open roof and down through the holes in the floors above sufficiently lit the destruction that lay before them. Burned doorframes, sodden plaster chunks, and twisted machinery from the upper floors were strewn across the now wide-opened first floor. Water still dripped from overhead, and the smell of smoke and charred wood was overwhelming. Charlie's tone was somber and pessimistic as he repeatedly pointed out fallen timbers and any other possible structural damage.

Emma, however, was not convinced. She knew that water and smoke damage could make fire scenes initially look a lot worse than they actually were. Often, once the debris was cleared, damage to the actual structural elements of the buildings was found to be minimal. Nevertheless, she forced herself not to interrupt Charlie's performance with her own preliminary speculations. She would wait until her experts gave her something more definite.

6

The group was back outside the mill in fifteen minutes, and the media personnel departed after collecting all their equipment. Emma started down Second Street to take more photographs of the site, but Joe motioned for her to hold up. She waited in front of the door of the warehouse, writing down a few notes while Joe continued talking with Charlie outside the mill. Five minutes passed.

Screw this, Emma thought to herself. She pulled out her camera and yelled to Joe. "I'll be around back near the rail shed getting some photos." She found the opening in the fence and trudged across the muddy rail yard. Along the way, she snapped several pictures of the heavily damaged eastern sidewall of the mill.

Near the partially collapsed rail shed, she stepped into the shadow cast by the grain elevator. When she stopped to adjust the light meter on her camera, she heard the faint sound of heavy machinery coming from inside the elevator. She trotted down to the other end of the rail shed where its roof was still standing and moved under the metal canopy. She saw the sliding door at the back of the elevator opened a crack. She tucked the camera back into her bag and peered in.

Faint daylight shone through the several ventilation louvers above the door. She could make out a small Bobcat idling in a far corner to the left of the door, where the wall of the multi-story, central room of the elevator met the interior cylindrical wall of the closest storage silo. A large hole, approximately six-foot by eight-foot, was cut into the concrete floor in front of the machine. A pile of debris sat beside the hole.

Emma was about to go inside to investigate further when, through a haze of dust, she saw Vicki Stephens standing ten feet behind the Bobcat near the rounded wall of the grain silo. She was still wearing the high yellow boots and was engaged in a heated discussion with a man who appeared to be the machine's operator. Even though they were speaking loudly, the noise of the machine engine drowned out most of their conversation, and Emma only caught snippets of their exchange.

"You idiot…" screamed Vicki. ". . . with TV cameras and the newspapers and even the fucking mayor crawling all over this place—"

". . . didn't know . . ." the man shouted in response. ". . . been in here the last couple of hours . . . sick of taking your abuse and tired of doing your shit . . . don't pay me enough—"

Vicki kept at the man. ". . . this about more money—"

But the man wasn't backing down. ". . . take the chances . . . where were you the other night—"

Emma leaned forward to get a better view. Her camera bag swung forward and hit the door, pushing it open another few inches. Daylight streamed into the elevator. Vicki and her companion suddenly stopped talking and stared at the entrance. Without hesitation, Emma rushed inside waving her free arm at the two of them.

"Turn that thing off," Emma screamed at the machine operator. The man reluctantly sidled up to the machine and killed the engine. Although he was already carrying a sizable potbelly, he looked to be only around thirty; and he badly needed a shave.

Emma approached him. "What do you think you're doing?" She noticed "Dave" embroidered on the chest of his Randolph Foods windbreaker and added, "Huh, Dave?"

"Chill out, lady."

Vicki shuffled across the several feet over to them. She was obviously not pleased to see Emma. "What the hell are you doing? You have no right to come snooping in here."

"Oh, don't I?" Emma snapped back as she nodded towards the hole. "Your man, Dave, has been digging up this floor. That's a violation of the Coalition's restraining order. You remember that court order, don't you? The one that says 'no demolition'?"

"He was just filling the hole with some of that useless mud outside. We want to set up a work area in here."

Emma stormed around the Bobcat and pointed at the hole, which was almost three feet deep and still littered with debris. "Filling the hole? Right! Looks more like digging to China!"

Vicki peered over the Bobcat at the hole near Emma's feet. "Gee, I guess Dave got a little carried away. I'll dock his pay and make a contribution to your blessed Coalition. Will that make you happy?"

Emma nodded angrily at the man. "What would make me happy is to get him and his wrecking machine out of here until all of us have a chance to do our assessments of the fire damage."

"Okay, okay," Vicki agreed. "We certainly want to keep the mighty Emma Randolph happy." She turned to Dave and pointed at the Bobcat. "Get this thing out of here and back to Bloomington."

Dave restarted the machine and left the elevator. Then Vicki turned to Emma. "Okay, he's gone. Now get out of here."

But Emma wanted to fully investigate the damage to the

elevator floor. *When I'm good and ready*, she thought to herself, relishing the opportunity to antagonize Vicki even further.

She pivoted away from Vicki and focused back down into the hole. In the corner closest to her, she saw a flash of green amidst the rubble. She dropped her camera bag and climbed down into the waist-deep opening. After kicking away several large chunks of debris, she uncovered the folded edge of a large green canvas tarp and stooped over to take a closer look.

"Now what the hell are you doing?" demanded Vicki, coming up behind Emma. "You just got done lecturing me on tearing this place apart. Leave that mess alone, and get out of here."

Ignoring Vicki, Emma cleared away more debris and turned back the corner of the tarp. Staring at her was the skull of what appeared to be a human being. She flinched, but continued pulling at the canvas. More skeletal remains came into view. She could make out the bony structure of a hand, and an old boot lay near the base of what looked like the long bones of a leg. "What in the . . . ?" Emma's voice trailed off as she looked down at her gruesome discovery.

Vicki was standing behind Emma and couldn't actually see what Emma had uncovered down in the hole. But she was fairly certain she knew what it was. As she stepped around Emma, her suspicions were confirmed. *Christ, this is all we need.*

Emma didn't linger long over the discovered remains. She quickly climbed up out of the opening and sprinted from the elevator. Vicki followed, but her clumsy boots slowed her progress. By the time Vicki tromped out of the elevator, Emma had raced past the Bobcat parked in the rail shed outside the steel door and was already halfway across the rail yard. Then she tore through the fence and ran towards the front entrance of the mill where Charlie and Joe were still talking.

Emma was excited and out of breath when she reached them. "Come quick. I think we found a body in there." She pointed back towards the elevator.

Joe reached for her arm. "Slow down, Em. What's this about a body?"

Vicki came into view. Emma pointed down the street. "Ask her. Vicki saw it too. Inside the grain elevator in a hole in the floor. A skull and a bunch of bones wrapped up in an old tarp."

Vicki tromped up to join the group. Charlie turned to her. "Is this skeleton for real?"

Vicki nodded. "Afraid so."

For a moment, no one said anything. Then Joe suggested to Charlie, "I guess we better go have a look."

Emma led the group back towards the rail yard. Before they arrived at the fence opening, a van, with "Randolph Foods" stenciled on the side panel and pulling a flat-bed trailer, pulled onto the property in front of them.

"Who's that?" Charlie asked.

"Dave Malone," answered Vicki flatly. "He's here to pick up the Bobcat."

Charlie stared at Vicki. "What Bobcat . . ." he began to ask, but then stopped. He waved to Dave to get his attention and then yelled through the chain-link fence, "Leave the machine, wherever it is, and get on back to the plant."

"Hey, I want to talk to him," Emma protested. But the man quickly backed out of the fence and drove away down Second Street. Emma turned to Charlie, but he ignored her and continued through the fence opening and over towards the elevator. Joe and Vicki followed him, and Emma could only do the same.

A few moments later, they were standing over the hole looking at the bones scattered on the tarp. "How'd you find this guy?" Charlie asked.

There were no interruptions during Emma's account of the actual discovery of the remains, but the decorum quickly broke down when Joe asked how they both had come to be in the elevator.

Vicki spoke first. "I asked Dave to clear a space—"

Emma cut her off. "Oh, give me a break. He was a one-man

wrecking crew in here. Just more damage to blame on the fire."

"What the hell are you implying?"

"Time out, ladies," Joe insisted. "Emma, grab your camera bag, and let's get out of here. We have to contact the police. Then you can sort it out with them." Back outside in the rail yard, Joe made the call on his cell phone. Then the group returned to the mill entrance to wait for the police.

7

Minutes later, two officers in a dark-blue, unmarked car pulled up and parked on Second Street. The driver was first to emerge from the car. Sergeant Don Lovich, a former all-state lineman, was still a monster of a man and Emma recognized him immediately. He dwarfed Lieutenant Sergio Suarez, who exited from the passenger side just a moment later, by more than six inches and a hundred pounds.

Sergio, or Serg as he was called, was an old friend of Joe's from high school. While Joe had waited out the draft at Dartmouth, Serg joined the Army. He came home from Vietnam two years later as a decorated war hero, but also minus an arm. Overcoming this obstacle with a lot of raw talent and hard work, he was now a first-rate homicide detective.

Emma had first met Serg three years ago during Joe's mayoral campaign. He had just transferred back to the Minneapolis Homicide Division after a five-year stint in Kansas City. Joe, preoccupied with the election, had asked Emma to help Serg get reacquainted with the city. Because Emma was curious to get to know one of Joe's few heroes and not very anxious to otherwise help in the campaign, she had spent a lot of time with Serg that spring as he waited for his family to move up from Kansas City. They had become good friends, and Emma had also hit it off with Serg's wife, Paloma, when she and their two daughters finally arrived back in Minneapolis.

Serg approached the group waiting in front of the mill. He had to bite back a smile when he noticed Vicki's rubber boots. *Well, this is quite the gathering,* he thought. He knew the players well enough to appreciate the feigned civility of their foursome.

After handshakes from Charlie, Vicki, and Joe, and a quick hug from Emma, Serg got right down to business. "Where's the body?"

Emma spoke first. "Vicki and I found what looks like a skeleton. It's in a hole in the floor back in the grain elevator. Come on, we'll show you."

"Hold up. I just need one of you to take us back there. We want as little traffic as possible until the crime scene team gets here and has a chance to go over the site."

"Charlie and I already took a look," Joe admitted.

"That's perfectly understandable," Serg assured them. "And when we take your statements, we'll want you to describe exactly what you did while you were in there." He turned to Don. "Let's go have a quick look, and then we'll come back here to get their statements. I'm sure all these people have places they need to be." Then he spoke to Joe. "If you can direct us to this hole, we'll be back in five minutes."

Actually, they were gone closer to fifteen minutes. Emma sat on the curb fiddling with her camera. Charlie and Vicki stood near the doors of the mill and said nothing to each other.

When Joe and the detectives returned, Serg walked back over to the police car and used the radio. Then he came back to the group and said to Don. "While we're waiting for the medical examiner and our crew, why don't you talk to Mayor Buchanan and Mr. Randolph? I'll start with Ms. Randolph and Ms. Stephens."

Don finished talking with Charlie and Joe at the same time that Serg wrapped up with Emma. Before Serg started interviewing Vicki, he told the others they were free to leave. "We may have a few follow-up questions once we look around," he said. "But for now, thanks for your help."

Emma still intended to continue with her photos of the site and started back down Second Street to the fence opening. Don stopped her. "Sorry, Miss Randolph. You'll have to leave. The entire property is off limits for the time being."

Emma looked at Don. "But I have a court order allowing me to be on this property. I won't go inside the elevator. I promise."

Don wasn't persuaded. "Sorry. No can do, Miss Randolph."

Joe knew how stubborn Emma could be. He stepped in to help Don out. "Come on, Em. I doubt your court order lets you interfere with official police work. If Don says so, you'll have to leave." His eyes begged her not to make a scene. "We're all leaving. I'll walk you to your car." He grabbed her arm lightly.

She shrugged off his hand and turned to face him. "I'm perfectly capable of getting to my car on my own. Besides, it's parked down along the river, and I wouldn't want you to get your shoes dirty." She tightened the grip on her camera bag and stomped off down the hill towards the river.

Joe yelled after her. "I'll talk to Serg and give you a call later to let you know when you can finish up with your photos." Emma kept walking and didn't look back.

8

As Emma came through her door, she heard the phone ringing. She kicked off her running shoes and dashed across the living room into the kitchen to pick up the cordless receiver.

"Hi, Em. Can you hold for a second?" It was Joe. He had this bad habit of putting people on hold after he called them.

She had just returned from a six-mile run—her long route from downtown through Loring Park and on up the hill behind the Guthrie Theater to Kenwood and Lake of the Isles. As an accommodation to middle-aged knees, she normally didn't run two days in a row, but she had made an exception after her extraordinary morning at the mill. She needed to distance herself from the fire's devastation and the discovered skeleton in the grain elevator.

Emma was still angry over Joe's treatment of her this morning and was tempted to hang up on him. But she needed to find out what was going on. She hoped he would fill her in. She grabbed a towel from the bathroom and wiped the sweat from her face as she walked into the living room.

She plopped down into a comfortable, rust-colored, uphol-stered armchair. Then she picked up a back issue of *Architectural Digest* from the coffee table and flipped through it while she wait-ed for Joe to return to the line. The chill of the morning was gone, and the early-afternoon sun was streaming through her large living room windows and across the floor of the room.

Emma lived on the ninth floor of an old L-shaped building in the Warehouse District of Minneapolis. Like many others of the turn-of-the-century brick warehouses in this downtown neighbor-hood, her building had been recently renovated. Condominiums had recently been carved out of the upper floors, and a coffee shop and deli occupied the street level.

Her neighbors were an interesting mix of young, single profes-sionals; affluent middle-aged gay couples; and adventurous seniors, who had opted to move back into the urban center after raising their kids. Notably absent were many of Emma's contemporaries. They were busy landscaping, carpooling, and barbecuing out in the suburbs and in the affluent family neighborhoods of Southwest Minneapolis.

Emma had consulted on the renovation of the building and applied her fees to the down payment on an unfinished unit. That was three years ago, when she had decided to permanently move out of Joe's house. Her condo was nestled in the inside back corner of the top floor with a partially obstructed view of the upper Mississippi River above St. Anthony Falls.

It had been nothing more than raw, open space when she moved in—with unfinished oak floors, an eighteen-foot ceiling, and four ten-foot by twelve-foot windows along the wall opposite the door. The exterior brick wall of the other wing of the ware-house was her most immediate view out the windows, but beyond that she could see the northern tip of Nicollet Island and on across Boom Island Park into northeast Minneapolis.

Slowly, as her cash flow had allowed, she built her home, doing most of the work herself. A short hall to the left of the door led to an enclosed bedroom and bath. All the other rooms were open to view from the front entry. A galley kitchen was along the far wall in front of the bedroom and bath. One of the oversized windows was at the end of the kitchen. Next to the kitchen, beyond a counter and breakfast bar, was the dining room with another of the windows. A buffet built into a half-wall separated the living room, with two additional windows, from the dining room.

In the living room, a large area rug in rich, multi-colored earth tones covered the refinished wood floors; and built-in wall shelves held books, stereo equipment, and a small television. Two large abstract watercolors, both painted by her mother, hung on the limited open wall space in the living room. Some of her furniture—like the handsome pine dining table—had been built by her father in his woodworking shop up at Lake Salish. The rest she had bought at antique shops and estate sales.

The high ceiling had allowed Emma to build an office loft across the far wall above the kitchen, bedroom, and bath. It was equipped with a computer, drafting table, fax machine, printer, and copier. Bookshelves along the back wall were stacked with client files and resource materials.

Folding steps and a ceiling trap door led from the loft up to a roof-top deck enclosed by a low parapet and edged with flower boxes. There was only enough room up there for a comfortable lounge chair and small table, but it was still a nice little hide-away in the city.

As she got up out of her chair to open the window closest to her, Joe came back on the line. "Sorry about that. And sorry about this morning."

Apologies, how Joe-like, thought Emma mockingly, before responding. "That little scene with Don Lovich?"

"Yes, but also the whole press conference thing. Charlie set it up, and I just assumed he'd invite someone from the Coalition."

"Never assume anything when it comes to dear Cousin Charlie," Emma teased, only half kidding. Then she said, "A formal invite would have been nice. But no harm done, since I showed up anyway."

Joe moved on. "I imagine you're heartbroken about the fire. I thought of calling you yesterday, but I knew you'd probably be up fishing with Sam."

She sat back down on the edge of the overstuffed chair and drew in her breath. "What? The mayor can't afford a long distance call to Ely! You know how hard I've worked on that mill."

"Of course, I know that," answered Joe defensively. "But I hate calling you up at your dad's. He always answers and gives me the third degree."

Emma continued chiding him. "You sound like a sixth grader."

"Well, I didn't know what you had told him about us breaking things off."

"Just that I couldn't live with a politician." Emma heard a moan from the other end of the line before she added sarcastically, "I skipped the part about some of your supporters still holding a sixty-year-old grudge against my grandfather."

Joe exploded. "Don't start on that again. You know one drunk at a Christmas party doesn't speak for all my union backers."

The labor unions were a huge base of political and financial support for Joe. But Emma's dealings with organized labor were very adversarial, mostly because of their constant opposition to her preservationist efforts, but also partly because of her family history. Sam's father had been sent to prison in the late 1930s for the killing of a respected local labor leader, Matthew Kelly. For both reasons, Emma rarely accompanied Joe to union events.

Last December, however, she had made an exception and attended a holiday fund-raiser hosted by the electricians' local. Late in the evening, some union political hack made a very loud and nasty comment concerning Emma's grandfather. The remark hurt, but it wasn't the thing that really bothered her. It was Joe's reaction, or lack thereof. In a perfect world, the obnoxious drunk deserved a good punch in the nose. But Emma would have been satisfied if Joe had even halfheartedly rebuked the guy. Instead, he simply laughed and walked away, leaving her alone to defend her family's honor.

After that night, she knew their relationship was over. She could no longer tolerate the personal compromises and moral accommodations apparently necessary for Joe to succeed in the political arena.

Emma immediately regretted her comment. There was no point in rehashing old history. "Okay, okay. Sorry I mentioned it." Joe breathed more easily on the other end of the line. Then Emma leaned back in her chair and asked, "Have you talked to Serg since this morning?"

"Yes, I talked with him right after lunch. They think your skeleton, and all that other debris, was packed in an abandoned shaft in the floor of the grain elevator."

Emma vaguely recalled a temporary underground tunnel marked on the original structural blueprints for the old warehouse. "I think I remember that shaft from some plans of the site. It was part of a tunnel running from that brick warehouse on Second Street under the rail yard into the elevator."

"You should let Serg know about that. He was wondering what it might have been used for."

Gee, we're actually having a productive conversation for a change, observed Emma, as she said, "Will do. I'll even dig out the plans so he can take a look at them." She leaned forward and grabbed a pencil and pad from the coffee table to write herself a note. "Any ideas on who this guy might be?"

"Not at this point; and it may take a while. Serg found the pair to that old boot loose in the rubble and thinks maybe parts of the skeleton could have been scattered as well. He's got a forensic crew over there now sifting through the debris and sorting out anything that might be bone or anything else of interest."

Emma put the paper and pencil back down on the coffee table. "Did anyone get the story on that yahoo, Dave? The guy Charlie made disappear from the site this morning?"

"I assume you're talking of Dave Malone. He's part of the Randolph Foods janitorial staff." The edginess had returned to Joe's voice.

"Why was he ripping open the elevator floor?"

"No one was 'ripping open' that floor, Em. It caved in during the fire."

Emma bolted from her chair and began pacing in front of the windows in the living room. "Says who?"

"Vicki Stephens," Joe responded firmly.

Emma groaned.

"Hey, it makes sense to me." Joe tried to explain. "That shaft would have been a weak spot in the elevator floor. And those collapsing timbers in the mill next door could have set off all sorts of vibrations." He kept talking and Emma kept groaning. "Anyway, Vicki sent Dave in there to fill the hole with some of the mud from out in the rail yard. They wanted to use the grain elevator for a work area. You know, sort of a temporary crisis-control center away from the more significant fire damage."

"I don't believe it," Emma said in disgust. "That's the same tune Vicki was singing this morning. But Dave wasn't filling the hole. He was excavating it. You could see that pile of debris next to the hole, and there wasn't even any mud in there."

"They hadn't brought it in yet. Dave was prepping the hole."

But Emma was too angry to listen. "Oh, and you just buy

everything that woman says. Incredible! Who knows how much damage Dave would have done if I hadn't come along? Or whether we would have heard about that body, either?"

Now Joe groaned. "Oh, come on, Em. That is pure conjecture. I suppose you think Vicki is somehow responsible for that body?"

"I tell you, it wouldn't surprise me! Vicki Stephens within ten miles of a dead body makes me suspicious." Emma was half-serious.

Cousin Charlie and Vicki were expert at working the Good Cop/Bad Cop routine with the Coalition and the city on the mill preservation issue. In Emma's opinion, Vicki's bad-cop role was a natural fit. In the preceding months, they'd had some now-legendary run-ins at city council meetings, court proceedings, and press conferences.

But those exchanges were nothing compared to some of their private conversations. Vicki had a sharp tongue. And once attacked, Emma seldom backed down. She had even got the best of Vicki a few times. That hadn't done much to improve Vicki's cordiality towards her.

"I know you don't like her, Em. But come on. You're being ridiculous."

Like always, Emma thought he probably wanted to add. She tried to calm down. "Well, maybe, but after this whole fire thing, that Bobcat really upset me this morning."

"Cool it, Em," Joe strongly advised. "The skeleton is Serg's problem. Let him handle things—"

"Hey, I've got no problem with Serg handling the skeleton. It's that Vince Shillings is supposedly handling the fire. He should have been kicked out of the department years ago. What's he doing investigating five-alarm fires?"

Joe took a deep breath and lowered his voice. "Just between you and me, I'm not happy about that either. I talked to Ken Johnson. Apparently, Vince is the only investigator who's around this weekend. Everyone else is fishing."

Emma dropped back down into her chair. "You can't be serious! Everyone else was fishing?"

"That's right. A lot of the guys take a few days for the Opener."

"And fires be damned?"

"That's just it," Joe said. "There usually aren't many fires this time of year when we've had a wet spring. The winter heating season is usually pretty much over, and furnaces and space heaters are shut down. And brush fires aren't a big concern. Even the homeless people help out by moving out of the abandoned buildings. Guess this cold snap caught the department a bit understaffed."

"So, let me guess. Vince Shillings isn't a fisherman?"

"Must not be. He's covered the Opener for the last few years."

"I still can't believe this," Emma muttered. "Will the chief replace Vince once the other investigators get back?"

"I doubt it. Not once he's on the case. That wouldn't look very good." Before Emma could comment, he continued. "Besides, there will be a lot of insurance investigators going through the mill looking over Vince's shoulder to make certain he does a thorough job."

Emma wasn't buying it. "He's had two days in that building already without somebody looking over his shoulder. Who knows what he's been doing in there!"

"Let it go, Em. He's staying on the case."

"Of course he is. Anything to smooth the path for the mighty Charlie Randolph."

Joe snapped. "That's unfair, Emma, and you know it," he said angrily. "Life is not one big conspiracy against you. Everyone's just trying to do their job."

With those words, Emma knew, Joe was defending himself as much as Vince Shillings and her cousin Charlie. *How many times have I heard that in the past few months?* she wanted to ask. But she didn't want to reopen the acrimonious discussion of their relationship. So instead, she accepted her scolding. "So, when can I get back into the mill?"

Joe moved on, too. "Serg says right away. They've cordoned off the area where the body was found, but your experts can have free rein over the rest of the place."

"Great! We'll get right on it."

Emma was ready to hang up when Joe cleared his throat and said, "Hey, Em, seeing you today was tough. It made me realize how much I've missed you."

Joe's unexpected intimacy made Emma blush. But she managed to keep her voice calm. "It was hard for me too. But we'll get used to it."

"I guess we'll have to." Emma could hear the sadness in his voice and was relieved when he then asked, "You'll be at the bridge dedication on Saturday, won't you?"

"Sure. I wouldn't miss it. The Coalition put a lot of energy into saving that old bridge."

"What a great project. Really a wonderful example of citizens and their government working together—"

"Hey, save the speech for your public on Saturday," interrupted Emma, trying to lighten up their conversation. "I'll see you then."

Clicking off the phone, she went over to a framed picture hanging on the kitchen wall. It was an old black and white photograph of the Stone Arch Bridge.

The Stone Arch Bridge was completed in 1883. It was the first rail crossing of the Mississippi River, carrying James J. Hill's St. Paul, Minneapolis, and Manitoba Railroad westward. This train connection across the river greatly enhanced access to eastern markets for Minneapolis milling products. It was also essential for the opening up of the vast wheat-producing regions in present-day

North Dakota, Manitoba, and Saskatchewan, thereby further spurring the rapid growth of the flour industry in Minneapolis.

Construction of the nearly half-mile bridge was an engineering marvel. Assisted by the use of steam-powered pumps to hold back the waters of the river during the setting of the platform foundations, the structure was built in just twenty-two months; and its piers and twenty-three arches, built with regional granite and limestone, successfully supported the weight of the heavy rail loads soon crossing over them. The dramatic location of the majestic span just downstream from St. Anthony Falls, together with the gentle curve at the bridge's western end, also added architectural distinction to the structure.

So, even though rail traffic over it had ceased in 1981, the bridge was recognized as historically significant and fortunately was never removed. Now it was being restored as a pedestrian walkway over the river, part of a planned walking tour of the historic milling district. The project was nearly complete, and rededication of the bridge was scheduled for Saturday.

If only our personal relationship could have been so satisfying, she mused, as she went back to the bedroom to get out of her sweaty running tights and long-sleeved T-shirt. After a shower, she put on her work clothes—well-worn Ely High School warm-up pants and a University of Minnesota sweatshirt—and went into the kitchen for a quick lunch.

She spent the next two hours up in her office loft on the phone with several structural engineers who were active in the Coalition. It was a tough sell to get a crew together for the following afternoon, because not only was she asking them to drop everything they were working on to help the Coalition survey the mill buildings, but she couldn't promise them any money.

The Coalition had a modest administrative budget provided by several generous donors, but most of the actual architectural and engineering work was done gratis by members of the organization. Emma herself had spent hundreds of uncompensated hours on the riverfront restoration. Obviously, no one had planned on the fire and this extra time commitment.

By the time Emma had assembled her team, it was nearly four-thirty and time to do some work for one of her paying clients. She had been retained to coordinate the restoration of a small carriage house behind a ninety-year-old mansion overlooking Lake of the Isles in the Kenwood neighborhood of Minneapolis. Bidding on the project was under way, and she had promised one of the competing contractors a few additional detail drawings of the entry door by tomorrow noon.

Emma sat down at her computer. Most of her original design work was still done by hand in her sketchbook and later at her drafting table, but she fully utilized her sophisticated Computer Assisted Design program when it came to production of detail drawings and other construction documents. She stared at the computer screen and tried to concentrate on the drawings, but all she could think of were the bones in the grain elevator. She stood up, walked over to her plan rack, and pulled out the Coalition's copy of the original plans for the Randolph warehouse. The brick building had been constructed on Second Street adjacent to the old mill in the late 1930s. It didn't take long to find the tunnel that had entombed the body. It was labeled "Temporary Construction Access."

The plans showed a wood-covered walkway leading twenty feet out of the back of the warehouse, which terminated at a shaft leading down through limestone to a sandstone layer fifteen feet below-grade. The tunnel then ran through the sandstone for a considerable distance under the rail yard and met another shaft located in the closest corner of the grain elevator, where a construction storeroom had been sectioned off. Ladders and dumbwaiters in the two shafts on either end of the tunnel facilitated traffic and material transport through it.

Emma tried Serg at his office. His secretary said Emma could still catch him over at the grain elevator. She went downstairs and changed into jeans and a sweater. She threw on her fleece jacket, grabbed the plans, and drove back to the riverfront.

9

Late afternoon shadows fell across the rail yard as Emma drove through the chain-link fence back to the grain elevator. The place was deserted except for an unmarked police car sitting just outside the rail shed. Emma parked her Subaru beside the vehicle and ducked under the metal canopy with the warehouse plans rolled under her arm. As she neared the door of the elevator, Don Lovich hurried out. He jumped when he saw Emma.

Emma laughed. "I didn't know big, tough cops scared so easily."

Don smiled. "Oh, Miss Randolph, it's you. I didn't expect to find anyone still out here."

"I just arrived," explained Emma. "I'm looking for Serg."

"He's inside. Go on in."

"Sure it's okay for me to be here?" Emma teased.

The man knew what she was joking about. "Sorry I had to ask you to leave this morning. But we gotta play 'em by the book until we know what we got." After a short laugh, he added, "And what we got is a bunch of old bones and not much else."

Emma made her way to the doorway of the elevator and then looked back at the sergeant. "Hey, no hard feelings, okay? I know you were just doing your job this morning."

"I appreciate you saying that. Don't worry about it." Don turned and headed for the car. "I'll be back in a bit. Just running back to the station for a few things."

The interior of the elevator was damp and musty, which Emma had barely noticed during all the excitement earlier in the day. She stopped just inside the entry to zip up her jacket and let her eyes adjust to the dimness. A human shadow, cast by bright spotlights, loomed on the cylindrical wall in the corner to her left. Emma slowly made her way over towards the glare and was finally able to make out Serg's figure standing with his back to her. She called, "Hey, Serg. It's me, Emma." Her echo bounced off the overhead concrete of the empty elevator.

"I know," Serg said, as she stepped into the bright circle of light. "I heard you talking outside to Don. It's nice that you two are friends again."

Emma flushed with embarrassment. "Oh, so Don reported on my little outburst this morning? I was a jerk."

Serg shrugged. "We all have our days. So what's up?"

"I talked to Joe earlier this afternoon. He told me that hole where we found the skeleton is actually an abandoned shaft."

"Take a look." Serg pointed at the gaping cavity Emma had discovered earlier that morning. "We uncovered some of the old vertical and horizontal support timbers down there. It looks like most of the shaft was filled with sand. Except for the few top feet where the tarp and the rest of that debris was found."

Emma edged closer to the hole. "Where's our friend?"

"Over at the medical examiner's office. Along with quite a pile of rubble."

"Guess you want to make sure you got all of him, huh?"

"Right. It looks like most of him was in that tarp, but we can't be certain. And we might also find some other helpful artifacts, like that second boot. Although, it's likely that the rest of his clothes disintegrated along with the body decomposition."

Emma bent and looked down into the hole, which was now six feet deep and had a sandy bottom. It was ringed with partially rotted wood columns. After studying it for a moment, she lifted her head and turned back to Serg. "I know where this shaft goes." She motioned to the roll of plans under her arm. "Here, I'll show you."

"Let's take a look."

Emma crouched down a few feet from the wall. Then she unrolled the warehouse plans on the elevator floor. Serg refocused one of the lights and squatted down beside her. Emma turned several pages and then pointed to a detail on the plans. "See, here's your shaft going down to the tunnel." She explained the passageway's use under the busy rail yard.

"Well, that clears up a big question—what that shaft was doing here." Serg said gratefully. "Do you know when the warehouse was built?"

Emma pointed down to the old blueprints. "These plans are dated September 24, 1936. But I don't think the actual construction was completed until mid-1937." Emma was a walking encyclopedia on the history of the milling complex.

"When do you think they would have sealed up the tunnel and filled in this shaft?"

Emma made an educated guess. "Probably right after the warehouse was finished. So they could tear down the storeroom and use this part of the elevator again."

Serg turned back to the hole. "I wonder if our guy's been in here since then?"

Emma shuddered, as she leaned down to take another look into the shaft.

"Perfect place to dump a body, huh?"

Serg laughed. "Hold on a minute with the stashed bodies. The whole thing could have been just a terrible accident."

Emma looked at Serg with raised eyebrows. "Come on, how

does someone get accidentally buried beneath a concrete floor?"

"Easy if no one expected him to be in there. He might have just picked the wrong place to sleep."

Emma still wasn't convinced. "And he just peacefully snoozed away while someone poured cement on his head?"

"Not necessarily. He could have been drunk and passed out in the partially-filled shaft. And then crushed by all that debris thrown down in there."

"But how did he end up wrapped in that tarp?"

"Maybe he was just trying to keep warm. There were a lot of people living on the street during those years. Even more than now."

Emma gave him another skeptical look. "You've been reading way too much Edgar Allan Poe."

"I know it sounds improbable, but I actually saw a similar case at a construction site down in Kansas City. One night some guy decided to use an empty structural form for a bed. It was a chilly night, and we figured he must have been looking for a warm place to sleep it off. Anyway, the footings were poured the first thing the following morning. And when the crew broke away the form later in the day, they saw this guy's hand sticking out of the set concrete. At that point, the drunk was beyond caring. But it really freaked out the construction guys. They checked those forms every morning after that."

"God, what a way to go!"

"But that's just one possibility," Serg conceded. "Your original theory could just as easily be true. Someone might have dumped the body into the shaft. Hopefully, someone over at the medical examiner's office will shed some light on it for us."

"Based on what? Just a pile of bones?"

"They've worked miracles with a lot less than what they have here," Serg said, before elaborating. "Of course, a big part of their job will be a final sort through that debris to isolate all the bones and bone fragments. But we know they have the skull and most of the pelvis. And those should give us the race, gender, and approximate age at death. We also might get lucky on dental work."

"What a job!" Emma remarked before asking, "So, do you buy Vicki's version of events in here this morning?"

Serg was very aware of Emma's opinion of Vicki Stephens. He took a deep breath. "Listen, my job is to stay focused on our long-dead friend. And regardless of what Mr. Malone and Ms. Stephens were up to in here this morning, I doubt it has much to do with him. He probably got buried in here long before their time. Probably long before even their parents' time. So I'm not much interested in Vicki's activities this morning or any other morning."

With raised eyebrows, Emma turned towards Serg. "Right. Joe explained the system to me earlier. You, being the genius, get corpses. And idiots, like Vince Shillings, pick up the arson."

"Simmer down, Em. I know Vince isn't exactly a star investigator, but so far no one has said anything about arson —"

"Well, everyone is thinking it," Emma blurted. She ignored Serg's deepening frown and pushed on. "And I heard from Joe of Vince's dislike for fishing. Sounds like the second weekend in May would be a great time for Charlie and Vicki to have a little fire. Just slip Vince a few bucks, and his crack investigative skills turn up a few homeless guys roasting weenies —"

Serg finally cut her off. "Em, I know you don't like your cousin and his sidekick, but you're way out on a limb on this one. And your wild hunches are going to get you in a whole lot of trouble if you're not careful. Leave the police work to the cops."

"This is more than not liking my cousin and his sidekick. I don't trust them, and the police shouldn't either." Serg repeated his admonition, this time with a more authoritative tone in his voice. "Just stay out of our way, and let us do our jobs."

"Yes, boss," Emma reluctantly agreed.

Serg saw that Emma was still upset. In an effort to lighten their exchange, he laughed and lightly jabbed her arm. "Now I see what Joe means about your active imagination."

Serg regretted his effort immediately. "Oh, wonderful," Emma exploded. "So now Joe's telling people I'm paranoid. He should focus on his own problems instead of worrying about mine."

"Come on, Em. I was just kidding. Besides, you should cut Joe some slack. He does still care for you."

"Oh, wonderful! He cares for me. That's the stuff of real passion."

"You know what I mean. He'd like to make it work with you. He just has too much else on his plate right now."

"No, it's more than that. He's changed. He's been pushing that political rock uphill too long. And barely notices all the fat cats and leeches along for the ride. He spends most of his energy courting people he used to despise. The 'silver spooners,' he always called them. People like Charlie Randolph."

"Come on, Emma. That's politics. He thrives on it, and you don't. Irreconcilable differences, as they say."

"That's right," Emma snapped back. "And that's why it's over, and he doesn't need to concern himself with my little paranoid obsessions anymore." Serg mimicked her earlier response to him. "Whatever you say, boss."

Emma took a deep breath and smiled at her good friend. A flashlight beam came towards them. "Hey, that must be Don coming back," she said. She was happy for the interruption and a reason to stop discussing Joe Buchanan. "I'd better quit monopolizing your time, and let you guys finish up so you can get out of here sometime tonight."

She crouched down to roll up the plans. "Listen, I'll run off a copy of this sheet that shows the tunnel and send it over to you."

"Thanks," Serg said, accepting Emma's peace offering. "Say, Paloma's doing one of her dinner things Saturday. Think you can make it?"

Emma ran her fingers through her hair and grinned sheepishly. "You're not afraid I'll rant and rave about fires and jerky politicians?"

"A little," Serg kidded. "But if you misbehave, we'll yank your plate and you'll have to go home hungry."

"I'll try to be good because I could really use the night out. It's shaping up to be a pretty crazy week."

"Work, work, work," scolded Serg.

"Gotta pay the bills somehow."

Serg smiled. "Listen, either Paloma or I will be in touch with Saturday's details."

"I'll hold the night," said Emma. "Now, get back to work. And thanks for the crypt tour," she added, as she headed back across the dark elevator to the entrance.

10

Peter still hadn't talked to Charlie since the fire. This morning, hung over, he vaguely remembered having left a ranting message on Charlie's answering machine late the night before. After choking down a cup of coffee, he had phoned back to apologize for his prior evening's likely insinuation of arson. But still he heard nothing back from his son. He suspected that Charlie was ignoring him, which only heightened his suspicions about the origins of the mill fire.

It was now late afternoon. He mixed himself a vodka martini and carried it out to the back porch off the kitchen to watch the local television news. Peter's mind wandered during the lead story covering the governor's fishing weekend, but refocused quickly when he saw a picture of the old Randolph grain elevator flash onto the screen. He heard the first few words of the newscaster's accompanying report:

"A body, really just a skeleton, was found—"

He punched the remote to turn up the volume, but hit "Mute"

by mistake. By the time he found the right button, the woman was on to another story. *I knew this day would come*, he thought as he anxiously flipped through the channels for more news on the discovered body.

He found no more coverage, turned off the television, and retreated to his library. First, he dialed Vicki's various phone numbers, but couldn't reach her. He left messages imploring her to call and then tried Charlie again, unsuccessfully.

For the next three hours, Peter sat at his desk staring out the windows, drinking successive martinis and periodically dialing Vicki and Charlie's numbers. His agitation mounted with every unanswered call, but especially with those to Vicki. She knew why he was calling and should appreciate his anxiety. She was probably enjoying his torment.

A little after eight, Peter staggered across the room to the bar to mix yet another drink. He couldn't remember if it was his fifth or sixth. Then he made his way over towards the fireplace, spilling most of his drink on the way. He drained what was left of the martini and fell back on the couch. Within a few minutes, he slouched down onto the cushions and passed out.

Charlie finally called him back at eight-thirty, and Berta answered. For a few minutes, he listened to his mother prattle on about some upcoming event at the club, but then interrupted, "Dad around? He's been trying to reach me."

Just before taking Charlie's call, Berta had found Peter slumped on the couch in the library. But as she had done for years, she tried to cover up his condition. "Your father is napping. He took a long walk this afternoon and was absolutely exhausted. Slept right through dinner."

Napping, that's a good one, Mother," thought Charlie. He knew Peter was probably passed out. But he also realized there was little point in questioning his mother's tiresome charade, which irritated him almost as much as his father's alcohol abuse.

"I can wake him if you want," Berta offered half-heartedly.

"No, let him sleep. Just tell him I called."

11

Emma finished the last of her Greek takeout and sat back in the chair to enjoy the final sips of her Pinot Grigio and the last strains of a Vivaldi oboe concerto on KSJN. The spanikopita and pilaf made up her first real meal since leaving Lake Salish the previous morning. And relaxing here in her living room was her first real break since she had heard of the fire. Lost in the music, she was startled by the ringing of the phone.

I don't want to talk to anybody tonight, she decided and let the ringing continue. But when the answering machine kicked in after four rings, she heard Sam's voice. She jumped up, ran into the kitchen, and picked up the receiver.

"Glad to hear I made it through your screening process," her father teased.

"Sorry about that. Things have been crazy around here, and one more reporter might have sent me over the edge." Emma walked back into the living room to turn down the radio.

"Any ideas yet on how the fire started?"

"Nothing definite. And we don't know if the buildings are salvageable, either. The war of battling engineers is just beginning." Emma fell back down in her chair. "But that's not the big news."

"What else happened?" asked Sam.

"A dead body showed up on the site."

Sam took a deep breath. "Someone died in the fire?"

"No," answered Emma. "We found a skeleton in the old grain elevator. It was in an abandoned shaft that led down to an underground tunnel."

"Where does the tunnel go?" asked Sam.

"Under an old rail yard over to a warehouse on the other side of the property. The shaft and tunnel were dug way back in the 'thirties when the warehouse was built."

"Oh, that warehouse."

"What?" Emma was confused. "How do you know about the warehouse?"

The answer came to her just as her father started to explain. "The groundbreaking for that warehouse was in the fall of 1936. It was the last time I was at the riverfront mill. I was only nine or ten. Shortly after that, Matthew Kelly disappeared."

"God, I've looked at the date on those plans a million times and never put those events together—"

"Don't be too hard on yourself. It was a long time ago."

Emma didn't know what to say to Sam. Over the years, she and her father had rarely discussed her grandfather's involvement in the labor leader's disappearance. There was silence on the other end of the line, too. Then, in a very serious tone, Sam said, "You know, he didn't do it."

Emma didn't hesitate now. She reassured him, "Dad, I've never doubted your father's innocence."

"And you never should. They never did find Kelly up at his house. And there's no way that jury should have convicted him without a body turning up—"

Emma gasped. "Wait a minute! Do you remember exactly

when Kelly disappeared?"

"It was a long time ago. But I'm pretty sure it was April of 1937"

"God, that's around the time the warehouse was finished."

"Yes, and?"

"Well, that's also when that shaft was probably filled in. And it's possible that our skeleton has been in there since then."

Now Sam got excited. "So you're wondering if it could be Matthew Kelly?"

Hearing Sam utter the possibility out loud, Emma immediately regretted sharing her crazy hunch with him. It would only raise false expectations. "Pretty farfetched, huh?"

But it was too late to backtrack. "Oh, I don't know. It has to be somebody, right? Why not Kelly? Do you think they could even tell after all these years?

No need to fuel this any more than I already have, thought Emma, as she chose not to share Serg's explanation of the medical examiner's identification efforts. Instead she answered, "Don't know. Skeletons are a little out of my area of expertise."

"Well, maybe you should mention Kelly to Serg Suarez."

"Hold on, Dad. It was stupid of me to mention Kelly and get you all excited like this." She remembered Serg's advice to her earlier in the evening. "We should let the cops do their job and not go jumping to all sorts of unfounded conclusions."

"You're right," agreed Sam, grudgingly.

Hearing the disappointment in Sam's voice, Emma couldn't keep from volunteering, "Listen, the medical examiner is supposedly working on this guy. I'll check with Serg in a day or so to find out if they've made any progress."

"Are you humoring the old man?"

"Well, maybe a little. But hey, this whole thing was my idea in the first place, remember?"

"Well, I appreciate it. But don't let it take you from your work."

"I won't," Emma assured him. "I can't afford to."

Sam, in his turn, tried to assure his daughter. "And don't worry.

I won't get my hopes up too high."

Emma knew this wasn't true. But there wasn't much she could do about that now. "I've got to go, Dad. I have some work to finish up."

After good-byes, Emma carried the receiver and her dishes into the kitchen. Then she grabbed a sweater from her bedroom and climbed up to the loft and her computer to work on the promised detail drawings for the Kenwood carriage house.

12

"Jesus, you're amazing," moaned Charlie as Vicki rolled off him onto her back. It was early evening, and the two of them were in Charlie's king-sized bed in the master bedroom of his Edina townhouse. The sweet trumpet of Miles Davis blared softly through the bedroom speakers. Charlie leaned over, brushed back the hair covering Vicki's face, and ran his index finger down between her breasts. "Five-alarm fires and decomposed bodies must really turn you on. You waltzed in here tonight hornier than ever."

"Oh, come on. We both needed it," Vicki said, as she pushed away her hand and eased out of bed. She slunk over to her clothes, casually piled on a chair across the room, and spoke back over her shoulder, "And you weren't going to get it from that uptight wife of yours."

Charlie sat up, stretched over to the left side of the bed, and switched off the music. He looked up to face her, and he wasn't smiling any longer. "Knock it off. I've told you before, my relationship with Joanna is none of your business."

Charlie's affair with Vicki Stephens had begun eighteen months ago, shortly after Vicki had been promoted to director of sales, when the two of them had started to work and travel more together. To Charlie, the attraction was entirely physical. And Vicki articulated the same limited feelings. She even jokingly compared their sexual encounters to Charlie and Taylor's weekly game of squash.

But Charlie never completely bought it. Vicki was an unusual woman, but still a woman. And for women, sex was always more complicated than squash. Periodic comments, like the one just made concerning Joanna, implied that Vicki might want something more than simple sport.

Joanna was Charlie's wife of fifteen years. By all appearances, theirs was a failed marriage. Joanna and his kids lived in a large house out on Lake Minnetonka. Charlie spent most nights at his townhouse closer to the office. Actually, however, Charlie and Joanna were perfectly happy with their marital situation. Together they were good parents to their twin thirteen-year-olds and, despite the lack of sexual intimacy, were still close friends. Both were in their mid-forties, and neither had any interest in remarrying or, therefore, divorce.

Joanna knew of Charlie's ongoing affair with Vicki and had repeatedly advised him to end it; not out of jealousy, she said, but because she didn't trust Vicki Stephens nor Charlie's ability to protect himself from her.

Vicki stood at the foot of the bed adjusting her half-slip and hooking her bra. "What's with you? Can't take a little après-sex banter?"

"Come on, back off," Charlie said. He sat up on the right side of the bed and pulled the sheet up over his legs and around his waist. "After these last few days, I'm not in the mood for your cute remarks."

Vicki laughed at him. "Having second thoughts about playing with matches, lover boy?"

"Maybe I am," Charlie shot back. "Christ, why did I ever listen to you in the first place? I should have let Emma have her way and just restored the old place."

"Right and spend an extra two million dollars in the process."

"If it really turned out to be that kind of money, we could have just called off the deal with the city and expanded out in the burbs."

"That would've looked great." Vicki sneered. "Can't get your way, so you pack up all your marbles and go home. You wouldn't have been able to stand the roasting you'd have gotten in the press. Besides, who is Emma to tell you what to do with that property? She lost her right to those mill buildings decades ago."

"Not as a member of Jane Q. Public, she didn't." Then Charlie smiled a bit. "God, she was pissed today."

"And that's worth a little something isn't it?"

Charlie nodded, but immediately got serious again. "But if we end up in jail or if we have to spend even more money also restoring this fire damage—"

"Neither of those things will happen." Vicki turned to look at him as she sat down to pull on her stockings. "Come on, trust me. Our preliminary engineering report is due early next week, and it will seriously question the structural integrity of those buildings. So will the city's report. We just have to ride this thing out, and we'll be under way with demolition and new construction in the fall."

"And do you plan to pay off the Coalition's engineers like you did Vince Shillings and our so-called experts?"

Vicki's eyes narrowed, and she let his question hang for a few minutes. She shook the wrinkles out of her skirt and slid into it, before marching back around the foot of the bed to his side. Charlie hunched forward and watched her approach. When she reached him, she leaned down. Her green eyes glared just inches from his face. "Listen, you thought all this sounded peachy-keen a month ago. Especially if I took care of everything, and you didn't have to get your fucking aristocratic hands dirty. You didn't want to know any of the details. Remember?"

"Yes, I remember," Charlie reluctantly agreed and looked away from her. Vicki pressed him. "If you want to take this thing over, be my guest. Otherwise, stop whining. You sound just like your chicken-shit father."

Charlie quickly turned his head to again meet Vicki's eyes. "What the hell does my father have to do with any of this?"

"Nothing, really," Vicki said casually, "except all this second-guessing sounds exactly like him."

Charlie's fists tightened under the sheet. "I am not my father."

Vicki kept at it. "Well, you're not your grandfather either. No wonder they nicknamed you Charlie. They knew you'd never be another Marcus."

"Shut up!" he screamed. His face reddened, and he fell back onto the pillows piled up against the headboard.

Neither of them said anything, and Charlie used the silence to collect his thoughts. No one in the world could infuriate him like Vicki could. Incensed as he was, however, he had to admit she was right. He was second-guessing himself, and it was getting him nowhere. He did need to be more like his grandfather. Marcus Randolph had never looked back.

So Charlie took a deep breath and turned to Vicki, who still stood beside the bed. "I'm sorry for giving you the third degree. Like I said, it's been a long few days. I don't really want to know who you've paid off or with how much. You just handle all that stuff like we originally planned."

Vicki patted him on the cheek. "That's my boy," she said mockingly before walking back across the room.

Charlie continued leaning back against the pillows and eyed

Vicki as she ran a brush through her hair. *God, how can something that beautiful be so much trouble?* After giving her the moment to savor her little victory, he sat forward again. "But I do have a question regarding something else."

Vicki glanced over at him. "Oh yeah? What is that?"

"I want to know what Dave Malone was doing in that grain elevator this morning."

Expecting his inquiry to bring on another of Vicki's tirades, Charlie was surprised by her reaction. She visibly flinched and stopped brushing her hair. "Hey, we didn't know that body was in there."

Charlie let out a short laugh. "Well, Christ, I hope not. I was talking about that idiot ripping the place apart while we were singing our preservation tune to the press and politicos. Malone, of all people, should have been miles away from there."

"Okay, okay, he shouldn't have been in there," Vicki answered defensively. "But how was I to know that your goddamn cousin would show up? That door was closed."

Charlie wasn't distracted by Vicki's mention of Emma. "So why was Malone in there?" he demanded.

"As I told the cops, Dave was filling in that hole—"

Charlie cut her off, as he reached down to the end of the bed to grab his robe. "Hey, don't feed me that bullshit you gave the cops. I happen to know you a lot better than they do." He got out of bed and tied his robe around him.

Vicki stuck by her story. She reached down to slip on her shoes and calmly said, "Believe what you want. But what I told the cops is true." She looked at her watch and then back over to Charlie standing at the bedside. "You have any more questions for me?"

He knew it was pointless to pursue the matter any further and just shook his head.

"Good. Because I have to fly if I want to catch the last Spin class at the club."

"What the hell is a Spin class?"

"God, where have you been? It's a group workout thing on high-tech stationary bikes. An hour of sweat and staring straight ahead at somebody else's rear end. Hopefully, it's a view worth the time."

"Sounds appealing," Charlie said skeptically. Mindless exercise classes weren't his style. He played games like hockey and squash to stay in shape.

Vicki grabbed her suit jacket from the back of the chair. She turned back to him when she reached the bedroom door. "You want me to come back later?"

"No, why don't you go back to your place. I'm going to take a steam shower and crash early."

"Whatever. I'll see you at the office tomorrow."

A few moments later, Charlie heard the front door close behind her.

Charlie laughed, as he walked into the bath off the bedroom. *Spin class. She really was incredible.* But after turning on the steam jets in the tiled shower stall, his smile disappeared.

Vicki scared the hell out of him. And for the hundredth time since Friday night, he kicked himself for not firing her when she first brought up the arson idea a month ago. *God, how could I be so shortsighted? So greedy? Even if we see that alleged two million dollars in savings, it was hardly worth risking the Company.*

He sat down on the edge of the whirlpool tub watching the shower fill with steam. *If the Company survives this, she has to go. Maybe in a few months when things settle down. But in the meantime, no more sex. That part of our relationship ends right now.* Somehow, that last resolution made him feel better. He stood up, opened the shower door, and stepped into the fogged enclosure.

MONDAY

Emma rolled out of bed just before eight after a night of tossing and turning, haunted by images of the mystery skeleton and, much to her surprise, by the possibility that after all these years, Matthew Kelly had finally reappeared.

She had originally planned to catch up on some billing before dropping the carriage house drawings off at the contractor's office at ten-thirty. But after her fitful night, she decided to take that time to do a little research on Kelly's disappearance. Maybe finding a few more details on the whole matter would help ward off further insomnia tonight. She showered, threw on a corduroy skirt and sweater, and was out the door just moments later.

She stopped in the small coffee shop on the first floor of her building, where she bought a muffin and a twelve-ounce cafe latte from a multi-pierced and earnest young man. Outside, it was a glorious spring morning, but chilly. It took her only ten minutes to walk the three blocks over to Nicollet Mall, the premier retail corridor of the city, and then south two blocks to the Minneapolis Public Library.

By the time she arrived at the library, the coffee and the crisp air had succeeded in clearing her head after the sleepless night. The doors were already open, but most of the other morning patrons were street people looking for a warm place to hole up until the day warmed. Emma was the only information seeker at the Periodical Desk.

After checking out two well-used microfiche cassettes, she made her way over to the readers, sat down, and loaded the machine. She scrolled through the *Minneapolis Tribune* for April of 1937. She squinted to read the blurry type rolling up on the screen until she spotted the headline: "Labor Leader, Kelly, Missing."

She stopped the film. The date was April 22. Underneath the headline in smaller print she saw: "Industrialist Wm. Randolph Held For Questioning." She perused the accompanying story, which was short on detail, probably because of the lateness of the events the night before.

"Matthew Kelly met with Will Randolph last night at Mr. Randolph's house on Hidden Lake. Mr. Kelly's driver, Thomas Lindgren, heard gunshots during the meeting and left to call the police. Mr. Randolph claimed to be asleep when the police arrived . . . Mr. Kelly was missing, but the police found his briefcase in Mr. Randolph's pantry . . . Mr. Randolph was being held for questioning."

Looking for more comprehensive coverage, Emma turned the reel forward towards April 23. But before she could get through *Sports* for April 22, her cell phone rang. The man who had just sat down at the next microfiche reader sneered at her as she reached into her backpack to retrieve her phone.

"Hello," she whispered.

It was Serg. "Where are you?"

"At the Library doing a little research." She glanced at her watch and saw that it was already nine-thirty. "But I'll be in my car in thirty minutes. Can I call you back then?"

"No problem. I'm in my office."

Emma returned to the microfiche. She found a special edition of the paper for the afternoon of April 22. It was devoted almost entirely to Kelly's disappearance and Will's arrest; not surprisingly, this was big news. She continued scrolling forward and saw that the story continued to be front-page news for weeks. She was certain there would be also be extensive coverage in the *Minneapolis Journal* and the other competing newspapers at the time. This additional research would have to wait for another day when she had more time.

Instead, she loaded the cassette for the last quarter of 1936 and scrolled forward to search for something else that her father had mentioned during his call last night. In the edition for November 6, 1936, Emma found a photograph of the groundbreaking for the new warehouse at the Randolph Mill. She hit the "Enlarge" button on the machine and studied the picture carefully.

Staring out at her from the photo was the face of her father as a young boy. Sam wore a handsome tweed suit and stood proudly in the front row between his father, Will Randolph, and his uncle, Marcus Randolph. Marcus's son, Peter, was barely distinguishable in the back row. Peter must have been close to twenty at the time.

This picture reminded Emma of a second photograph stored in the Coalition's file on the milling complex. It had been taken several months later at the warehouse dedication in June 1937. Her grandfather and father weren't in that second photo. By that time, Will was probably already in prison and Sam was on his way to Lake Salish with his grandmother.

Emma looked at her watch again. It was going on ten. No further sleuthing today; a paying client was waiting. Emma rewound the reel, returned the microfiche cassette to the desk, and walked the several blocks back to her building to pick up her car.

14

Emma emerged from the parking garage below her building, pulled into a vacant parking space along Third Avenue North, and called Serg back. "Hi, it's me. Sorry I had to hang up earlier, but cell phones are frowned upon in the public library."

"Believe me, I understand. Paloma complains about them all the time." Serg's wife, Paloma, was a librarian at the University. "I was just calling you with details for Saturday's dinner. How does seven sound?"

"Sounds great. Count me in." After accepting the invitation, Emma asked, "Anyone I don't want to see going to be there?"

Serg understood her question perfectly. "No, Joe is not invited. We can't afford what he's charging people to eat with him these days."

Emma laughed. "Ain't that the truth!" Then, trying to keep her voice casual, she asked, "So we learn anything about our mystery body yet?"

"I don't normally discuss open cases with civilians. But since you did find the old guy and help me out with those plans, I guess it's okay to indulge your morbid curiosity. The examiner's office has only had him for twenty-four hours, but they've given us some preliminary determinations. Laura Finney is the medical examiner on this one, and she says our guy is an adult Caucasian male, probably somewhere between thirty-five and forty-five when he died. And even though her staff is still sifting through that rubble looking for some missing bone pieces, she's begun reassembling the skeletal torso and is certain all the bones we do have belong to the same person."

Emma looked in her rearview mirror and saw a car waiting for her to vacate her idling space. She waved the driver past as she commented, "Pretty impressive, but that still doesn't tell us much about this guy."

"Well, we have more. We got lucky on some dental work on a couple of upper molars. Apparently it was an inexpensive, crude bridge technique not used much after the early 'thirties. And the Minnesota Historical Society also took a look at those boots first thing this morning. They were a popular low-cost brand worn by working-class men during the Depression years."

"Anyone know how old that tarp is?"

Serg chucked. "Good idea, Detective Randolph. But there's nothing really special about it. Heavy canvas tarps like that one were common all during the first half of the century before plastic replaced them in the 'sixties. But we did find discarded shards of the warehouse brick in all that debris down in the shaft with the skeleton."

Emma's pulse quickened. "So the guy has been in that shaft since it was closed up in 1937?"

"Looking more and more likely," answered Serg. "And given the boots and dental work, we're speculating that he was a blue-collar worker or was unemployed."

Emma tried to hide her excitement. "But can you know any of that for sure?"

Serg sighed. "Not at this point. That elevator has been empty for years, and the top few feet of that shaft could have been reopened at any time."

Emma considered mentioning Matthew Kelly, but she wasn't ready for another crack ridiculing her active imagination and decided not to bring it up. Instead she asked, "Any support for or against your sleeping drunk theory?"

"Not really. But there are signs of trauma to the right parietal bone of the skull—"

"Hey, come on Serg," Emma interrupted. "Biology 101 was more than twenty years ago."

Serg smiled. "Okay, I'll skip the technical jargon. The back of his skull was partially crushed on the upper right side. Laura thinks the guy took a pretty good shot to the head, either shortly before or shortly after he died."

Emma remembered the supposed cause of Kelly's death. "A gunshot?"

"No, bad choice of words. Laura has definitely ruled out a gunshot based on the condition of the bone fragments. It was some sort of blunt trauma, which then caused an intracranial hemorrhage." Serg paused. "Or brain bleed, as it is known by the scientifically challenged."

"Very funny," drawled Emma. "But it still could have been foul play, right?"

"It could have been. But we're not treating it that way yet. Remember, that shaft was also partially filled with old construction materials. Any of that stuff could have accidentally crushed someone when it was thrown in there."

"I suppose that's right," Emma agreed.

"But enough speculation. As I said earlier, all these findings are still preliminary. Laura still has a lot of torso work to do, but she promised me a final report by the end of the week. In the meantime, I'm having one of my staff go back through the missing-persons files from early 1937 forward for ten years or so."

Again, Emma resisted suggesting Kelly. She knew they would review his file as part of their routine search. "Well, it sounds like quite the mystery."

"Sure does," concurred Serg. "Listen, I have to run. Make it seven o'clock on Saturday. And casual, as always."

"Can I bring anything?"

"Some wine if you want to."

"Okay. I'll see you then." Emma slipped the phone back into her pack and eased out into traffic. She took a few deep breaths to switch her mental gears back to the 1990s, contractors, and carriage houses.

Peter awakened shortly before six in the morning with a splitting headache. Morning doves cooed noisily outside the library windows, and he rapped on the glass to quiet them. Having spent the night on the library couch where he had passed out ten hours earlier, he was still dressed in the casual slacks and wool crew neck sweater he had worn the previous day.

At some point during the evening, Berta must have removed his shoes and covered him with a blanket because both had been piled on the floor in front of the couch when he awoke. He swallowed a couple of aspirin from the bottle in his desk drawer and stumbled upstairs to his bedroom for a few more hours of sleep.

He woke again at ten and still had quite the hangover. He showered, which calmed the pounding in his head somewhat, and put on fresh clothes. Then he dragged himself downstairs to the kitchen.

He found the morning *Star Tribune* on the center island and scanned through an article on the fire in the front section. There was no mention of the body. He turned to the *Metro* section and found a short four-paragraph article about the discovery in the grain elevator. Not much was added to what he had learned on television the night before. The police didn't seem overly interested in the body, but that gave him little comfort.

Peter found a message from Berta on the counter. It said that she was at the hair salon, and that Charlie had returned his call the evening before. He tried Charlie at his office, but once again he had to leave a message. Peter knew he should try to eat something while he waited for Charlie's call. He fixed himself some scrambled eggs and toast and carried the plate into the library to eat at his desk. He looked over at the bar and thought of mixing a weak Bloody Mary, but he resisted.

Charlie got back to him just before noon. "Early night last night, Dad?" inquired Charlie, knowing full well his father had passed out.

Peter perpetuated the game he'd played for years. "Yes, I've had a bit of a bug this week."

"I would have called earlier, but yesterday was a crazy day. The fire was bad enough, but then that body showed up. I assume you heard that on the news?"

"Yes, I did. Do the police have any ideas on who it is?" Peter was trying to sound only casually interested.

"No. But whoever he is, he's been there a long time. Just a pile of bones at this point. Probably some drunk who had his last drink a long time ago."

"Probably," Peter said, wishing that was true.

"Anyway, Dad, I have been getting your messages—the good and the bad. I accept your apology of yesterday morning, and it's probably best if we just forget your call on Saturday night."

Peter had expected Charlie to blast him for his incessant calls and unfounded allegations. When Charlie so readily brushed them aside, Peter's suspicions about the origins of the fire were more or less confirmed. But he just answered, "Okay. Fine by me."

"Was that all you wanted yesterday?" Charlie asked. "You seemed pretty anxious to get hold of me." Charlie knew how fixated Peter could get when he drank, but he had been even more persistent in his efforts yesterday than usual.

"Something has come up, and I need to talk to you right away. But not on the phone. Can you come up here?"

"Is it an emergency?" Before Peter could answer, Charlie added, "Is Mom sick or something?"

Peter hesitated a moment. "Well, no. It's not that kind of emergency. But it's really important."

Having lived through many of Peter's crises, Charlie had learned long ago not to rearrange his life to cater to Peter's needs. "I'm sorry, Dad, but it's going to have to wait until Wednesday. Our East Coast distributors are in town for meetings. We'll be going late tonight, and I'm hosting a party for all of them at the townhouse tomorrow night."

"I was hoping you could come up sooner."

"Dad, it's going to have to wait."

"Okay," Peter agreed reluctantly. "What time can you be here on Wednesday?"

"We plan to wrap up by five to allow everyone to catch their evening planes. So I could probably be there by six-thirty."

"I guess that works. I'll arrange for a light dinner." Peter had gone back and forth on including Vicki in this meeting with his son, but had finally decided he did want her there. She hadn't returned any of his calls from the previous day, and Peter wanted to know what she was up to. "Oh, and why don't you ask Vicki Stephens if she can join us? It might be good if she were here."

Charlie was more than a little surprised by Vicki's inclusion. "Vicki Stephens? You're inviting Vicki Stephens to your house for dinner? I thought she was no longer welcome at Chez Randolph."

"I want her to hear what I have to say," answered Peter with considerable gravity in his voice.

"This isn't about the fire again, is it?"

"No. As we agreed, nothing more on that."

"What is it then?" This invitation to Vicki was definitely sparking Charlie's interest.

"We'll talk on Wednesday night."

Charlie knew he was late for a lunch appointment, so he curbed his curiosity. "Okay. We'll see you Wednesday night."

Peter walked out into the hall towards the kitchen and back entry. The breakfast had calmed his stomach, and he decided to go out for a short stroll along the lake. *Wednesday will be difficult, but now Charlie will know the whole story,* he thought, as he reached for a light jacket and opened the door.

Emma's afternoon had been exhausting. The job manager for the carriage house cornered her at the contractor's office when she went in to drop off the plans, and she couldn't escape until two-thirty. By the time she had grabbed a late lunch and stopped back at her condo to change from her skirt and loafers into old clothes and work boots, she was a half-hour late for her Coalition meeting at the mill.

She had joined the inspection already under way. The Coalition's three engineers and two restoration contractors each had a considerable amount of experience in preservation, including previous work on the mill buildings. They knew each other well, with a familiarity that encouraged a friendly and open exchange of ideas—and also made for a long inspection. They crawled into every corner of the damaged buildings; the tour itself took more than three hours. At the end of the ordeal, Emma was tired and dirty.

After leaving the site, the six of them had retired to a dingy nearby bar to continue their discussion. The combined odor of stale beer and cigarettes was even worse than the dank smell of the charred mill. But the group's preliminary structural assessment had been mildly encouraging. They agreed that although the structural damage to the mill and warehouse was extensive, the buildings were not beyond repair. Ultimately, the outcome would be determined, as always, by money—whose, and how much?

Emma arrived home well after dark. She immediately stripped off her filthy clothes and jumped into the shower. Once clean, she played back her phone messages and was pleased to learn that Marv Flood had space on a charter flight to Ely the following morning. She could keep Athena Bergen happy and herself solvent.

Next Emma surveyed the mostly empty cupboards and refrigerator. She settled on granola for dinner. *Pitiful*, she thought as she carried the bowl into the living room. *Life is out of control.* She was more than competent at whipping up Asian stir-fries and hearty soups, but she hadn't been to the food co-op or farmers' market for weeks. As she sat and ate the uninspired meal of rolled oats and skim milk, she vowed to make more time for cooking and a healthier diet.

She drank up the last of the milk from her cereal bowl, carried it into the kitchen, and called Sam to let him know she was coming up tomorrow. He had been waiting to hear from her. "Anything?" he asked hopefully.

Of course, Emma knew exactly what he was asking about. "A few interesting developments." She told him of the dental work and boots that linked the skeleton to the mid-1930s. Then she launched into Serg's report on the crushed skull.

Sam cut her off. "It's him! I knew you were right."

"Dad, please calm down, and let me continue." Emma sat down on a stool and leaned on the breakfast bar.

"Okay, no more interruptions."

Knowing this probably wouldn't be the case, Emma returned to Serg's account of the crushed skull. Sure enough, just as she was beginning to explain that the trauma could have been accidental, Sam jumped in again. "So he was murdered!"

Emma imagined her father pacing off laps around his dining table, as he often did while talking on the phone. "Not necessarily, Dad," she said. "Serg is keeping an open mind until the medical examiner's office finishes its work. In the meantime, he's going to have someone go back through the old missing-persons files."

"Did you tell him to take a look at the Kelly file?"

"No. I thought the suggestion would sound too self-serving. Besides, it won't take them long to get to Kelly's case."

"I suppose not," conceded Sam, although it was clear from his voice that he would have done otherwise.

Emma was reluctant to let Sam know she was checking up on his painful recollections, so she didn't report on her morning trip to the library. Instead, she shifted to her main reason for calling. "Dad, are you going to be around tomorrow?"

"Sure. Why?"

"Marv Flood is letting me hitch a ride up on a morning charter. I need to get out to Athena's property. Needless to say, she was not too pleased with my non-profit priorities this past weekend."

Sam laughed. "Two visits in one week. I feel honored."

"Can I borrow the pickup to drive over to her property?"

"It's yours to use. I've been using the sedan now that the weather is nice. What time will you be getting in?"

Emma glanced at a note she had written earlier after listening to Marv Flood's phone message. "Between ten and ten-fifteen. Can you pick me up?"

"No problem," answered Sam. "When are you heading back?"

"Not until Wednesday morning. I should be finished at Athena's property by five. So let's plan on a good dinner back at your house tomorrow night. Maybe Ginny and the gang could join us."

"I don't think Jack and the kids will be able to make it. They've got a soccer tournament or some darn thing going on."

"Well, maybe Ginny could join us," suggested Emma.

"I'll give her a call. And I'll see you tomorrow."

Emma rinsed out her cereal bowl and then trudged up the stairs to her office. She wanted to draft a short report to Judge Flynn, who had issued the Coalition's restraining order against Randolph Foods, outlining her suspicions of the Company's violations in the grain elevator at the mill. The fire damage would only contribute to the Company's demolition argument; and Emma didn't want Vicki's version of events in the elevator to become the official story without at least offering a protest.

She typed a few lines, but was too tired to focus on her computer screen. She went back downstairs and made herself a cup of chamomile tea. She sat in the living room and stared out the windows, watching the waning quarter-moon rise over the river. It was after eleven when she drained her cup and stumbled into bed. Despite the calming tea and her exhaustion from the day's activities, she again slept fitfully.

TUESDAY

Emma awoke early to another clear, brisk day. She popped out of bed, slipped on her running clothes, and took a short half-hour run along the river and over to Nicollet Island. Returning to her condo, she ate some breakfast—the same granola as at dinner the night before—and packed for her short trip up to Lake Salish. She drove out to Flying Cloud Airport in Eden Prairie shortly after eight o'clock toting her overnight duffel, camera equipment, and sketch-pad. She was already wearing a roomy turtle-neck and fleece pullover with her jeans and hiking boots, the better to start out for Athena's property as soon as possible after landing.

The charter plane carried four early season fishermen back in the small cabin. Emma sat up in the cockpit with Marv Flood in the empty co-pilot's seat. Through the lightly scattered clouds, she monitored the flight's progress out of the densely built metro area, up across the still unplanted fields of the mid-state farms, to the lakes and pine forests of Northern Minnesota. After passing over the city of Virginia on the Iron Range, Emma recognized Bear

Island Lake and then spotted the squat tower and single runway of the Ely airport. The plane landed and taxied up to the terminal building.

Emma was surprised to see Ginny waiting for her as she descended the steps from the plane to the tarmac. Her sister was dressed in faded climbing pants and a sweatshirt that read "Ely Timberwolves." She waved Emma through the fence enclosure and gave her a light hug.

Emma noticed that Ginny had cut her wavy auburn-brown hair since they had last seen each other. The shoulder-length hair of the past twenty years, which Ginny usually wore pulled back into a pony-tail, was now several inches shorter. Emma ran a hand over her older sister's head.

"We look like twins," Ginny said, parroting what the two of them had been told repeatedly when they were little girls, even though Emma had darker eyes and sharper, more striking facial features than those of her sister.

"Where's Dad?" asked Emma after the two of them had hopped in the front seat of Ginny's ancient International Scout and were driving north on Highway 1 towards Ely.

"Oh, Darryl Soderberg called him this morning. They're over at Olson Bay trying to impress Mrs. Polsky." Olson Bay was on the northwestern shore of Shagawa Lake, just outside of town.

"Janet Polsky?"

Ginny nodded. "Her husband died last year, and Dad and Darryl help her out from time to time. This morning they're supervising the spring installation of her dock. Bobby Horner and some of his buddies from the high school football team will do the actual work. But Darryl and Dad will be right there making certain it's done right."

Emma chuckled. "More like getting in the way, I'm sure."

Ginny nodded. "You've got that right. Mrs. Polsky is more than capable of handling this little project herself. But she seems to encourage their attentions. Freshly baked cookies will probably figure into the morning somewhere."

Just as they entered the city limits of Ely, Ginny turned left at Pattison Street. "No rhubarb muffins from the Moose?" asked Emma, referring to the Chocolate Moose, her favorite local restaurant. It was several blocks away up on Sheridan Street, the extension of Highway 169 running through Ely and the center of canoe outfitting and tourism in the small town.

"No, I'm on a tight schedule. I have to be back at school for third-hour gym class." She drove west by the high school football stadium and then turned south on Highway 21, heading away from town.

"Well, I guess trying to help Mrs. Polsky keeps Dad and Darryl off the streets."

Ginny saw her opening. "And is probably more constructive than this little Kelly fantasy you've got him going on."

Shit, Dad's told her, Emma thought. Trying to avoid an argument with Ginny, she calmly admitted, "Okay, I know it was a mistake to mention the Kelly possibility to him."

But Ginny wasn't going to let it go at that. She turned and looked at Emma. "You're darn right it was a mistake. Now he's completely obsessed with this guy being Matthew Kelly. He's talked so little about Grandfather Will and all this over the years, I'm a little surprised it still riles him up so much—"

Emma lost her calm. "It was his father, for Christ's sake."

Ginny's eyes were back on the road. "Well, I know, but it was a long time ago."

"So what? It only changed Dad's whole life. I'm sure he's thought of it a lot over the years."

"Well, whether he did or not, he's certainly thinking about it now. And I don't think that's so great. I don't want him getting totally absorbed by this thing. It'll do nothing but frustrate him," explained Ginny using her best big-sister and parental tone of voice.

"Okay, how exactly do we stop him from wanting to believe his father wasn't a murderer?" asked Emma sarcastically, her usual responsive tone to her sister's lecturing.

"Oh, you know what I'm getting at. I just don't want you encouraging him with false hopes. This may be a big exciting mystery to you, but it's a lot more to him. You said that just a minute ago."

"Hey, I'm not encouraging him. I'm just telling him what I find out." Then she took a deep breath and said to Ginny, "Listen, I don't want him disappointed by this either. But he's my father, too, and he's an adult, and I'm not going to hide the truth from him when he asks."

"All I ask is that you tread carefully."

"Request noted," Emma answered and said no more.

After driving past several miles of scattered businesses and houses along the highway, Ginny slowed the Scout and turned left onto a black-topped road. Two towering white pines, one on each side of the pavement fifty yards in from the intersection, graced the road's entry back into the forest. Much to Emma's relief, with the change of scenery, Ginny also changed the subject. "Who's this client with the property up here?"

"Potential client," Emma corrected. "A woman named Athena Bergen. Gretchen introduced us. They're on some foundation board together."

"How's Gretch doing?" Ginny only knew her cousin through Emma.

"Working too hard, just like the rest of us. But she and Taylor are really enjoying the new house over in Wisconsin."

"What does she think of your ongoing battle with her brother over that mill?"

"Don't know," answered Emma truthfully. "It hasn't ever come up."

Emma had first met Gretchen Randolph ten years ago through their mutual involvement in Friends of the Boundary Waters, an environmental group committed to the preservation of the canoe wilderness in Northern Minnesota. On first impression, Gretchen appeared the direct opposite of her second cousin; she was tall and fair, and her demeanor was thoughtful and steady. But the friendship between the two women formed quickly after the discovery of their shared love of outdoor adventure.

Emma always marveled at Gretchen's dedication to medicine. With her sizable trust fund and patrician breeding, she easily could have spent her life clad in tennis togs and swapping lunch-hostess responsibilities with her childhood girlfriends at their various exclusive clubs. Instead, Gretchen poured herself into her medical practice and was more likely to do her recreating wearing Lycra bike shorts and a polypropylene T-shirt.

On their countless canoe, bike, and ski trips over the years, the subject of Randolph Foods had come up occasionally—but only because Gretchen's husband, Taylor Alexander, worked there. These conversations were very casual, however, and the two cousins had never really discussed their respective family connections to the Company. This remained the case even when the preservation battle had heated up, and Charlie and Emma started publicly butting heads.

"So Gretch introduced you to this Athena Bergen?"

"Right. Ms. Bergen has decided she needs a little getaway in the north woods. Something modest, I've been told. Absolutely nothing more than four thousand square feet."

Ginny laughed. "She sounds like a piece of work."

"That she is. Her husband was Dr. Erik Bergen, a bigwig at the University of Minnesota heart institute until he died two years ago.

Athena was wife number three. She has turned the spending of his fortune into a full-time job."

"So you still don't know if you have the job?"

"Not definitely, but it's looking good. Athena likes the fact that Gretchen has only just recently discovered me, and that I'm a woman. She apparently prides herself on being a patron to unknown female artisan types. Besides, she really liked the photos of Gretch and Taylor's farmhouse. She's meeting me over in Wisconsin later this week to walk through the place. Hopefully, by then I'll have knocked out a few preliminary-concept drawings for her to review. If that meeting goes well, it's a go. If not, Athena pays me for my time." Then Emma truthfully added, "But I hope it's a go. I could use the work over the next few months."

"Well, if you do get the job, you'll be assaulted by all the contractors up here."

Emma glimpsed Lake Salish glimmering though the trees. "It won't be pleasant picking among them. We grew up with most of those guys."

"The good ones will become obvious once you've reviewed their work. But I'm not going to point you in any particular direction. I have to live up here," Ginny said, as she left the county road and started down a short, steep driveway to the lake

"Hard to blame you for not wanting to play favorites. But I am your sister! I hope you'll at least steer me away from the real turkeys."

The Scout reached the bottom of the hill. Ginny pulled into a small turn-around area at the back of Sam's house and pointed the vehicle back uphill. Coming to a stop, she said, "The door is open so you can drop your things off before you head out. The keys should be in the pickup, as usual."

'You coming by later?" asked Emma.

"I'll check back, but I probably won't be able to stay much past six-thirty or so. Jack and the kids will be home by eight, and I promised them a proper home-cooked meal for a change."

"Well, it's just thirty miles over to Athena's property. I should be able to make it back here by five-thirty." With that, Emma hopped out of the Scout. After grabbing her things from the back seat, she stuck her head back in the passenger-side window. "I'll see you then. Thanks for the lift." She waved as Ginny pulled away, and then she went into the house to leave her duffel and throw together a bag lunch.

18

Emma arrived at Athena's property on Lake Vermilion just before noon. It was on a heavily wooded peninsula jutting out towards Ely Island in the middle of the lake. She spent the next couple of hours walking and photographing the eight hundred feet of shoreline and the ten forested acres running gently uphill from the water. There was an obvious house site with direct southern exposure down near a small creek that entered the lake at the western edge of the acreage. Several patches of newly blooming marsh marigolds marked the spot, and Emma noted that on the property survey Athena had given her.

Emma took a break at two o'clock to eat the lunch she had packed at Sam's. Then she spent the latter part of the afternoon down near the water, taking more photos and making rough sketches to explore potential elevations and sight lines. Shortly after five, she loaded up the pickup for the return trip back to Lake Salish. Satisfied with her day's work, she was looking forward to a relaxing evening with her father.

Sam and Ginny heard the approaching pickup and were outside the back door to greet Emma as she emerged from the cab of the truck. Sam, dressed in worn corduroys and a faded red-plaid Pendleton shirt, announced, "Just in time to slice vegetables for Sam's famous marinara sauce. And we have homemade ginger cookies for dessert."

Emma grinned at Ginny as she pulled her camera equipment out of the pickup. "Oh, and where did those come from?"

"Didn't Ginny tell you? Darryl and I were over helping Janet Polsky with her dock today. We like to be neighborly. Besides, she promised us the cookies."

"They must be the world's best ginger cookies for you and Darryl to commit to a morning of physical labor."

"Well, we did have some help with the physical labor part," Sam admitted. "A few of the high school boys showed up. But they were in a hurry to get going. So Darryl and I ended up with most of the cookies."

Ginny winked at Emma. "And that's probably fair. I bet you two did most of the work."

As they strolled into the house, Sam asked Emma, "Any more news on the skeleton in the elevator?"

Emma was tired and hungry from dragging her equipment around all afternoon. "Dad, we just talked last night, and I've been up here most of the day. Why would I know anything more?"

"Oh, right," Sam acknowledged, quietly.

Emma knew she had hurt his feelings. "Let me get cleaned up, and then I'll be right back."

Emma stashed her gear in her old bedroom and washed her hands and face in the bathroom. Then she changed out of her jeans and boots into some old running tights and tennis shoes she kept in the closet and rejoined Ginny and Sam in the kitchen. Sam was opening a bottle of Chianti and directing Ginny on the cutting of the tomatoes, parsley, and garlic piled up in front of her on the counter between the kitchen and dining area.

Emma pulled off the green pullover she'd been wearing all day. She walked around the counter and draped it over the closest of the ladder-back chairs surrounding the dining table. As she pulled a stool up to the counter across from Ginny to join the vegetable brigade, she kidded Sam about his supervisory role in the dicing effort. "Reminiscent of Mrs. Polsky's dock, I see."

Sam raised his eyebrows, pretending not to understand Emma's chiding. Then he offered each of his daughters a glass of wine. Ginny declined hers. "None for me. I still have dinner to make when I get home."

"I guess I'll have to drink it, then," Sam said, as he began to collect the vegetables and throw them into a saucepan. After stirring his secret assortment of spices into the sauce, he turned to Emma. "Everything went okay today?"

"Absolutely. That is one beautiful piece of property. I hope I get to work on the house. It would be good exposure for me up here."

"Well, she'd be crazy not to use you," offered Sam.

"Thank you for the completely unbiased endorsement," Emma said, "And, Dad, I am sorry I snapped at you earlier. I really don't know anything more abut that skeleton than what I told you last night. It could be a few days before I hear anything more from Serg."

"Okay, then, enough said about dead bodies," Ginny strongly suggested in that same parental tone of voice she had used with Emma that morning.

God, now she's bossing Dad around, Emma thought. *We're adults, and we can talk about whatever we want.* So she forged ahead with her father. "You know, Ginny and I were saying this morning that you've never said much about all that stuff with your father—"

"And I thought that was just fine. It all happened so long ago," interrupted Ginny, glaring at Emma.

Feeling Ginny's disapproving eyes, Emma continued. "If you're up to it, I'd like to hear some of your recollections of 'long ago,' as Ginny puts it."

"What do you want to hear?" asked Sam.

Emma sat forward on her stool. "The circumstances surrounding Kelly's disappearance. And the investigation and the trial. Anything you can remember."

"Oh, I don't know. Ginny's probably right. It does seem kind of pointless to dredge it all up again." Sam took a sip of his wine. "Especially since I spent most of the last forty or so years trying to protect you girls from all of it."

"Okay, Em, you heard him," said Ginny. "Let it drop."

Still ignoring Ginny, Emma assured Sam, "Whatever you want to do, Dad. But if you ever want to talk, I'll listen."

Sam thought for a moment as he took a sip of wine. "Oh, hell, you're both full-grown women. Maybe it's time you heard the whole story."

Ginny frowned at Emma and then grabbed her sweatshirt from the coat rack. "I'm going to pass. You know me, not much interested in the past. I've got too much going on in the present."

Both Sam and Emma tried to hide smiles. Ginny saw that and knew she was laying it on a bit thick. Finally, she smiled too. "Besides, Jack and the kids will be home before I know it. I'll leave you two to marinara and mystery."

Emma slid off her stool, stepped around the counter, and made her way over to a cupboard next to the stove. She pulled out a large pot for cooking the pasta. "Right. We can't forget dinner. Let's get that on the table first, and then we can talk."

Ginny stopped on her way out the door. "Em, what time do you leave tomorrow?"

"Marv's got a spot for me on the early flight tomorrow morning," answered Emma, as she stood at the sink filling the pot.

"Want me to drop you off before school?"

Sam cut in. "Don't worry. I'll drive her over."
Emma breathed a sigh of relief. *No more lectures this trip.*

19

Dinner was ready twenty minutes later. Two plates of steaming linguini, topped with tomato sauce, sat on the table, along with a loaf of garlic bread. Sam, in his customary chair with his back to the corner of windows that looked out over the lake, started in on his pasta and said nothing. Emma, sitting in the chair to his right, knew he was collecting his thoughts. She used her spoon to twirl the noodles onto her fork, and she also ate without speaking. She was tempted to put on some music to ease the quiet, but she resisted the urge and stayed seated.

After a long few minutes, Sam pushed back his plate with only half of his dinner eaten. He stood up and walked slowly back into the kitchen. Crossing to the coat rack next to the back door, he pulled off it an old brown cardigan sweater that Ellen had knitted for him years ago.

"You want me to build a fire?" asked Emma.

Sam shook his head. "No, this will be fine." He put on the

sweater and made his way back to the dining area, stopping at the counter to pour himself a second glass of wine. He seldom had more than one glass with dinner, and Emma noticed the refill. She continued eating her dinner, waiting until Sam was ready to begin.

Sam sat back down at the table. "You'll have to remember I was only ten at the time. And Grandma Kate really shielded me from the worst of it. I only got bits and pieces during the trial by eavesdropping whenever I could and by digging out a few discarded newspapers. I learned most of the story much later from Kate and several conversations with my father."

Emma nodded, encouraging him to continue.

Sam shifted in his chair. "Since Kelly was a labor leader, I guess it all goes back to the labor troubles in the mid-'thirties. That's why Will asked him up to his house that night. To try to settle the strike that—"

"Wait a minute, Dad," Emma interrupted, between bites of bread. "Back up."

"What do you mean?"

"Before you get to Will and Matthew Kelly, give me some background on the Company and the family. You know, the good guys and the bad guys."

Sam chuckled. "You really want me to go back through the whole cast of characters?"

"Yes, please. Start at the beginning."

"You want the sanitized version or the truth?"

"I want the truth. The dirt and everything." Emma rose from the table and went over to the stove to add another spoonful of marinara sauce onto her linguini. On her way back, she grabbed the bottle of Chianti and brought it over to the table. The evening sun had fallen to just above the tree line across the lake. It shone brightly through the windows behind Sam and cast blinding rays across Emma's chair. Wanting to watch the sunset, Emma decided not to close the curtains and instead sat back down in another chair on the other side of her father. She reached across the table for her plate and silverware.

"Let's see. Where should I begin?" Sam sipped at his wine. "I guess with Henry Randolph, my grandfather. You know, he's the one who founded the Company back in the late 1800s. It was called Randolph Milling during those early years. His first wife was the daughter of one of his original business partners. As far as I know, it was sort of an arranged marriage. She and their second child died in childbirth just a few years after they were married. Their first child, Marcus, was three at the time. Henry was extremely busy getting the Company off the ground, so he pretty much turned over the raising of Marcus to nurses and tutors."

Emma held a forkful of pasta over her plate. "That's how he met Kate, isn't it?"

"Yes. As you know, your great-grandmother was from Northern Minnesota, not too far from here. She moved to Minneapolis after high school to attend the U of M and was hired as a tutor for Marcus, who was then eight. She and Henry fell for each other immediately, even though Kate was nearly twenty years his junior. Kate always told me that Henry promised her the world, but that there was only one thing she ever really asked him for."

"What was that?"

"This property. She asked him to buy Lake Salish shortly after they were married. The shore was just raw land at that point, but they cleared this site and built the cabin shortly afterwards. At first it was just a small kitchen, this space—" Sam pointed to the dining area,"—a screen porch where the living room is now, and the front bedroom. No bathroom, just an outhouse out back."

"Did they spend much time up here?" Emma asked, trying to help her father recall the family history.

"Quite a bit during the summers; but the fireplace was the only heat, so they shut the place up in the fall."

While spearing her last few noodles with her fork, Emma

asked, "Henry was able to leave his work?"

"Apparently. From what I understand, Henry was less consumed by the business after their marriage. He still worked hard, but he loved spending time with Kate and took much more of an interest in Marcus. In fact, he often took Marcus to work with him even though he was still just a young boy at the time."

"What was the mighty Marcus Randolph like as a kid?"

Emma's questions were triggering a flood of memories for Sam, and conversations with his grandmother and father came flowing back. He thought for a minute before he answered. "Well, Kate remembered him as being kind of strange. As far as she could tell, the only thing he ever really enjoyed was going to the office with Henry. And there, he quickly tired of the attempts by the secretaries to entertain him and just sat quietly in the corner of his father's office, observing the ebb and flow of the business. After just a couple of years, he started to articulate his own ideas concerning the Company. And by the time he was just a young teenager, he had already developed strong anti-labor feelings after watching his father and other owners break a city-wide strike in the mills."

"When was that?"

"Early years of the century. Maybe 1902 or 1903. The workers had all sorts of radical demands—like an eight-hour workday and overtime pay," Sam commented sarcastically. "Anyway, young Marcus was enthralled by the events. And when labor was defeated, he delighted in the outcome. Grandma Kate found his fascination somewhat appalling. But Henry was only amused by his son's precocious behavior."

Emma pushed her cleared plate to the side. Then she grabbed her fleece top from the back of the chair beside her. She pulled it on and reached for the bottle of wine and poured herself another glass. "So had Will arrived by that time?" She remembered only that her grandfather had been born in the early part of the century.

Sam relaxed back in his chair, now more comfortable in his

storyteller role than he had been at first. "Will was born in 1902, three years after Henry and Kate were married. Marcus was thirteen when his half-brother was born. Kate was only twenty-three." Sam chuckled ruefully. "And that's when the happy family really started to show some cracks."

"How so?"

"From the beginning, Marcus resented Will. A second son meant possible competition for future control of the Company. And his behavior towards his step-mother changed considerably after Will's arrival. He constantly accused Kate of promoting Will's favor with Henry."

"Was that true?"

Sam shook his head. "I doubt it. But you know, it didn't matter. Marcus eventually poisoned the household. He bullied Will until Kate finally did have to step in to protect the boy. And even Henry's relationship with his jealous older son eventually soured somewhat. Nevertheless, Marcus joined his father at the office after his formal schooling ended. That must have been when he was eighteen because he never went to college. He proved himself to be a valuable addition to the Company and quickly became Henry's right-hand man. Kate said, though, that Marcus was sometimes more ruthless than his father would have preferred."

Sam turned in his chair to look out the windows at the sun dropping below the treetops. Then he buttoned up his sweater before continuing. "But Will was the golden boy and Marcus knew it. Apparently, everything came easily for Will. Athletics, grades, friends. You name it. By seventeen, he was an accomplished and self-assured young man, and Marcus hated him more than ever. But then Will announced he planned to study medicine at the University of Wisconsin. Marcus, who was nearly thirty at the time, was relieved by Will's departure for Madison and by his apparent lack of interest in the family business. That is, until he heard of Will's shift in studies."

"Didn't he end up in chemistry or something?" Emma asked.

"It was agri-chemistry, or whatever it was called in those days. He did a lot of work with some professor who was researching grain combinations for specialty flours. Not exactly music to his big brother's ears."

Sam reached for his wine and sat in thought, trying to decide where next to take his story. After a moment, he put his glass back down on the table, without having taken a sip. "Anyway, Will finished his studies with a master's degree and returned to Minneapolis and the Company in the mid-'twenties. He was a product of the times. He was full of new ideas, which was good because the milling industry was going through a lot of traumatic changes."

"What kind of changes?"

"Well, the biggest change was that Minneapolis was no longer the undisputed flour capital of the country. More competitive railroad rates shifted a lot of business to Kansas City. And then hardier wheat strains opened up wheat farming in Canada; and Buffalo, as an international port, could avoid the American railroads altogether. The population was also much more prosperous, so the country's diet diversified and people used less bulk flour. And," Sam added, "there were also shifts in the Minnesota political climate."

"You mean with the rise of the Farmer–Labor Party?"

Sam laughed. "Gee, an architect with a sense of our state's political history. You must have had very good high school history teachers."

Sam had taught Minnesota history to Ely's ninth graders for thirty years, and his alumni included his two daughters. Emma rolled her eyes at her father's feigned self-aggrandizement, but she was relieved to hear him joking.

"The Farmer–Labor Party didn't really hit its stride until the late 'twenties and early 'thirties, but one of its forerunners, the Non–Partisan League, had been very active in North Dakota and Minnesota during the during the years shortly before the country's entry into World War I. Their efforts led to state inspection of the mills and even some federal regulation of the bulk grain trade." Sam shifted in his chair and asked, "Am I boring you? Is this the kind of stuff you wanted to hear?"

"It's absolutely what I want to hear. Please, go on."

"Okay. So anyway, both Henry and Marcus were overwhelmed by the pace of these changes, and Will returned home from college to find them in something of a panic. In contrast, Will was excited by all the opportunities presented by these changes. He helped to refocus the Company and, within the next several years, his suggestions helped to launch many new products for Randolph Milling."

"Like what?"

"They introduced some pre-mixed and pre-packaged cereal products," Sam recalled from his father's accounts. "And, because fewer women were making their own bread, the Company started selling five- and ten-pound bags of flour for home use instead of the old fifty- and hundred-pound bags. They also developed specialty flours for doughnuts, pastry, and different kinds of bread, and marketed them to the many new commercial bakeries."

The eerie evening call of a loon sounded out on the lake. Both Emma and Sam looked out the windows. The sun had set and only its red afterglow was visible below the horizon. Emma reached behind her and switched on the lamp sitting atop the buffet to the right of the windows. Then she turned back to Sam. "Isn't Marcus usually credited with those innovations?"

Sam took a sip of his wine before answering. "Well, in all fairness, Marcus did do his part. He was a shrewd businessman. And as much as he resented Will, he did recognize the value of Will's ideas and effectively implemented many of them. Besides, Will was perfectly willing to let him take the credit. What excited Will were the ideas themselves, not the recognition."

Emma nodded in understanding as she propped her feet up on the center pedestal leg of the table.

Sam returned to his chronology. "Their joining of efforts was a huge relief for Henry. For Marcus as well. He had found a niche for Will, one that still allowed Marcus to keep effective control over the day-to-day running of the company. Marcus actually encouraged his father to agree to Will's idea for a new research facility. They renovated the top floor of the old mill, and that's where Will and his team of researchers puttered with their new product ideas during the late 'twenties."

Sam leaned back from the table and folded his arms across his chest. He sighed before continuing. "Then, in 1930, Henry suffered a fatal heart attack. He was in his early seventies, but his death still seemed sudden because he had never been sick a day in his life up until then."

"Was that hard for Kate? She would have been only fifty or so."

"I'm sure it was hard. But being so much younger than Henry, she always expected to be widowed at a relatively young age." Then Sam added, "Besides, she had plenty of things to keep her busy. My mother was usually down with her tuberculosis and needed help with me. Kate spent a lot of time with Peter, too, even though she was only his step-grandmother. Marcus and his socialite wife never had much time for the kid."

"How old was Peter then?"

Sam thought for a moment. "Oh, he would have been twelve or thirteen, I guess."

"So, what was the deal with the Company after Henry died?"

"Henry's probate instructions split the ownership of the Company evenly between Marcus and Will. According to Kate, Marcus wasn't happy about the arrangement. But he learned to live with it. This neutrality continued throughout the early 'thirties until the Depression really set in."

"That's when the labor troubles heated up again, isn't it?"

"Yes, and things were especially hot in Minneapolis. The Depression threw a lot of people out of work and tempers were short. In fact, martial law was declared in 1934 after people on both sides were killed in riots during some teamsters' organizing strikes. But the situation in the milling industry managed to stay relatively calm until early 1936. That's when the local representatives of the AFL began organizing in the mills."

"AFL?" queried Emma.

"American Federation of Labor."

Emma nodded. "As in AFL/CIO. I get it now."

Sam paused and then said, "Actually, let me back up a few years because a lot had already changed in the mills by 1936. During the 'twenties and early 'thirties, the Farmer–Labor Party and the Democratic Party had won many concessions for Minnesota laborers. That was before the two parties merged into the DFL Party of today. The mill owners had grudgingly conceded the eight-hour workday, the six-day week, and some pension and medical benefits."

Emma smiled at the familiar tone of one of Sam's history lessons. "So what was the issue in 1936?"

"The strikers now wanted the right to unionize—with collective bargaining and open union elections. But Marcus and most of the other employers were vehemently opposed to labor organizations. They believed that only the employer could successfully balance the rights and needs of the company and its employees. So they dug in on the issue of union recognition. By fall of that year, picketing had forced the shutdown of several mills, including two of Randolph's facilities. Intervention by the governor finally reopened the mills near the end of 1936. But the contentious negotiations over union recognition dragged on."

"And where was Will on all this?" Emma asked.

"Pretty much in direct opposition to Marcus and the other mill owners. Will thought that the owners' paternalism was out-dated, as well as insincere. But he had his own ulterior motives, as well. Earlier in the year, he had convinced Marcus to undertake a major expansion of their packaged food line to put the Company in a more competitive position when the economy improved. That fall, the Company had started building the new warehouse that would contain the packaging operation, and the construction was being slowed by the labor unrest."

"So I imagine that Will's support of the union didn't make him any too popular with his older brother."

Sam smiled. "That's an understatement. Will's backing of the strikers' demands was a major embarrassment for Marcus, and the brothers' relationship was pretty stormy during this time."

"Hold on for a sec," requested Emma. She picked up her dinner plate. "You done?" she asked Sam.

"Yes, go ahead and take it. I wasn't as hungry as I thought."

Emma carried the dishes to the sink in the kitchen. Looking back over the counter, she saw Sam sitting alone in the dim light at the table. She was reminded of many evenings when she and Ginny were teenagers. They would clean up in the kitchen after dinner while Sam and Ellen sat at the table lingering over their coffee and rehashing the events of their days. Sam smoked a pipe then, and Emma could still conjure up the smell of his chicory-scented tobacco, even though he had given up the habit years ago.

20

While Emma was up, she made a quick trip to the bathroom. Upon her return, she grabbed the cookie tin on the counter and brought it over to the table. "Time for dessert."

Sam had continued mulling over the past while Emma was up. But once she returned, he interrupted his reflections. "I have ice cream to go with the cookies. Vanilla and chocolate-strawberry swirl. And I've got some of that herbal tea that you like. It's up in the cupboard behind the coffee."

Emma licked her lips. "Chocolate-strawberry swirl and chamomile tea. Can't get much better than that. Any ice cream for you?"

"Bring me two scoops of vanilla."

Emma walked over to the refrigerator and opened the upper freezer compartment. "Order's on its way."

After pulling out the two cartons of ice cream, Emma put on water for her tea. Then she looked back across the counter at Sam.

"Go on, Dad. You were telling how the union negotiations were dragging on after the mills reopened."

Sam picked up his story where he had left off a few minutes earlier. "Well, so that was the situation in late April of 1937 when Will set up his secret meeting with Kelly. Matthew Kelly was a mill worker who had been tapped by the AFL as one of the local union organizers."

"Did he work for Randolph?"

"No, for one of the other mills. At least he had until he was hurt on the job, and one of his arms had to be amputated just above the elbow. In those days, that kind of disability cost you your job. Shortly after his firing, Kelly joined the union effort and went to work organizing for the AFL. And he developed a strong following from among the workers, even though he was apparently one of the few reasonable voices within the movement."

Sam's eyes followed Emma, as she returned the ice cream cartons to the freezer. Then he continued. "Will believed that the formal union negotiations were being sabotaged by extremists on both sides, so he invited Kelly up to our house on Hidden Lake to discuss the recognition issue in an informal setting." Sam paused. "You know the house, don't you?"

Emma returned to the table with the two bowls of ice cream. "Yes, I do. It's just down the lakeshore from that Gothic monstrosity that Peter lives in."

"Hard to believe that Will and Marcus built those two places within a year or two of each other, isn't it? They're as different from one another as were the brothers."

Emma stood looking at her father. "Will's house is still considered one of the most beautiful examples of Prairie Style homes in the upper Midwest. It was one of the last houses that Elmslie designed in this area."

"Who?"

"Ah, now it's time for me to be the expert," said Emma, grinning. "The architect, George Grant Elmslie. He was a contemporary of Frank Lloyd Wright. In fact, early in their careers they worked together for Louis Sullivan down in Chicago. Elmslie eventually moved to Minneapolis to partner with another noted Prairie School architect, William Purcell, and they went on to design many notable houses in the upper Midwest up through the early 'twenties."

Emma handed Sam his dessert. "In fact, the Minneapolis Art Institute owns one of them and gives tours through it. We'll put it on the agenda for your next visit." She put her own bowl down on the table, before concluding her tutorial. "But Elmslie worked on Will's house after the Purcell partnership had dissolved. I think he was back living in Chicago at that time."

"Have you ever been inside Will's house?"

Emma nodded, as she sat back down. "I toured it at an open house when it was on the market several years back. It was gorgeous, especially the quarter-sawn woodwork and the terra-cotta detailing. Must have been quite the place to grow up in."

"From what I remember, it was. Although most of my real growing up occurred right here." Sam motioned to the walls around them.

Emma smiled at her father. "And here is a gorgeous place in its own right."

Emma dug into her ice cream, and Sam continued. "Anyway, what happened during that meeting is the great mystery."

"That's the night Kelly disappeared?"

"Right. The meeting was set for seven. A guy named Thomas Lindgren drove Kelly up to Will's, because there was no automatic transmission in those days, and Kelly couldn't drive with just the one arm. Lindgren waited in the car while Kelly and Will talked in Will's study inside the house. According to Will, the meeting went well and, although nothing concrete was agreed to, the two men were civil and made plans to meet again. Will always insisted that Kelly had left the house before eight o'clock and that Lindgren had then driven him away."

Emma swallowed the first spoonful of her ice cream. "I take it Lindgren told a different story."

"Vastly different." Sam paused for a spoonful of his dessert. "Lindgren claimed he sat in his car outside the house until nine-thirty when he heard gunshots from the direction of the house. Lindgren said that when Kelly didn't appear after several minutes, he panicked and left. He called the police from an all-night diner somewhere out on the main road. The police arrived at the house a few minutes before ten o'clock. They found Will in his study, where everything appeared normal. You know, no sign of struggle or anything. Will gave them permission to make a quick search of the house, and they found Kelly's briefcase in the kitchen pantry."

Emma continued leading her father. "What did Will say about the gunshots?"

"He had also heard them around nine-thirty. He said they came from the woods out towards the road. Will attributed them to nighttime coon hunters."

"Hunters around Hidden Lake?"

Sam laughed. "Probably hard to believe today, but that area was still undeveloped in the mid-1930s. Marcus and Will were practically the only people living on the lake."

"So what did Will do after hearing the shots?"

"He remembered going into the kitchen to make some coffee; that's when he noticed Kelly's briefcase on the front hall bench. He picked it up and carried it into the kitchen with him. Then he put it in the pantry near Mrs. Terry's shopping bags, reminding himself to instruct her to return it to Kelly on her next trip into town."

"Mrs. Terry?"

"She was our housekeeper."

"Where was she through all this?"

"There at the property. And her story could have supported

Will's. But for some reason, it seemed more consistent with Lindgren's."

"What was her story?"

"Mrs. Terry testified that she let Kelly in shortly after seven. After serving a light dinner and drinks to the two men in Will's study, she retired to her quarters in the cottage behind the main house at seven-thirty. She didn't remember seeing Kelly's briefcase in the front hall before she left the main house. Asleep before nine, she was awakened a half-hour later by the same gunshots Will and Lindgren had heard. She wasn't certain from which direction they came, but wasn't terribly concerned because she was used to hearing gunfire in the area. She then drifted back to sleep, but was reawakened by the police knocking on her door shortly after they arrived at the main house."

"You're right. Not much help from the faithful servant." Emma leaned forward in her chair to eat another spoonful of her colorful ice cream. "And where were you and your mother?"

"Down in Rochester at the Mayo Clinic with Grandma Kate for one of Mother's medical appointments. We didn't get back until late the following day."

"So what happened after the cops found the briefcase and talked to Mrs. Terry?"

Sam finished eating his first scoop of ice cream while he collected his thoughts. "The police took Will down to the station for questioning and ended up holding him overnight. That was initially more for his protection than anything else because, by midnight, word had already spread among the mill workers that Kelly was missing after a secret meeting with Will Randolph. When Kelly didn't show up by morning, the cops returned to Hidden Lake with a warrant and tore apart Will's property looking for any sign of the labor leader. They found a blood smear on the outside handrail leading down from the front door. It was Type B Positive, which was Kelly's blood type. And of course, Kelly's fingerprints from his one hand were also on the railing, and in the hall and study inside the house."

"But those prints are consistent with Will's story," Emma protested.

"I know, but the proximity of those outside prints to the blood smear was strongly suggestive. Remember, police work in those days was pretty crude."

"How did they match Kelly's prints?" asked Emma.

"I don't know, maybe military records." Sam continued with his account. "There was no other sign of Kelly anywhere on the property. But still, Will's detention at the station turned into a formal arrest."

The kettle started to whistle, and Emma got up to pour her tea water. On her way to the stove, she asked, "Do you remember if the police ever looked for Kelly's body anywhere other than at Will's?"

"They might have, but after they found that blood smear, Will became their prime suspect and most of the focus was on his place." Sam turned to Emma who was standing at the sink while her tea steeped. "With only thirty minutes between Lindgren hearing the gunshots and the cops arriving at ten, they figured there wouldn't have been enough time for Will to dump Kelly's body anywhere else. When he didn't show up in the woods, they assumed he was in Hidden Lake. The ice had gone out just a couple of weeks earlier."

"Did they drag the lake?"

"They dragged for weeks, both before and after the trial. But that's not an exact science, especially if the body has been weighted down in some way."

Emma thought for a moment. "How about the family? Do you know if they ever undertook an expanded search for Kelly?"

"Actually, they did. Marcus hired several private investigators to help out. But I don't remember Kate or Will saying exactly where they looked." Then Sam asked, "Why are you so interested in whether there was a broader search?"

"Oh, I was wondering if anyone checked the warehouse construction site down on the river. If they did, that tunnel surely would have been searched. And that would probably wipe out the slim possibility that our mystery skeleton is Kelly."

"Seems unlikely that Marcus would have searched his own mill property. But like I said, I don't know where the police looked. Would there be some kind of record of their investigation?"

"There might be something in the old police file about the scope of the official search. I think those records are available to the public. I can check when I get back."

"Only if it's not a big deal. I really don't want you wasting a lot of time on my account."

Emma carried her mug over to the table and settled back into her chair. "Dad, it won't be just on your account. I want to know too. You keep forgetting I initiated this whole Matthew Kelly thing. Now, let's get back to 1937."

Sam ate a few more spoonfuls of his vanilla ice cream. During the short lull in their conversation, they could hear a chorus of croaking frogs from outside in the darkness. Then Sam started up again. "They held Will for a couple of days, but then the prosecutor had to either charge him or let him go. Feeling the pressure of public sentiment, but also being without a body, he settled on a charge of first-degree manslaughter. With no corpse and the weak evidence, Will's attorney took a gamble and pushed for a quick trial."

Sam inhaled deeply. "And, as it turned out, that was a big mistake. He would have been better off trying to delay the trial until the whole city cooled off a bit. The trial started in mid-May and was over quickly. Took only two weeks. Will was convicted and sentenced two days later. Twenty-five years with possibility for parole only after fifteen."

Emma sat up in her chair. "But he was a leader in the community. And a labor supporter. How could they convict someone like him on such flimsy evidence?"

"Those were weird times," Sam reminded her. "Tempers were short, and just his being a mill owner was damning enough for most people. The union organizers really kept the heat on. They turned Kelly into a martyr and promised chaos if Will was exonerated. The police and prosecutor knew that. So did the jury. And look at that harsh sentence. Even the judge must have felt the political pressures of the day."

"But where was the motive? What did Will have to gain by killing Kelly?" Emma felt like she was cross-examining her father.

"That question never came up. The prosecutor didn't need premeditation to prove manslaughter. He just speculated that Will lost his temper over something or other, and Kelly ended up dead."

"Didn't Will's attorney appeal the conviction?"

"Yes, of course he did. But he was shot down on all counts."

"What was brother Marcus doing through all this?"

"Well, he hired those private investigators. And then once the trial had begun, he stood by his younger brother in a big way. He gave interviews, wrote letters, and used whatever other influence he had at his disposal to rant and rave about malicious prosecution and the like. Kate thought his support was counterproductive, though, especially since part of Will's defense was to distinguish himself from the other mill owners. She asked Marcus to back off, but he refused. Marcus was just being Marcus. Never one to fade into the background. Anyway, it all worked out just fine for him."

"You mean, with Will out of the way?"

"Yes. Not only was Will sent to prison, but he also forfeited his interest in the Company. Old Henry always worried that Marcus might cross the lines of legality, so he put a provision in his will that directed forfeiture of Company ownership if Marcus were ever convicted of a felony. For the appearance of equal treatment, he put in a similar provision concerning Will's activities. After Will's conviction, Marcus sued for enforcement of the provision."

Emma shook her head in disbelief. "What a bastard!"

Sam laughed halfheartedly. "Oh, Marcus claimed he was just honoring Henry's wishes, and he wept when he told Kate that he regretted having to do so. She didn't believe him for a second. Anyway, he won, and we were left with nothing. The whole thing was too much for Mother. The tuberculosis worsened with all the stress, and she died just a couple of months after Dad went to prison. I was practically an orphan."

"Except for Grandma Kate, right?"

Sam nodded. "That's when she moved us to Lake Salish. She had some money saved and figured it would go a lot further up here. And she was anxious to escape all the publicity down in the Cities. So we moved north and rebuilt our lives up here. Starting with the cabin. During that first summer, we insulated the walls and roof and closed in the porch to make the living room. And added the bathroom. The two back bedrooms didn't come until a couple of years later when I got too old to sleep with Kate in the front bedroom. I started school in the fall, and Kate went about renewing most of her old girlhood friendships. Before long, we were just regular Ely folks, and everyone around here pretty much forgot about our prior lives."

Emma's eyes narrowed, as she asked, "And meanwhile back in Minneapolis, Randolph Milling was thriving, right?"

"Eventually. The warehouse, with the packaging operation, opened in June. And the mill owners finally recognized the union later in the summer of 1937. The Company went through a couple of lean years at the tail-end of the Depression, but it was in a perfect position by the time World War II broke out to secure huge defense contracts for K-rations and other dehydrated foods. Then came the booming post-war years, and the Company broke into the packaged-food market that was expanding rapidly throughout the 'fifties and 'sixties. Again, Marcus was brilliant and ruthless in his realization of Will's vision."

Sam finished the last little bit of ice cream in his bowl before concluding. "Will died in 1951, shortly after your sister was born. He was eligible for parole the next year, but his heart just gave out. Too many years of prison food, cigarettes, and limited fresh air and exercise. He died before he was fifty. What a waste."

"He always sounded like such a fascinating man—"

"He was," Sam commented before she could finish. "Kate and I made the long trip down to Stillwater on the first Saturday of every month to visit him. I loved those visits. When he wasn't working in the prison laundry, Will spent most of his time reading everything he could get his hands on. Scientific journals, historical treatises, novels, drama—you name it. And so he always had something new to tell me. Those tutorials were like pieces of him that I'd take home with me at the end of each visit." He looked down at his hands folded on the table for a moment. Then he stood up and carried his now-empty bowl to the sink. He turned back to Emma. "So that's the whole story."

"Well, I know that wasn't easy for you. I appreciate it."

Sam looked at his watch. "Oh my, it's after eleven. No wonder I'm exhausted. I can't keep up with you younger folks."

"You should be exhausted. You did all the talking." Emma rose from her chair and joined Sam in the kitchen. She gave her father a light kiss on the cheek. "Go on to bed, and I'll clean up."

"I won't argue with that. What time is your flight in the morning?"

"It's at eight-fifteen. We should leave here by seven-fifteen. I know you'll be up first. So give me a call once the coffee is made."

Emma watched her father head down the hall towards his bedroom. Her eyes filled with tears as she imagined him at the age of ten, following the proceedings of his father's trial from discarded newspapers and overheard conversations.

WEDNESDAY

It was a cold, gray morning. Upon arriving at the airport, Emma discovered that her flight was delayed due to the low cloud cover. Sam parked the car and came inside to wait with her. Emma left him sitting in the small reception area and went to check her phone messages.

The first call was from Gretchen Randolph—Emma's second cousin, good friend, and rambling answering-machine user:

"Hi, Em. Calling to wish you good luck with Athena on Thursday. Don't panic if she's late. She's usually running at least an hour behind. And if you're planning on serving her something to drink, she prefers a dry white. And, hey, why don't you just spend the night out there? After an evening with Athena, you'll need some relaxation in the Wisconsin countryside. I'm working into the wee hours on Thursday, but give me a call first thing Friday morning to let me know how things went. Should be up by seven. Talk to you then."

Thursday night at the farm sounds great, Emma thought. *I'll head back to Minneapolis first thing Friday morning.*

There were several other calls, all from clients, including Athena Bergen. She was confirming their meeting for Thursday evening. She also sounded a little peeved that Emma had forgotten to call her last night after the Lake Vermillion site visit. Emma kicked herself for not calling. Athena was a prima donna, like many of Emma's better clients who needed constant attention and pampering.

On her way back over to Sam, Emma stopped at the coffeemaker to talk with Marv and to pick up the front section of the outstate edition of the *St. Paul Pioneer Press*. When she returned to her seat, her father reached for the paper without saying anything. In fact, he had been unusually quiet ever since leaving the house.

"Not very talkative this morning," probed Emma. "The weather have you in a bad mood?"

Sam put down the paper. "No, I've just been thinking."

Emma sensed something was really bothering him. "Nothing wrong with that. Want to tell me about what?"

"Not really. But I know I should."

"This sounds serious. Are you sick or something?" Emma asked with a note of slight panic in her voice.

"Simmer down, I'm fine. Strong as an ox. But there is something I've been meaning to tell you. That is, until you got caught up in this Randolph mill issue. And then I didn't want to put any pressure on you."

"Dad, what is it?"

"More family history." Sighing, he added, "Actually, I wish it was history."

"Enough with the riddles. Just tell me."

"Okay, here goes." Sam took a deep breath. "Grandma Kate never owned Lake Salish and neither do I."

Emma gasped. "What?"

"Henry only left Kate a life estate, with the land and improvements reverting to the Company when she died. Of course, he never anticipated that it would become her primary residence and only real asset."

"This is incredible!" Emma couldn't quite believe what her father had just told her. She couldn't imagine her life without Lake Salish. Or Sam's either. "How'd you stay there all these years? And all the additions to the house and everything?"

"Peter told me I could stay. And he agreed to compensate me for any improvements I made."

"When? How did that happen?"

"It just happened. He called the day after Kate's funeral, and I remembered that she was effectively his grandmother, too. He hadn't actually seen her since the trial, but I knew he always sent her birthday and Christmas cards. It sounded like he'd been drinking. He went on and on saying how wonderful she was. And near the end of the conversation, he brought up the life estate and told me not to worry. So I mostly haven't. I kept the place up and paid the taxes just like I was the owner."

"Did Mom know about this?"

"Of course she did. We never had any secrets."

"God, why didn't Peter just sign Lake Salish over to you, if he was so concerned about honoring Kate's memory?"

"I think he always meant to. But he kind of lost track of things there for a while. Years slipped by and, before he knew it, Charlie took over, and Peter lost the right to convey any of the Company's assets, including Lake Salish."

"Pretty easy to lose track of things when you're drunk by noon most days," Emma commented angrily.

"Don't be so hard on Peter. He did call me several months after he retired, when things had calmed down a little for him. Told me he'd taken the Lake Salish file from the Company offices, and that the whole thing would remain our secret." Then he added, "You know, he's not really a bad guy. Which has always been his problem. Only the bad guys win in that family."

Emma shifted in her seat. "Well, his drinking doesn't help."

"Have you ever wondered why he drinks?" Sam posed rhetorically.

Emma returned the conversation to Lake Salish. "And you never thought to pursue this with Charlie?"

"Remember, he doesn't know anything about this. Besides, what is there to pursue? Charlie's a businessman. He would want me to pay fair-market value. Where am I going to get the kind of money it takes to buy a private lake surrounded by two hundred acres of prime timber?" Sam paused for a moment. "And that was before all this mill stuff."

Emma stiffened in her chair. "What does the old mill have to do with any of this?

"Well, Peter called me a few months ago."

"When?"

"Right after you got that judge to stop their demolition."

"Did he know anything about that when he called?"

"Of course. He mentioned it when he called."

"Shit! Those assholes. Why didn't you tell me?" Emma was furious.

"Calm down. And watch your language. Let me finish."

"Okay, okay." Taking a sip of her coffee, Emma tried to relax and let Sam continue.

"Peter asked if I ever told you about Lake Salish. I said no. He said he figured as much, given how hard you were coming at Charlie on the mill. Anyway, he thought maybe he could broker a deal—you convince the Coalition to withdraw the lawsuit, and Charlie considers a below-market conveyance of Lake Salish."

Unbelievable, thought Emma. "So, what happened? Obviously, you decided not to tell me."

"Right. I told Peter I couldn't put you in that position. Besides, his whole scheme counted on you selling out. And I knew you'd never do that. Your work and your integrity mean too much to you."

"God, that would have been awful," Emma admitted, reaching for Sam's hand. "Lake Salish is who we are. The thought of you anywhere else is unimaginable." Then she pulled back from her father. "So was Peter surprised by your refusal to drag me into this whole thing?"

"Not really. I think he kind of expected my response."

"Don't you think Peter will eventually tell Charlie anyway?"

Sam shook his head. "I don't know. I get the sense that Peter isn't Charlie's biggest fan."

"Well, it's just hard for me to believe that Charlie won't find out somehow. He is the president of the Company!"

Sam laughed. "Well, I'm not planning on telling him."

Emma smiled at her father. "Me, neither." Then she got serious again. "But, if Charlie does find out, he'll hardly be able to wait to serve up his revenge." Emma took a sip of her lukewarm coffee and moaned. "Oh, Dad, I'm sorry. This mill dispute has really mucked up your life."

Sam shrugged. "Not really. As I just told you, the problems with Lake Salish date back to long before your run-in with the Company."

Marv Flood came over and interrupted their conversation to tell them they'd been cleared for takeoff in five minutes. He then led his three paying passengers across the tarmac to the waiting plane. Looking at her watch, Emma turned to Sam. "Why'd you tell me all this now?"

"I don't know. After last night, I decided you should have the whole story. And, as you said, Charlie will probably find out someday. I didn't want you to first hear all this from him."

"I'm glad you told me."

"Besides, Ginny and Jack have been talking about finally building that dream home on the east bay of the lake. I'm going to have to tell them the score before they get too far along. They should be looking for other land."

Emma's heart sank. She and Ginny had been designing their respective houses on Lake Salish since they were kids. They even had the locations picked out—Ginny on the east bay and Emma up near the flat rocks overlooking Sam's house. She thought of all the times Sam had heard them dream, and she was swept by the realization of how much it must have hurt him to know none of it was possible.

"Oh, Dad—"

"Go on. Get on the plane." Sam picked up her duffel and accompanied Emma over to the door at the end of the reception area.

"Dad, I love you." Emma hugged Sam. As she started to leave, she turned and added, "We'll figure something out." She exited through the door and hurried across the tarmac in the rain towards the waiting plane. The dreary day weighed heavily on her as she mounted the stairs and ducked inside.

22

The plane touched down on the runway in Eden Prairie shortly before ten-thirty. One of the charter passengers had wanted to sit in the co-pilot's seat, so Emma had been relegated to the back cabin where she made small talk with the other two fishermen during their trip south. They had hit an occasional rough spot due to the weather, which turned out to be only slightly better in the Twin Cities.

Once back at her downtown condo, Emma unpacked her things. Then, after leaving a message for Gretchen accepting her offer to stay out at the farm Thursday night, she called Athena Bergen with her long-overdue report on the site visit. Athena was glad to finally hear from Emma and seemed placated by the promise of at least a few preliminary sketches at their meeting on Thursday evening.

Emma knew she should start working on Athena's project, but she was eager to review the old police file on the Kelly disappearance. She had been truthful with Sam last night when she offered to continue her research. This thing had taken hold of her, and her father's revelation of this morning, that Charlie controlled Lake Salish, made her appreciate even more how those long-ago events affected her family still today.

Convincing herself that any work for Athena would be premature until she had photographs of the site, she decided to make a quick trip to City Hall while the film she had shot out at Athena's property yesterday was being processed. She gulped down some yogurt for lunch and was back out the door just after noon.

She walked over to First Avenue North and strolled up several blocks of restaurants and bars to Fifth Street, where she cut over through the lower portion of the city's financial district to City Hall. On the way, she stopped at a one-hour photo mart in the lobby of an office tower to drop off the film.

Even though it was cool and drizzly, the walk lifted Emma's spirits slightly. She continued mulling over an idea that had occurred to her on the plane back from Ely. Could she possibly ask Gretchen to intercede with Charlie to convince him to transfer Lake Salish to Sam, in spite of Sam's limited resources and her own preservation efforts on the riverfront? It would be a terrible abuse of her friendship with her second cousin, but might be necessary.

Fifteen minutes later and still undecided about approaching Gretchen, she arrived at Police Records in Room 31 on the first floor of City Hall. The Kelly file was stored in the basement, and it took twenty minutes for Ms. Kron, the primly dressed archivist identified by the polished nameplate at the counter, to finish up with two other people and have a chance to retrieve it. The file was stored in two oversized accordion envelopes covered with dust, and Ms. Kron was not happy to have to lug them upstairs.

As soon as Emma had picked up the envelopes and started for one of the viewing desks on the far side of the room, the clerk made an announcement to the room. "I have a doctor's appointment at three-thirty, and my assistant is at computer training all week. So we will be closing early this afternoon, at three o'clock sharp."

Then she looked sternly at Emma. "And in case you're wondering, we do not check out files overnight. If you don't finish up before three, you'll have to come back tomorrow."

"Understood," Emma responded and wandered over to her table.

She began her research by shuffling through the reams of police notes in the file. Sam's recollection of the case had been fairly accurate. The only damning pieces of evidence against Will were, in fact, the blood-stained handrail, the stashed briefcase, and the gunshots heard by Thomas Lindgren and the awakened Mrs. Terry. *Incredibly circumstantial*, Emma thought.

As she read through the housekeeper's account of the gunshots, Emma recalled the remains discovered in the grain elevator. Serg had told her there were no gunshot wounds to the head. *But what about the rest of the body?* She would have to wait until Serg heard the final results from the medical examiner.

An hour later, Emma reached for the second over-sized envelope. It accidentally fell to the floor and landed with a loud thud. Ms. Kron, still unhappy about having to drag the dusty file up from the basement, shot her a disapproving look. Emma grimaced towards the clerk and tried to look apologetic. Then she retrieved the envelope from the floor and opened it. In the interest of time, she skipped over most of the investigation into Will's motive and focused on the unsuccessful search for Kelly's body.

After finding the briefcase and the blood smear, the police had spent days ripping apart Will's house and his surrounding property. They had dragged the lake and scoured every inch of the grounds with bloodhounds and search parties. But, just as Sam had speculated last night, the police never widened their search for Matthew Kelly.

Emma pushed back her chair. *But weren't the cops right?* There wasn't enough time for the body to be anywhere else. Certainly not in the shaft if the abandoned tunnel down at the mill property. Even today with much better roads, it would be impossible to get back into downtown, dump the body, and get back to Hidden Lake within thirty minutes. Broader search or not, the skeleton couldn't be Kelly.

Suddenly, Emma remembered Sam's protestation of earlier in the week. *You know, he didn't do it.* She'd just fallen into the same trap as the cops had sixty years ago—the trap of assuming Will's guilt. *What if she assumed instead that someone else killed Kelly?* Then the body could have been disposed of anywhere, including the unsearched tunnel in the old grain elevator.

God, if only that was Matthew Kelly in the floor of the grain elevator. Unconsciously, she finished her thought aloud. "Will would be in the clear." She sheepishly looked up and caught another glare from Ms. Kron. Quietly pulling in her chair, she took a notebook out of her backpack and made some notes.

A short while later, Ms. Kron came around the counter and made her way over to Emma's table. "It's two-fifty-five. We're closing in five minutes." Then she brusquely reminded Emma, "And remember, none of this material may leave this room."

Emma took a deep breath, trying to hide her contempt for the woman. "I was just finishing up." She packed up the file and returned it to the counter.

As she came out of Police Records, Emma spotted Vince Shillings, the arson investigator assigned to the riverfront fire. He was standing outside the men's bathroom just a few feet down the hall. Emma was hoping he wouldn't notice her, but she had no such luck.

Vince approached her. "Well, if it isn't Miss Randolph. What brings you to Police Records?"

"None of your business," Emma snapped. "I was just leaving." With that, she turned from him and marched away. "Damn," she muttered, descending the steps to the street. *That man gives me the creeps. I wish he hadn't seen me snooping around in there. Oh well, not much I can do regarding that now.*

Emma started walking back towards the photo shop and home. The weather had cleared, and patches of blue sky reflected in the pools of rainwater scattered on the sidewalk. But her mind was still muddled. She tried to refocus on Athena's project, but couldn't stop puzzling over the possible identity of the mystery corpse and Sam's devastating news of earlier that morning. Still completely lost in her thoughts several blocks later, she stepped off a curb without looking. A bicycle messenger swerved to avoid plowing into her.

"Hey, lady, watch where you're going," the young woman screamed back at Emma before racing off up the street.

Emma bristled. Even at the ripe old age of thirty-nine, she hated being called "lady."

God, I have to let this thing go, she thought. It was all too crazy. Nothing she had found so far even remotely suggested that the corpse in the grain elevator could be Matthew Kelly. And whether she was humoring her father or herself, she was wasting a lot of time and not doing her dwindling bank account any favors. *It's only my preservation work and my paying clients from now on. No more distractions,* she vowed to herself.

"Well, maybe I'll just make it my business," Vince Shillings said aloud to himself immediately after Emma was out of earshot. After using the men's room, he detoured into Police Records and asked to see the file Emma had been reviewing.

"Sorry, sir, but you know I can't do that. The rules say that all information requests by citizens are confidential," the ever-bureaucratic Ms. Kron responded.

"Not if that request might be critical to an ongoing police investigation."

Ms. Kron wasn't easily intimidated. "Well, then, bring me a

search warrant in the morning. I'm already closed for today."

Vince knew that any further efforts to bully Ms. Kron would be pointless. "Fine, you're the boss. I'll be in touch tomorrow if I'm still looking for that information."

As Vince left the office, he made a mental note to call Vicki Stephens from his home that night. Vicki had warned him of Emma's likely suspicions concerning the fire and had asked to be notified if Emma contacted him to discuss the investigation. This chance meeting wasn't exactly "contact," but Emma Randolph's activities were clearly of interest to Vicki Stephens. And Vince Shillings never passed up an opportunity to further ingratiate himself with one of his special clients.

23

Emma returned to her condo after picking up her photos. Walking home, she had remembered that she still needed to finish her report to Judge Flynn concerning the damage to the grain elevator floor. She went up to her office to get that out of the way before turning to Athena's work.

As she sat at her computer outlining her version of Sunday morning's events, she realized she had no idea how long Dave Malone had been working inside the elevator before she interrupted him, or how extensive his supposed clean-up work had been. She looked at her watch and saw that it was still before four. Maybe she could catch him at work; not that she expected much cooperation, but it couldn't hurt to try. She opened her drawer and pulled out the phonebook.

As Emma was looking up the number for Randolph Foods, the phone on her desk rang. She picked up the receiver. It was Taylor Alexander, the Company's chief financial officer, calling from his office. Even though Taylor was her good friend and client—and

145

Gretchen's husband—Emma was momentarily taken aback by the coincidence of his call. But she quickly regained her composure when she heard Taylor ask, "Hey, I heard you're driving over to the farm tomorrow."

"You heard correctly. I have a meeting with Athena Bergen tomorrow evening."

"When do you plan to go out there?"

"Between three-thirty and four before traffic gets too bad. Besides, I need time to commune with my creation before the big presentation."

"Would you be willing to make a short detour on your way out there?"

"Sure. What's up?"

"On our way back to town last weekend, Gretch and I picked up the landscape plans for the entry drive out at the farm. We've made a few changes, and I want to get the marked-up plans back to the nursery so they can get going on the work just as soon as the weather warms up. It's that place there on the right as soon as you exit from the freeway, Laducer Nursery."

"I know the place. And I'd be happy to stop."

"Thanks, Em. I've got that fishing trip with my nephews this weekend, but I can drop off the plans tomorrow afternoon before I pick the boys up. I should be able to make it to your place just before you leave. Does that work for you?"

"I'll wait for you. See you then."

Emma hesitated for a minute to mentally separate Taylor's call from her next one. Then she dialed the general number for Randolph Foods and asked for Dave Malone. Emma still didn't know exactly what she was going to say to him, but it didn't matter because after several minutes the receptionist returned and announced that Dave Malone was out sick for the day. Emma didn't leave a message.

As she disconnected the line, she grabbed the phonebook

again and looked up the home number for Dave Malone. Emma dialed the number as she jotted down his address.

After six or seven rings, a man finally answered. "Malone," he roared into the receiver.

There was a lot of noise in the background from what Emma thought sounded like construction power tools. Emma tried to sound friendly, yet businesslike at the same time. "Hello."

"Who the hell is this?"

Charming, thought Emma. She jumped right in. "We met briefly Sunday morning at the old Randolph Mill—"

"Are you from the newspaper? I already told you people everything I know."

"No, I'm not from the newspaper or TV or anything like that. I was there when you found the body. My name is Emma Randolph."

"Oh, yeah," he drawled, in what Emma thought might be a slightly friendlier tone. "I remember you." But then his hostile attitude returned. "And I got nothing to say to you, lady— except stay out of my business."

"Whatever," Emma stated calmly. Then, hoping to get a rise out of Dave Malone, she added, "I guess I'll just have to take my questions to your boss, Ms. Stephens."

The man laughed, which surprised Emma. "Go ahead. Take your questions to 'Ms.' Stephens. I'm sure you'll find her much more cooperative."

Emma heard the receiver slam on the other end of the line. *So much for my interrogation skills*, she mused.

Before returning to the report, she went downstairs to use the bathroom and continued thinking over her phone conversation with Malone. His flippant attitude regarding Vicki Stephens was surprising. It suggested a familiarity between them beyond what she would expect Vicki to have with a company custodial worker.

On her way back through the living room, she stopped dead in her tracks as she suddenly recalled Dave and Vicki's fractured conversation in the elevator on Sunday morning. In all the excitement surrounding the discovery of the skeleton, she had completely forgotten about it. The tone of that overheard exchange had also seemed very familiar.

Phrases came pouring back to her. *Doing your shit...about more money...the other night...* Then Emma muttered aloud, "Christ, he could have been talking about Friday—the night the fire started."

She ran upstairs and grabbed the piece of paper with his address written on it. She now wanted to know more about Mr. Malone. She would start by checking out where he lived. Just ten minutes later, she pulled her Subaru out of the garage. She made her way northwest for several blocks to the entrance ramp onto I–94. Once on the freeway, she drove towards Fridley, a tidy suburb of mostly blue-collar workers just north of the city.

24

It took her just fifteen minutes to reach Fridley on I–94, but then another quarter-hour to find Dave Malone's address. She finally stopped across the street from his modest bungalow. A brand new Ford pickup truck was parked in the carport, with the dealer plates and price information still proudly displayed. Three men were working on the house roof, ripping off old tarpaper, and several piles of new shingles were stacked on the driveway behind the new truck. A painting contractor's truck sat out at the curb in front of the house.

The new truck and home improvements certainly suggested more income than just a custodial salary. But maybe Dave Malone did more than janitorial jobs for Randolph. *Like arson,* thought Emma. *Or whatever other special job Vicki ordered him to do in that grain elevator on Sunday.* She doubted she would get a more detailed job description from Dave Malone by ringing his doorbell, so she drove on up the street.

Back on the freeway and crawling south in heavy rush-hour traffic, Emma calmed down and told herself that her arson theory was every bit as crazy as her obsession with Matthew Kelly. She was fabricating a whole conspiracy out of a few overheard conversation fragments, a new truck, and a few home improvements. And she probably was paranoid when it came to Vicki Stephens. Nevertheless, when she reached downtown, her arson suspicions were still nagging at her.

Emma considered trying to learn still more about Dave Malone. As she thought longer, however, she realized that the Randolph janitor probably wasn't the key to this puzzle. If Vicki was involved, she was calling the shots. But Emma knew almost nothing of Vicki—other than that she was smart, utterly ruthless, consumed by Randolph Foods, and probably sleeping with Charlie. Until now, that was all Emma had ever needed to know.

25

Charlie and Vicki were driving north on Highway 100 back into the city for their evening meeting at Peter's house on Hidden Lake. Late rush-hour traffic was only moderately heavy, but the glare of the evening sun was slowing their progress somewhat. They were coming directly from work, and both were still dressed in their tailored office attire—Vicki in a pale-green silk pants suit and Charlie in a subtly striped dark wool suit.

Consistent with his new resolve to end their personal relationship, Charlie had planned to drive up separately. But he flagged down Vicki in her Range Rover just after his car stalled out as he was leaving the executive garage. He spent the first ten minutes of the drive on the phone with the Jaguar dealer, arranging for an early morning tow and loaner. The car was his third Jag, so he knew the drill. They tended to be temperamental, like racehorses, as the dealer never failed to point out.

During the rest of the drive, Charlie kept the conversation focused on work, which wasn't hard because they had barely talked since Vicki had rushed out of his place on Sunday night. She had offered to stay last night after his party for the distributors, but Charlie pleaded exhaustion and asked her to leave. When she didn't seem upset in the least, Charlie suspected that she probably had managed to solicit at least one backup invitation over the course of the evening's party.

He wasn't looking forward to their later trip back to his townhouse. Vicki never wandered for long and probably planned on spending tonight with him. He would have to tell her otherwise and knew she wouldn't buy the exhaustion excuse again. It would be the start of an ugly game between the two of them. This wasn't really about sex, and Vicki would be very quick to see that. She was on her way out. And it wasn't likely to be a graceful exit. Charlie shuddered at the unknown severance cost he and the Company would have to pay—monetary and otherwise.

Vicki turned and looked at Charlie from over the top of her dark sunglasses. "Why do you think your old man wants to see us?"

Charlie shook his head. "No idea. I was hoping you could tell me. He was so insistent that we both be there. I thought you might know."

"Why would he tell me?"

"I don't know. It's just strange that he wanted you there."

Vicki smiled sardonically. "Oh, you mean because he hates my guts?"

Charlie winced. "Well, yes. If you want to be so blunt."

"I call 'em as I see 'em." Vicki turned into Peter's long circular drive. After switching off the engine, she turned down the vanity mirror to touch up her lipstick. "Charlie, your father is a hysterical old man. God only knows what he's come up with now."

"This better not be more accusations about that damn fire."

"One way to find out. Let's go." Vicki slipped the lipstick back into her handbag and started to get out of the car, indicating that the discussion was over.

26

Berta greeted them at the door and, much to Charlie's surprise, did not make her usual fuss over his arrival. She gave Charlie a quick hug and Vicki a strained handshake. Then Berta immediately led them down the hall and into the library where Peter was waiting at his desk, vodka martini in hand. After just a few minutes' exchange of small talk about the weather and spring gardening, Berta excused herself and retreated to another part of the house.

"What's with Mom?" asked Charlie, after Berta had shut the heavy library doors behind her.

Peter stared at his son. "What do you mean?"

"I don't know. She seemed to be in such a hurry to get out of here."

Peter was well into his second drink and had been impatient through even the small amount of social chatter with Berta. "Oh, that. She's off tomorrow for a few days of shopping in Chicago. She went up to pack. Besides, I asked her to leave us alone."

"Sounds serious, old man," said Vicki, leaving the doorway

and crossing over to the bar. "I might need a little something to get me through this. Any decent Scotch over here?"

"Yes, yes, help yourself," mumbled Peter.

Vicki put her purse down on the bar, picked up a bottle of Glenlivet, and turned to him. "I knew I could trust you to have a well-stocked bar—"

"Vicki, drop the smart remarks," Charlie interrupted. "Just pour yourself a drink, and sit down over there in front of the fireplace. It's been a long couple of days, and I just don't have the energy to sit here and listen to the two of you sniping at each other."

Charlie shot Vicki a glare to indicate that he really meant it. Not giving her time to retort, he turned to his father at the desk and addressed him similarly. "Dad, grab a couple of those sandwiches. The food will soak up some of that vodka." He pointed towards the tray of food sitting on the end of the bar.

For some reason, both Vicki and Peter did exactly as Charlie directed. A few moments later, Vicki was slouching in the green-leather club chair closer to the fireplace, and Peter was sitting on the nearby couch with a plate of food in front of him on the walnut coffee table. Charlie poured himself a seltzer water over at the bar and joined the silent duo.

"Why did you want to see us, Dad?" prompted Charlie, as he sat down in the second chair between his father and Vicki.

Peter shot a quick look at Vicki and then stared down into his drink. "I've got something to tell you. I should have told you years ago, but I was too busy trying to forget. It's all so horrible." Still not looking at Charlie, Peter stumbled on. "Anyway, now you need to know because this thing can't be mishandled."

"Dad, get to the point." He wasn't in the mood for his father's usual convoluted tales or misguided business advice.

"It's about that body," blurted Peter.

Charlie sat forward in his chair. "What body?" Vicki also straightened up, but kept quiet.

"You know, that body found down in the elevator after the fire."

Charlie stood up. He angrily tore off his suit coat and threw it over the back of his chair. "Damn, I knew we'd get back to that fire. You promised me—"

Peter cut him off. "Son, I don't care about that two-bit fire. You two can torch the whole city for all I care." He was visibly agitated. "We've got bigger problems and, if you'll let me explain, you'll know what I mean." He rose from the couch and walked past Charlie over to the bar to freshen his martini.

Vicki nodded at Peter. "Good idea." She gulped down her first drink and also got up to pour herself another.

"Okay, I'm listening," said Charlie, settling back into his chair.

Peter returned to the couch and sat down before speaking. "I know who the guy is."

Charlie was confused. "What guy?"

"The skeleton in the grain elevator. I know who it is."

Charlie was stunned, and it took him a moment to ask, "Who?"

Peter looked down into his glass and then turned his eyes up to meet Charlie's. "It's Matthew Kelly."

Charlie stared back at Peter. "What?"

"You know, the labor leader who disappeared back in the 'thirties—"

"Dad, I know who Matthew Kelly is, or was." Charlie had first heard the gruesome details surrounding Kelly's disappearance from his grandfather Marcus when Charlie was only eight, and the old man had repeated the story many times after that.

Charlie looked over towards the bar to see if Vicki knew what they were talking about. She assured him, "I also know the family history, Charlie. It's all part of being a loyal Randolph employee."

"Right," responded Charlie, matching Vicki's sarcastic tone. He turned back to Peter. "So that's where Will stashed him. How long have you known?"

Peter felt Vicki glaring at him from across the room, defying him to continue. He refused to make eye contact with her. "A long time. And Will didn't stash him anywhere. Will had nothing to do with Kelly's murder."

Charlie shook his head. "I'm confused. Go back and start at the beginning." But before Peter could begin, Charlie added, "No, wait. I think I'll have a drink after all." He made his way over towards Vicki and poured himself a healthy bourbon and water. Then they both returned to their chairs in front of the fireplace.

Peter faced Charlie and started to explain. "You know that meeting that night between Kelly and Will?"

"Yes," Charlie answered slowly.

"Well, it really wasn't such a big secret. Marcus knew everything that was going on."

"How was that?"

"Through Kelly's driver, Thomas Lindgren."

Charlie thought for a moment. "The guy who testified against Will at the trial?"

"Yes, that's him. He was some tough hired by Marcus to report back on all of Kelly's activities." Peter looked over at Vicki as if he expected her to say something. When she didn't, he took a big gulp of his drink and turned back to Charlie. "Will told the truth about their meeting that night. It was over in less than an hour, and Kelly and Lindgren did leave the house shortly before eight."

"Where'd they go?"

"Lindgren took Kelly to the mill. For another meeting—this time with Marcus. When Kelly refused to give Marcus a report on his earlier meeting with Will, things got a little rough. Marcus shoved the man, and he lost his balance. Maybe because he was missing that arm. Anyway, Kelly fell backwards and knocked the back of his head on the edge of Marcus's desk. He was pretty badly hurt, but Marcus refused to call for help. I don't know if it would have made any difference in the long run, though, because Kelly was dead within minutes." Peter stopped speaking and stared back down into his drink again.

"And how do you know all this?" Charlie inquired, even though he had already guessed the probable answer.

"I was there," Peter replied quietly.

Charlie said nothing.

Peter stood up with his drink and wandered over to the windows. The sun had partially set behind the hill on the far side of the lake. For a moment, Peter stared out at the darkening sky, and then he turned back to look at Charlie. "When Kelly died, I tried to convince your grandfather that we should call the authorities. After all, the whole thing was just an accident. He said that would be crazy, given the ugly mood of the city. And I must say, after seeing how Will was railroaded right into prison, he was right." Peter slowly pivoted to face the windows again. He watched the evening shadows spread across the garden.

A few moments went by before Charlie broke the silence. "I assume Marcus came up with the notion to hang the whole thing on Will?" Charlie knew how his grandfather had felt towards his younger half-brother.

Peter took another sip of his drink and put the glass down on his desk, before turning back to the room. "That's correct. And he actually came to relish the plan. You know, getting rid of both Kelly and Will with one masterstroke. He was a very frightening man—"

"Skip the family commentary, and get on with the story," Charlie interrupted. "Kelly's dead and bleeding on the floor of Marcus's office down at the mill. That's a long way from Will's house up here. What happened next?"

"Well, it was all quite simple. Marcus never touched the body after that fatal shove. He just gave orders to Lindgren and me. I didn't want to go along with it, but I didn't have the courage to object. And Lindgren didn't care as long as he got paid."

Peter hesitated, again expecting Vicki to comment, but she remained quiet. "We wrapped the body in an old tarp, stashed it in a closet in an unused office, and cleaned up the mess in the office. Then, because Marcus didn't trust Lindgren to keep his mouth shut, I returned alone later that night and moved Kelly."

"To the grain elevator, I presume?"

"That's right. We were using that tunnel as a construction passageway during the building of the new warehouse. But by late April, it wasn't needed anymore. Most of it had even been filled in by that time, and I knew the floor in the elevator was going to be sealed off the following morning. I moved the body and buried it in the shaft under some old construction debris that had been thrown down there. Everything went according to plan, and Matthew Kelly remained missing for sixty years—until this past Sunday."

"And the evidence against Will?"

"Oh, Marcus orchestrated that as well. Lindgren drove back up to Hidden Lake and parked down the road from Will's place. He hiked the rest of the way into the house and smeared that blood on Will's handrail. It came from one of the bloody rags we used to clean up Marcus's office. Then he returned to his car and shot off several rounds from an old shotgun Marcus had given him. Those were the shots that Will and the housekeeper heard at nine-thirty."

"And the briefcase?" asked Charlie.

"Pure circumstance," Peter said ruefully. "Kelly must have actually left it at the house, just like Will said."

Charlie had heard enough. "It all just fell into place for Marcus, didn't it?"

Peter nodded and reached for his glass.

Charlie sat in his chair watching the pitiful man standing over at the windows draining the last of his martini. "Dad, this is unbelievable."

"I know, I know. I always planned to clear up the whole thing once Marcus died. But when that finally happened, there didn't seem to be much point, since Will had already been dead for twenty years."

"And what did you think would happen when we got around to demolishing the mill and that elevator?"

"I would have told you the whole story before demolition ever got under way."

"Right," sniped Charlie. "Christ, why didn't you tell me about this earlier? When it would have been a lot easier to dump old Kelly for a second time. Now we're stuck."

Peter had started across the room towards the bar, but he stopped midway and looked over at Charlie, his eyes narrowing. "Listen to yourself! I just told you that I watched your grandfather kill a man, and that everything concerning this family is a goddamn lie. And all you can think about is the precious Company."

Then Peter stared down into his empty martini glass. "Try thinking about Will rotting away in prison. That's what I think of. Everything changed that night Kelly died. Nothing was the same after that."

27

"Christ, spare me the melodrama of your miserable life," Vicki finally interjected. She stood up and worked her way over to Peter. "Things haven't been so rough for you. Drinking yourself to death in this mausoleum surrounded by servants and shit-loads of money. What about Thomas Lindgren? With just his one-way ticket to Ohio and two thousand bucks?"

Peter said nothing and finished making his way over to the bar. After pouring a glass of seltzer water, he turned to look back at her and finally answered. "I never gave a damn about what happened to Mr. Lindgren. He was a hustler who'd been snitching on Kelly for months. He took the money and ran, didn't he?"

"Lindgren didn't run. Your bastard of a father pushed him out of town. And he took a lot less money than he deserved. He was terrified of Marcus, just like you. Dragging his wife and kid to Ohio was better than ending up with the murder pinned on him, which was the threatened alternative, from what I understand."

Charlie, still seated over by the fireplace, interrupted their exchange. "Did I miss something here?" His eyes fixed on Vicki. "What the hell does any of this matter to you?"

Neither Vicki nor Peter said anything right away. They glared at one another, and each waited for the other to speak. Finally, Vicki said, "Go ahead, tell him. Tell him why you and I have always been such buddies."

Peter brushed past Vicki and stumbled back over to the fireplace. He took a deep breath before answering Charlie's question. "She claims to be Lindgren's granddaughter."

Charlie's jaw dropped. "How can—"

Peter didn't let him finish. "Vicki's father was supposedly Lindgren's son. Whether she is Lindgren's granddaughter or not doesn't matter. She knew most of the story when she arrived in town. Why do you think she came to me looking for a job?"

Charlie turned to Vicki. "Is this for real?"

"As real as it gets. I heard the whole story from my granddaddy right before he died. I left home shortly after that and eventually worked my way up here to collect on a few old family debts."

"You are incredible!" Charlie shot up out of his chair and stormed over to face Vicki. "And just what are those family debts? How much has he paid you?"

"Not a dime I haven't earned." Vicki nodded towards Peter. "Go ahead, ask him."

"It's true. I tried to pay her off. You know, make her disappear. But she wouldn't take it." He shrugged. "All she wanted was a job. So I recommended her to you. But she really didn't need me. As I recall, her resume was fairly impressive on its own."

Vicki laughed and turned back to Charlie. "I've never been big on regular channels. Patiently climbing the corporate ladder isn't really my style. So I used your daddy and our little secret to kind of give me a jump-start. I doubt I would have been hired as an account manager without a good word from my friend here."

Smiling insincerely, she glanced over at Peter.

"And now you're director of sales. And development. What's next? My job?"

Vicki shook her head and shrugged her shoulders. "I'm happy with the status quo." Then she left Charlie standing in the middle of the room and sidled over to the bar.

Charlie followed close on her heels. "Like hell! You're only happy if you're causing trouble. And that, you've managed just fine. How could you be so stupid? The fire? With that body in there?" He stopped a few feet from her and waited for an answer.

As usual, she was ready with one. "When we set that fire, I had no idea that Kelly was in that grain elevator. You heard your father. He moved the body without Lindgren. That was the one piece of the story I didn't know."

Charlie and Vicki were so involved in their screaming at each other that they had forgotten about Peter standing in front of the fireplace. When Vicki mentioned setting the fire, Charlie suddenly felt his father's eyes. He couldn't meet them.

He did, however, manage to regain his composure and lower his voice. "Well, not much we can do about any of that now. Right now the police are chalking up the fire to vagrants. And their likely candidate for the skeleton is another bum from an earlier day. So we just continue cooperating with the police on both investigations and not give them any reason to change their suspicions."

Vicki laughed at him. "Oh, that's a swell plan."

Charlie didn't respond to her remark. Instead, he retreated back towards the fireplace to rejoin Peter.

With Charlie back at his side, Peter spoke again. "I hope it is that simple. Because if they can prove that skeleton in the elevator is Kelly, Will is off the hook. There wasn't time for him to hide the body downtown before the police took him into custody."

"Christ, that's right. Why didn't you just dump Kelly in the lake up here? Isn't that where everyone assumed he was anyway?"

"That was the original plan. But the lake was crawling with cops for weeks. Once it became apparent that Will was going to be convicted even without a corpse, Marcus decided to just leave Mr. Kelly in the elevator. Which was fine with me since I would have been the one to reopen that floor and move the body. I didn't think I could stomach all that."

"So," Vicki said in disgust, "you've always been spineless."

Peter ignored her and continued talking to Charlie. "Can they identify people after all these years? Do you know?"

"I don't know. But it probably depends on how much interest the cops show in this guy. Hopefully, they won't be that interested."

Vicki marched back to her chair and sat down. She sneered at Charlie, who was still standing at the fireplace with his father. "Who are you trying to kid? Serg Suarez is on this case, and he's a homicide detective. You know, one of the guys who are paid to be interested in dead bodies." As she pushed on, Vicki noticed Peter's hands were shaking. "Besides, don't forget your snooping cousin. She was there in that grain elevator when Kelly reappeared, and she seemed mighty interested in the whole affair."

Peter's whole body flinched when he heard that Emma had been present at the mill when the body was discovered. In a panic, he grabbed Charlie by the arm. "I knew it as soon as that skeleton showed up. We've got big problems. Emma's smart, and if she starts poking around in all this—"

Charlie shook off his father's grasp. "Calm down, both of you. You're both freaked out because she's Will Randolph's granddaughter. But that's only coincidence. It doesn't give her any extra psychic powers here. That body means nothing to her. It's that damn mill she's so attached to, and she's convinced we tried to destroy it."

He turned to Vicki. "And so, even though you've assured me she'll never hang that one on us, I think it would be a good idea to give Emma what she wants. Now that the two of you have decided to cut me in on your little secret, I realize there's a lot more at stake here than just those damn buildings."

"I hate to cave in to that bitch, but you might be right," conceded Vicki.

Remembering his father's glare at the previous mention of the fire, Charlie didn't want to get into the details in front of Peter. He went over to the bar and retrieved Vicki's purse. Then he walked back over to her chair. "Why don't we discuss it all later. Right now, I'd like a minute alone with Dad. Would you mind waiting for me in the car?"

"Yeah, sure. I know when I've been dismissed," quipped Vicki as she stood up and reached for her purse. "Let me just grab a few of those sandwiches to sustain myself during your big Randolph power chat."

28

Peter heard the front door slam. "I'm glad that woman left. She makes me so furious."

"Yes, Vicki certainly does have that talent," Charlie readily agreed and then turned to his father. "Dad, we'll deal with all this. Everything will be just fine."

"God, I hope you're right. But I've got a bad feeling regarding all of it."

Charlie led his father to the couch, sat him down, and returned to the bar to mix him another vodka martini. When he handed the drink to Peter, he said, "You know, Dad, there's no way Emma could have any notion of all this Kelly stuff."

"I know, I know." Peter took a big swallow of the fresh drink. "There's one more thing I should probably tell you. Something Vicki Stephens knows nothing about."

Charlie grimaced and sat down in the chair beside his father. "More secrets? Lay it on me. How much worse can it get?"

"Hold on. You might find this one useful. And that's exactly why I haven't told you all these years and especially the last few months. But it seems the stakes have suddenly gone up, and now it would be best for you to know."

"Come on, Dad, we've already had enough cat and mouse this evening. Just spit it out."

Peter set his drink down on the coffee table and deliberately paused for a moment. "It's concerning Sam Randolph, Emma's dad. You know he lives up near Ely on that Lake Salish property?"

"Yes, and?"

"Well, he doesn't own that property. We do. Or rather the Company does."

Charlie bolted forward in his chair. "Since when?"

"Since forever," answered Peter. "Katheryne Randolph, Sam's grandmother, had only a life estate. At her death, the property was to revert back to the Company for use as a corporate retreat. Obviously, our grandfather's estate was set up long before Will got tied up in the Kelly thing and lost his share of the Company."

"Katheryne Randolph died years ago. Why is Sam still living there?"

Peter pulled himself up out of the couch, stepped around the low table in front of him, and turned to face his son. "Because I let him stay after his grandmother died. He was raising his family up there and not bothering anybody. It was the least I could do after all that stuff with his father. I was hoping that you would eventually agree to a below-market sale, or at least to some sort of long-term lease."

"And how was I going to do that when I didn't know about any of this? You live in la-la land."

"I was going to tell you everything. But only when you needed to know."

Charlie stood up and shouted, "I am the president of Randolph Foods and the only person in this fricking family that cares a hoot about the Company. Everything that you've told me tonight I needed to know yesterday. Last week! Last year! Instead, I'm the last to find out because you didn't think the time was right. Christ almighty!"

"Calm down. Your mother will hear you," Peter implored. "Besides, you're probably not the last to learn of this. As of several months ago, Emma didn't know anything about it either. Probably still doesn't."

"And how do you know that?"

"Sam told me. I called him and offered to broker a deal—he gets Emma to call off the Coalition, and I talk you into a below-market sale of Lake Salish."

"You did what?" Charlie stared at Peter. "Thanks for the vote of confidence. I'm plenty capable of dealing with the Coalition without your help."

Peter took a few steps towards Charlie. "I wasn't trying to help you. I was trying to help Sam." Then he added, "Even though, as it turns out, you could have used the help."

"Not from you," blurted Charlie, momentarily looking away from his father. "I just underestimated Emma and the Coalition. Or I overestimated my courting of the city leaders. I didn't think they'd do anything to jeopardize the new jobs we promised to bring back to the city."

"Oh, you can't tell me that if I'd come to you with the Lake Salish information, you would have refused to use it."

"Okay, okay. If you had told me about Lake Salish before Emma got that restraining order, I probably would have agreed to use it. But hard to tell how much good it does us at this point." Charlie took a deep breath. "So what did Sam say?"

"What do you think he said?"

Charlie played along. "I would guess Sam refused to put Emma in that position by telling her about Lake Salish."

"That's exactly what he said."

Charlie chuckled. "Too many damn scruples run through that side of the family."

Peter sat back down on the couch. "Well, maybe our side

could use a few more."

Charlie ignored his father's comment. He walked over to the plate on the bar and picked up a sandwich, before asking, "So now I know it all, right? No more dirty little secrets."

"No more secrets. That's all of it." Peter stared at his feet. "Will you throw Sam off Lake Salish?"

As he returned to the couch, Charlie answered between bites of his sandwich. "I might have before I heard all this tonight. But now I have to shift everyone's focus, including Emma's, off that damn body."

"How are you going to do that?"

Charlie thought for a moment. "The only way I can, given the circumstances. The Company will agree to restore the damaged mill in compliance with the Coalition's guidelines and, in a considerably more private transaction, I'll offer Sam a long-term, below-market buyout of Lake Salish. Emma and everyone else will be doing nothing but singing our praises."

"Don't you think Emma might be a little suspicious of your sudden generosity?"

"Maybe, at first. But she'll come around. Her father and that mill preservation are too important to her."

"Well, you certainly have it all figured out, haven't you?" Peter commented quietly as he reached for his martini glass with his trembling right hand.

God, he's pathetic, Charlie thought as he watched his father. *But I can't have him falling completely apart now.* He sat down on the couch next to the old man. "Dad, you may not believe this. But given everything else you told me tonight, I can understand and respect your decision to let Sam and his family stay on at Lake Salish. I really can."

Peter was skeptical that Charlie was being sincere, but answered, "I appreciate your telling me that. It's one of the few good things I did in my life."

Charlie rose from the couch, grabbed his suit coat from the

back of the chair, and started towards the door. "Listen, I better be going. The dragon lady awaits me, and she's not exactly the waiting type."

Peter smiled for the first time all evening.

Charlie walked out into the hall and called up the stairs to say goodnight to his mother. Then he stuck his head back into the library. "As I said earlier, Dad, don't worry about any of this. I'll take care of everything."

Peter, sitting on the couch with his back to the door, didn't speak until after Charlie had left. Then he said aloud, "That is what I'm worried about."

29

Outside, night had fallen. Charlie crossed under the dimly lit portico and climbed into the passenger side of the Range Rover. The vehicle was idling with its headlights on, and Vicki was talking on her cell phone plugged into one of the two mobile jacks on the dashboard. Her right hand clutched the phone tightly, and her eyes were wide and unblinking.

But her voice was calm and measured, hiding her obvious anxiety from whoever it was on the other end of the line. "It's probably nothing, but it's always good to know what that woman is up to. You did the right thing by calling me. Keep in touch, if you know what I mean." Vicki clicked off the phone and hung it up.

She turned to Charlie. "We might have a problem."

"Why? Who was that?"

"My buddy Vince Shillings from the Arson Squad. Guess who he bumped into down at Police Records this afternoon?"

Charlie groaned. "Just tell me. I'm not exactly in the mood for games."

"Okay. It was your dear Cousin Emma."

"What? Where was this?"

"Police Records. Where they keep all the old police files. Vince tried to find out exactly what Emma was looking at, but apparently citizen requests are confidential."

Charlie looked over at Vicki suspiciously. "Why the hell did Vince call you? You're not having Emma followed, are you?"

"No, don't panic. I asked him to call me if Emma tried to contact him regarding the fire investigation. So when he bumped into her at Police Records, he had a hunch I might be interested in her poking around down at City Hall. He's just that kind of guy—naturally helpful."

"Naturally sleazy is more like it."

"Call him what you want, but it doesn't change the situation. Emma's looking at old police files. That's our problem, not Vince Shillings." Vicki reached across her body to pull down her seatbelt shoulder strap. "Vince thinks he can get the name of that file, but he has to get a search warrant first."

Charlie shook his head in disbelief. "Oh, right! And let the whole world know we're particularly interested in old police files right now."

"You're right. That might look odd. I'll just tell Vince to forget the whole thing."

"And will he?"

"Sure. He seems eager to keep me happy."

"Must be hoping for repeat business."

Vicki sneered at Charlie's last remark. Then she looked up and saw Charlie's mother standing in the hall light at the open front door. Berta was watching the two of them. Vicki waved at the peering woman, put the Range Rover in gear, and pulled out of the circular drive. Once she was on her way, she returned to the subject of Emma's afternoon research. "Other than Kelly, can you think of any reason why Emma would be interested in old police files?"

Charlie thought for a minute before calmly answering. "We shouldn't assume it's a big deal. She's probably doing research for some other Coalition project. Lots of old buildings have unsavory pasts. And as we know only too well, Emma usually does her homework before tackling a new preservation effort."

"What if it was the Kelly file?"

"Hey, relax. There's no way Emma could possibly figure out the whole Kelly story. The only people who know what really happened are you and I. And Dad, of course. Right?"

"Right," Vicki conceded. "But don't underestimate your cousin."

Charlie laughed. "Trust me, I'll never make that mistake again." Then he shrugged. "Whatever she was doing at City Hall, there's not much we can do about it now. But agreeing to restore the mill is something that we can do. And that should keep Emma focused on the building instead of other aspects of our family history. I'm calling her tomorrow to set up a meeting with the Coalition."

"That should thrill her." Vicki obviously wasn't convinced that Emma could be dismissed so easily. "But what if she doesn't go away when we toss her your little restoration bone? What if she knows more than we think she does? Then what do we do with Cousin Emma?"

Charlie didn't like the tone of Vicki's questions. He grabbed her right arm from the steering wheel. "You're not going to do anything with Emma. Just stay away from her."

Vicki pulled her arm away. "You obviously haven't focused on what could be at stake here."

"What do you mean?"

"The Company." Vicki knew she was one step ahead of Charlie on this one, and she relished breaking the news to him. "You could lose Randolph Foods if the truth came out about Kelly's murder. Remember how Marcus ended up with the whole works because of that weird provision in Henry's will? Well, think of

Emma teaming up with some hotshot corporate lawyer once Will is exonerated. She and her family would probably sue for the whole works and end up with at least half."

Charlie knew Vicki was hoping for hysterics from him, but he refused to take the bait. "Spare me the doomsday scenario. This thing will be dealt with long before it comes to that." Charlie wasn't planning to share his father's last piece of family information with Vicki. "Just leave Emma to me for the time being. You've got plenty else to do."

Vicki didn't push him. "Okay, okay. You deal with her on the restoration. Less time I have to spend with her, the better."

"And I'm certain she won't miss you much either."

They drove for several minutes in silence. Charlie shut his eyes and was happy for the quiet, but Vicki was still agitated by Vince's call. She resumed the conversation just as they turned onto the entrance ramp to Highway 100 to head south, back to Charlie's townhouse. "Your old man is losing it. He could be a real problem."

Charlie opened his eyes, sat up in his seat, and screamed at Vicki, "Leave him alone. He'll be fine. If anyone's a problem, it's you." Charlie had restrained himself in front of his father, but now his exasperation with her came pouring out. "You never stop long enough to think through anything. That arson was a crazy idea from the beginning. I never should have agreed to it."

Vicki glanced over at him. "But you did agree to it. Remember?"

Charlie kept at her. "But I wouldn't have if I'd known what I heard tonight. It doesn't surprise me that Dad kept his mouth shut. But you should have told me about this whole thing a long time ago. Christ, now the whole Company is at jeopardy."

"Back off," Vicki demanded. "We already went through that back at your father's. Even if I had told you my part of the story, we still wouldn't have known that Kelly was buried in that tunnel."

"Well, I might have stopped to wonder where he was buried. And the mill buildings would have been high enough on my list that I certainly wouldn't have risked torching the place just to settle a score with Cousin Emma."

"Oh, don't be so sure," snapped Vicki.

"Besides, once I heard your part of the story, I would have asked Peter about the body."

"Yeah, and he might have told you where it was if you got him drunk enough."

Charlie let her last comment go. They drove on for a few more minutes without talking. It was Charlie who broke this silence. "Wait a minute. Maybe you're not so stupid. What sweet revenge to bring down the mighty Randolphs."

"Don't be ridiculous. I've worked too hard to make the Company what it is today. If I wanted to destroy it and you, I could have done it by now." Vicki hesitated a moment before continuing. "Revenge isn't what I came looking for seven years ago. Your father was right about one thing. Thomas Lindgren was a loser. Just like my daddy, my step-daddy, and my ma. But that wasn't the life for me. I came looking for this life." She motioned to her fifteen hundred dollar suit, and next to her car, and finally to him. "Why would I want to destroy it?"

"Rags to riches. How touching."

"What would you know? You were born with a silver stick up your ass."

Charlie didn't bother to answer. Instead, he thought, *God, how do I get rid of her? It's more important now than ever.* He knew what old Marcus would have done, but that was way out of his league. He'd have to come up with something else.

Vicki read his mind. "I bet you'd like me to disappear, huh? Well, I'm not going to."

"No, I didn't think so. I couldn't be that lucky." Charlie leaned back in his seat.

Vicki saw she was pushing too hard. With her right hand, she tried to run her fingers through his hair. "Listen, Charlie, I know your father laid a lot on you tonight. But let's not let it come between us."

Charlie pushed her hand away and straightened his hair. "What? There is no 'us'."

Vicki decided to back off. Neither of them said anything more for the rest of the drive. When they arrived at Charlie's townhouse, he didn't utter even an insincere good night. He went inside alone.

THURSDAY

30

Emma had gotten home from Fridley at five-thirty the evening before, and she didn't think any more about Vicki Stephens for the rest of the night. First, she finished up her report for Judge Flynn; and then, after another quick dinner of granola, she had retreated upstairs to her office to begin work on Athena's project.

With the site photographs and preliminary location drawings spread out on the table, she had started by roughing out a site plan of the property, noting the elevations and required setback limits shown on the survey provided by Athena. Next she sketched several possible design concepts for the house that had been percolating in her brain since the site visit on Tuesday morning. Athena didn't have a budget—or at least not one she had shared with Emma—because she didn't want to stifle Emma's creativity. Spared the usual constraint of a client's pocketbook, Emma freely dabbled with new excesses in rustic luxury and had a lot of fun doing it.

Three feasible designs had finally taken shape, and she worked on them until well past midnight, when she quit for the night. She had slept soundly for several hours—dreaming about monstrous lakeside chateaux in place of sixty-year-old murders.

She awoke refreshed at six-thirty and went out for an early-morning jog, taking her shorter loop along the river. When she returned to her condo, she brewed a half pot of Sumatran coffee and carried it up to the loft. There she settled in, reviewing her previous night's work and tinkering with the drawings.

When she finished, she walked back downstairs to retrieve the morning newspaper from the hall outside her door and climbed up two flights of stairs to her roof deck. The morning sun was peaking over the wall of downtown office towers, and Emma positioned her chair with her back to the warmth. Before turning to world and local events, she spent a few minutes mentally planting annuals in her dirt-filled flower boxes. The actual planting would have to wait for another ten days until after the last chance of frost had passed.

She chuckled when she picked up the *Metro* section of the *Star Tribune* and saw a feature article discussing fires in abandoned buildings. Emma knew the public relations personnel at Randolph Foods most likely had suggested the story. Other than that, there was no other mention in the paper of the fire investigation or the mystery skeleton, which probably meant there were no new leads on either front.

As Emma was folding up the local section, an idea popped into her head. *That's it. That's how I discover more about Vicki Stephens.* Gathering up the newspaper, she descended the folding stairs. She snatched a pen and pad of paper from her office desk and proceeded down to the kitchen. Munching on a toasted bagel, she wrote down and rehearsed a few lines.

Fifteen minutes later, she returned to her office and looked up the number for Randolph Foods for the second time in as many days. She called the Company and asked for Vicki's secretary or assistant. Emma was extremely nervous when she was transferred to a very efficient-sounding woman by the name of Sherry Collins, who identified herself as Vicki's executive assistant.

"Hi, Sherry," Emma opened, in an overly friendly voice. "This is Barbara Michaels from the *Star Tribune*." After these first few words, Emma relaxed a bit and continued with her introduction with more confidence. "I'm gathering some background information for a story we're doing on up-and-coming young business executives. Your boss, Vicki Stephens, is one of the profiled people. Would you mind answering a few questions?"

"You'll have to contact our Public Relations Department," Sherry answered. "They handle all inquiries from the press." Sherry Collins was Vicki's ninth assistant in eight years. Because she held her tongue, worked efficiently, and didn't take Vicki's diatribes personally, she had survived and had negotiated a nice bonus from the human resources director for her agreement to continue the assignment. So even though she was very tempted to let this reporter in on a few of Vicki's flaws, she stuck to the protocol.

Shoot, thought Emma. She was hoping for someone less professional and more cooperative. She knew she didn't stand a chance with the trained media experts in the Public Relations Department. They knew most of the reporters and wouldn't talk anyway until they checked out the validity and slant of the story. She wouldn't be able to bluff her way around them.

Using the name of a Randolph employee she had bumped heads with in the past, she gave Sherry one more shot. "I already talked with Roger Milstein over in PR. He gave me a lot of resume information. You know, where she went to school, professional affiliations, and the like. He said it was okay to ask around to get some impressions from her colleagues." Emma hoped this last lie wasn't a mistake. Anyone who knew Vicki would probably never encourage solicitation of personal testimonials from her staff.

"I'm not exactly her colleague. An executive assistant is really more like a secretary. And with Ms. Stephens, that doesn't amount to colleague."

Emma chuckled, as she thought, *Surprise, surprise! Sherry Collins doesn't like Vicki.*

Sherry quickly added, "I didn't mean that the way it sounded. It's just that Ms. Stephens is very busy, and we don't spend a lot of time chit-chatting."

"I understand," Emma assured her. "But sometimes an assistant's insights can be helpful. You probably know her better than you think. Mr. Milstein didn't have much personal information on Ms. Stephens. Like, where did she grow up? Does she have any family living in the area? You know, background details."

"I really don't know much about her. Except stuff you probably already know. College at Duke. Business degree from Stanford. Joined the Company in June 1984." Sherry paused for a moment. "Oh, and I know that her mother lives in Ohio."

Emma scribbled the details down on her pad, but also continued prompting the woman. "Really?"

"Yes, Akron, I think. Ms. Stephens sends her some money every few months. At least, I think it's money, but I don't know for sure. I mail the envelopes, but they're already sealed when she gives them to me. I never paid much attention to the address other than its being in Akron." Sherry Collins paused before going on. "Her mother called once. But Ms. Stephens told me to tell her mother that personal calls weren't allowed at work. That's not true, but I told the woman what Ms. Stephens had asked me to. And she never called again. I don't think they're close. She's never mentioned any other family. But that doesn't mean a lot. Like I said, we don't chat much."

"Well, this helps," assured Emma. "Maybe I'll try to contact her mother. You know, include a couple of cute childhood stories. Do you happen to know her mother's name?"

"She has a different last name. It's Schorr. The first name starts with 'D'. Della or Daphne or something like that." Then Sherry said, "Listen, I really shouldn't be talking to you."

Emma knew she wouldn't get anything more from Sherry Collins. So she brought the conversation to a close. "Thanks a lot, Sherry, you've been a big help. If we run the story, it should be within the next few weeks. You know, when we have a slow news day."

"Yes, certainly, Ms. Michaels." After Sherry hung up, she felt uncomfortable about the whole exchange even though she really didn't think she had told the reporter anything important or confidential. So she put a call into Roger Milstein to cover herself. The last thing she wanted was to get in trouble with Vicki. She didn't want to jeopardize her job or that hazardous-duty bonus.

On the other end of the terminated phone conversation, Emma was also feeling a little guilty about tricking Sherry Collins. She could imagine Vicki's tirade if she ever found out about their conversation. Emma hoped she never would.

Because she was allowed only two numbers per directory-assistance call, it took Emma four calls to compile listings for six "D. Schorr" and for two "Della Schorr" in the Akron area. On her fifth call, Emma requested "Daphne Schorr." An unusually helpful directory-assistance operator suggested "Danielle Schorr" when the requested search turned up no listing. Emma took down the number for Danielle Schorr and began calling through the numbers.

Three of the "D. Schorr" listings were definite dead ends. One was a man. Another was only nineteen and the third was an elderly Hispanic-American woman with five sons. The other three weren't home. One of the no-answers just rang. The other two had answering machines. Their messages were not encouraging. Each speaker sounded far too young to have a daughter in her mid-thirties.

Even so, Emma made a note to call the three numbers later in the evening after the usual work hours. "Della Schorr" was no more fruitful. One of the numbers was disconnected, and the second reached another discouraging answering machine.

31

Emma sat at her desk and dialed her only remaining number, the one for Danielle Schorr. "Hello," sounded a raspy voice on the other end of the line. A television was blaring in the background.

"May I speak with Danielle Schorr?" Emma asked loudly.

"You got her. Who's this?" slurred the woman.

Emma thought the woman sounded drunk and looked at her watch. It said 11:40. *I guess it is after noon down in Ohio.* She cautiously continued. "Hi, my name is Barbara Michaels. I'm a reporter for the *Star Tribune* newspaper in the Twin Cities."

"Fancy that! My kid lives somewhere up there."

Bingo, thought Emma, flipping her pad open to a new sheet of paper.

"Hold on. I gotta find my clicker so I can turn down this damn TV." After a couple of minutes, the woman returned to the line. "Okay, now we can talk without screamin' at each other. Like I said, my kid lives in the Twin Cities."

"Yes, I know. I'm actually calling concerning your daughter."

Emma tried to sound very businesslike. "That is, if your daughter is Vicki Stephens."

"Yeah, she's my kid. She in jail or something?"

Emma was taken aback by the question. "No. Should she be?"

"Wouldn't surprise me. That kid's always been too smart for her own good." The woman's speech was uneven and slurred. "Well, if she's not in jail, what do you want?"

If not drunk yet, definitely on her way, thought Emma before answering the woman's question. "I'm a business reporter for the local paper up here, and we're thinking of doing an article on some of the up-and-coming young business executives in the community, profiling their paths to success. Your daughter is one of the people we've chosen."

A coarse laughter came from the other end of the line. "Is this some kind of joke? Why would you want to write about her?"

"Well, her career does fit our project description."

"Not the way I see it. My kid's just a part-time manager at some convenience store. I never considered that much of—what'd you call it—an executive position?"

"There's some confusion here. The Vicki Stephens I'm interested in is sales director for Randolph Foods, which is headquartered here in Minneapolis. She's in her mid-thirties, approximately five-foot-seven, attractive, blond hair, green eyes—"

Danielle Schorr interrupted Emma's description. "Why that little bitch—"

"Excuse me?"

"How much money would you say this Vicki Stephens makes?" Danielle Schorr suddenly sounded very sober.

Emma thought for a moment. "Oh, I don't know, two hundred grand or so. Probably some stock options on top of that." While speculating on Vicki's salary, Emma had reached for the phone-book again and quickly looked up "Vicki Stephens." She found just two listings, both for the Vicki Stephens with whom Emma was acquainted, one for her Mount Curve condominium in Kenwood and the other for her office at Randolph Foods. There was no listing for a second Vicki Stephens, the supposed manager of a convenience store.

"So she's been lying to me?"

"Not necessarily. Maybe you're just confused." Emma knew immediately that the last comment had been a mistake. She cringed and waited for Danielle's response.

"Listen, lady, I may have my problems, but I still listen plenty good." After a deep breath, Danielle continued. "Vicki told me Randolph Foods was the name of the convenience store where she worked. Says she can't afford to send me but a few measly hundred bucks every few months or so." Emma remembered Sherry Collins's speculations about the periodic check sent by Vicki to her mother. "That little ingrate. I'm livin' in this dump, while she's leadin' the good life. Where's this place she works? I'm gonna call her."

"It's Randolph Foods." Then Emma tried to buy herself some time before Danielle Schorr could contact her daughter. "Vicki's out of town for a couple of weeks. I've been trying to set up an interview with her and was told that she's in Europe on some kind of business trip."

"Europe, now isn't that hot shit? Well, when she gets back, she's going to hear from me."

Emma heard Danielle pouring something into a glass. A splash of ice cubes and long gulp followed. Emma forged ahead. "Ms. Schorr—"

Danielle cut her off with a snarl, "Don't 'Ms.' me. I'm not one of those feminists."

Smiling, Emma tried again. "Okay, Mrs. Schorr, I've answered your questions. Now could you answer a few of mine?"

"Sure, I got nothin' better to do. Fire away."

Emma opened with a general question. "What was Vicki like as a child?"

"As a kid?"

Emma elaborated. "Was she a good student? Did she have many friends? What kind of activities did she enjoy? That sort of thing."

"I knew what you meant. I was just tryin' to figure out a nice way to answer your question, but there isn't any. That kid was never any good. She might have fooled you people up there, but I would guess she's still no good. You see, she was always real smart and quick to put on airs, but trouble through and through. Left here twenty years ago—"

"Wait a minute," Emma interrupted. "Twenty years ago she would have been only in her mid-teens. Did she run away?"

"More or less. She cleared out when she was sixteen, after she graduated from high school. She was in a big hurry to get away from the 'white trash,' as she put it, and she finished a year ahead of her class. We didn't even know where she was until some college down in North Carolina tracked us down a few years later when she got behind in her tuition payments."

"Was it Duke?" Emma suggested.

"Yeah, that's it."

"Thought so. That's where Vicki graduated from."

"Graduated! Well, that's news to me! I just assumed she got kicked out when I told 'em we didn't have that kind of money. They were pretty snooty on the phone. Actually, it sounded like the perfect place for Vicki," Danielle laughed. "Well, I guess the kid must have figured out some way to come up with the money. She was real creative in that area."

"How so?"

Danielle was quiet for a moment before continuing. "I don't think that's something you should hear."

Emma wanted to scream, *But I do, I do.* Instead she said, "Listen, Mrs. Schorr, my job is not to dig up dirt on your daughter. The article will be very complimentary regardless of what you tell me. But a few colorful childhood stories might assist me in giving her profile a slightly more personal flair." Emma knew she was babbling, but she was counting on the woman being too inebriated to notice.

"So if I tell you this particular story, you'll promise not to write about it in your paper?"

"That's right, I promise." Then, feeling guilty about taking advantage of the drunken woman, but also a little cocky at her apparent success, Emma added, "But I don't want to pressure you, Mrs. Schorr. Tell me only if you want to."

"Oh, I want to. Vicki's got it coming after cheatin' me all these years. It's just that she'll have my head if this shows up in the newspaper."

"But it won't," Emma reiterated.

"Okay, here goes. You know how I told you she cleared out of here after finishing high school?"

"Yes."

"Well, she took our life savings with her, along with a two days' receipts from the heating company where she did some part-time bookkeeping. Same place my husband worked. He came close to losing his job over it until he agreed to take a cut in pay until it was all made up."

"How much did she take?"

"Counting our money, it was nearly eleven thousand. Like I said, we didn't know where she was until we got that call from North Carolina."

"Did you try to reach Vicki after you found out where she was?"

Danielle Schorr laughed. "Hell, no. At that point, I figured good riddance. Didn't get in touch with her until a couple of years later, after my second husband died. I called that Duke place, and they told me she moved to a different school. Some place in California."

"Stanford?"

"Yeah. Guess you know all that, huh? Anyway, I tracked her

down through them and gave her a call."

"What year was that?"

"God, when was it that John died?" Danielle paused to think. "March of 1983, I think."

"And what did Vicki say when you phoned her?"

"Well, not much, cuz Vicki was out. I got her roommate. I think her name was Jackie. A nice sweet-sounding sort of girl." Danielle chuckled. "Don't know what she was doing living with my daughter. Anyway, I was upset about John and all that. And I probably had a little too much to drink. I told her I was Vicki's mother. She said that was impossible because Vicki's parents were killed in a car crash when she was just fourteen."

In her most sympathetic voice, Emma offered, "That must have hurt."

"Don't worry, I got even. I told Jackie all about Vicki's past, including her stealing that money before she left town." The woman laughed again. "See, you're not the first person to hear that story."

"What did the roommate say?"

"Not much. She told me she would pass my message along to Vicki, and then she got off the phone as quickly as she could."

"And did she?"

"What?" Danielle was apparently having trouble staying focused on their conversation.

"Tell Vicki that you called?"

"Oh, yeah. Three hours later, I heard from my long-lost daughter. She was not amused by my little conversation with her roomie. Told me never to call their place again. Promised to send me money, when she could swing it, if I just disappeared from her life. Sounded good to me since I was broke at the time. So I agreed to the money."

Danielle stopped for a moment. Not knowing if the woman was going to continue, Emma prompted, "And did you ever see any money?"

"Yeah, but it was never much. At first, a few bucks would show up only every once in a while. Then the checks started comin' in more regularly. From that place up there called Randolph Foods."

"Do you remember what year that was?"

"I don't know for sure. A year or so after I talked to her, I guess."

Emma glanced back at her notes of her conversation with Vicki's assistant. "That would be about right. As I recall from her bio, she began working for Randolph Foods after finishing her MBA at Stanford in 1984."

"Her what?"

"Oh, sorry. A master's degree in business administration. It's a 'hot-shit' deal, as you would say."

Danielle laughed. "You're okay." But then Danielle's chuckles trailed off. "Since I've been getting on in years, sometimes I think it might be nice to see the kid. But I need her money too bad to make myself a nuisance. So mostly I just let her be."

Emma didn't know what to say to Danielle and simply returned to her story. "So when you called Vicki in California, was she upset at all over her father's death?"

"Her step-dad, actually. Her real daddy died in Vietnam in 1966. I married John a year later when Vicki was nine. He was a good man. He tried everything with that kid, but she never gave him a chance."

"Well, I imagine losing her real daddy at eight was tough on her."

"Maybe, but I always thought she was better off. Her daddy had a real temper. He never hit her cuz she was just a kid, but he'd come after me when he was home on leave. I don't think Vicki would have put up with that when she got older, and there would have been real trouble." Danielle sighed. "The Marines is all he was ever good at. He'd been in for twelve years when they sent him to Nam. He thought he was some kind of superman, but he lasted only three months over there. I always figured we were real lucky when that sniper picked him off."

So much for fond memories, thought Emma, writing down the information provided by the woman.

"Hey, what time is it?"

Emma looked at her watch. "Just before noon up here. Guess that would make it close to one where you are."

"I gotta go then," Danielle announced abruptly. "My program's coming on. *All My Children.* You ever watch it?"

"No, I have to work most days."

"Too bad, it's a really good show."

Hearing that the volume of Danielle's television had already increased again in the background, Emma raised her own voice and concluded the call. "Okay, I'll let you go. But here's my number, and you feel free to call me back collect if you think of anything more to tell me about your daughter."

"Well, thank you. I just might do that."

Emma sighed, as she switched off her phone. Danielle Schorr certainly didn't sound like a model human being, but Emma rather liked her. She also felt extremely sorry for her.

32

Charlie and Taylor were wrapping up their meeting in the small conference room adjoining Charlie's office. Taylor Alexander provided a stark physical contrast to the sophisticated Charlie. Bear-sized and bearded, his hair was unfashionably long and, as usual, his office attire was casual and wrinkled. As chief financial officer, Taylor was indispensable to Charlie and the Company. But he avoided the complications and intrigue usually surrounding Vicki and Charlie.

Nine years ago Taylor had married Charlie's sister, Gretchen, but the brothers-in-law were not close. However, their business relationship was friendly enough. The prior month's income statements left both of them in a good mood, and they chatted as Taylor collected his papers and packed away his laptop computer.

"Good note to end the week on," Taylor said.

"Hey, it's only Thursday."

"I know. But your sister dragged me to some high-society shindig at the hospital last weekend, and I missed the Opener." He rolled his eyes at the thought of the black tie event the previous Saturday. "I have lots of fishing to catch up on this weekend, and it's going to take tomorrow and Monday to bring me even. I'm going into the Boundary Waters for a few days. Taking my sister's boys up with me. They just moved back here from Phoenix last fall and, at thirteen and fifteen, it's time someone taught them to fish. We're all looking forward to it."

Charlie winced. "Sounds like my idea of hell." Although he could dress the part if the occasion called for it, he wasn't much of an outdoorsman. And, other than his daughters, he considered kids a nuisance.

Taylor laughed. "Gee, and I was going to ask you to come along."

There was a knock at the door of Charlie's office. Vicki, dressed in a tight red skirt and cream-colored blouse, came in without waiting for a response. As she charged through the office to the open door of the conference room, she pointed at Charlie. "We have to talk."

She was obviously agitated about something. The coolness of the night before was replaced with her usual fiery intensity. She stopped short in the doorway when she saw Taylor in the room. "Oh, you're not alone?"

"No, he's not. That's why we call this the conference room," Taylor chided, even though Vicki didn't appear to be in the mood for teasing. "Actually, I was just leaving. So he's all yours."

Vicki inhaled deeply and collected herself. She picked up the report Taylor had left on the table for Charlie's further review. "You guys reviewing last month's sales? Not bad, huh? I beat our projections by five percent."

Taylor winked at Charlie. "We were so impressed, we raised this month's projections by ten percent."

"You're an asshole, Taylor. And I don't care if you are sleeping with the boss's sister."

"Oh, as usual, the conversation deteriorates when Ms.

Stephens enters the room." He and Vicki often used humor to cover up their actual mutual dislike for one another.

Taylor closed his briefcase and looked at his watch. It said 12:20. "I better get going. I've got a twelve-thirty lunch meeting with my staff."

As Taylor was heading out the door, Charlie said, "I'll take a closer look at these numbers after lunch."

Taylor paused in the doorway. "I'm leaving early this afternoon to get a jump on traffic. So if you have any questions, catch me before I go. Otherwise, they'll have to wait until I get back next week."

"When are you leaving?"

"Three-thirty." But then Taylor corrected himself. "No, actually more like three. I have to swing by Emma's before picking up the boys. She's heading out to the farm for the night, and she agreed to drop off some landscape plans at our nursery out there."

At the mention of Emma's name, Vicki dropped the income statements back down on the table and tuned in to the men's conversation.

"Is she doing more work for you out there?" Charlie inquired.

"No, she's showing it off to a prospective client early this evening and then spending the night. The client is Athena Bergen. You know her?"

"She's on some board with Gretch, right?"

"Right. And more important for Em, she's loaded."

"Well, sounds like a perfect client. Your place will blow Ms. Bergen away." Personal feelings for his cousin aside, Charlie had to admit that she had done a spectacular job on the house.

"Em hopes so."

"Anyway, give my best to dear Cousin Emma," Charlie said sarcastically. "I'll give you a call before you leave if I have any more questions on the statements. Otherwise, see you on Tuesday. Have fun."

Vicki shut the door as Taylor disappeared down the hall. She turned back to Charlie, who was still seated at the conference room table. "Christ, I thought he'd never leave. We've got a big problem."

"And now the whole world knows about it. You can't just come barging in here shooting off your mouth."

Vicki leaned angrily across the table towards him. "Listen, I'm getting a little sick of you telling me what I can and cannot do. You need me now more than ever. So once and for all, lay off the high-and-mighty routine."

"Okay, relax. What's going on?" Charlie got up to pour himself a cup of coffee.

Vicki paced back and forth across the room. "More trouble. Someone's been checking up on me."

"What do you mean, checking up on you?"

"Some woman, Barbara Michaels. Supposedly a reporter from the *Star Tribune*. She called my office this morning and had a long chat with my assistant." Vicki let out a sinister chuckle. "My ex-assistant, now."

"So? Maybe they're doing a story on you." He laughed. "How exciting for you. Your name in the newspaper."

"Very funny," sneered Vicki, whose name and face regularly showed up in all sections of the *Star Tribune* except *Sports*.

"Well, I still don't see why you're so upset over a routine phone call."

"That's just it. It wasn't a routine call. First of all, this so-called reporter lied and claimed she had gotten clearance from PR before calling my assistant, but Roger Milstein doesn't know anything about it. Next, I talked to a friend of mine on the editorial staff at the paper. He checked with the business and news groups, and neither has a Barbara Michaels working for them. No one from the *Star Tribune* made that call."

"Did your assistant get the right paper? Maybe it was the *Pioneer Press*."

"Maybe, but that still doesn't explain the PR thing. Besides, this woman's questions were really strange. Concerning my mother and where she lives."

Charlie stared at Vicki. "Isn't your mother dead?"

Vicki stopped pacing and plopped down into one of the conference room chairs. "No," she confessed. "I only pretend that she is. Trust me, you wouldn't claim her either. Some day I'll give you all the horrid details."

"Whatever," Charlie mumbled and returned to the table and sat down across from her. "So you think this phone call is a major problem?"

"Well, maybe."

Charlie shook his head. "I think you're over reacting. It sounds to me like some enterprising young reporter doing background work on a potential story. Her editors probably don't even know about it yet."

"I don't know if we should just assume that. We have a lot of dicey stuff on our plates right now. I don't think it hurts to be a little bit paranoid."

"Okay, so call your mother, and tell her not to talk to this mystery woman if and when she calls."

Vicki shot up from her chair and started pacing again. "I already tried her right before I came in here, but there was no answer. Besides, it's not that simple. If this person manages to get hold of her, Ma's liable to be half in the bag."

"Just tell her to steer clear of discussing your grandfather."

"But then she'd just blab about other things."

Charlie smiled mockingly. "What? There are more deep dark secrets buried in your past?"

His question caught Vicki by surprise. She stopped pacing and hesitated for a moment before answering. "Oh, you know, just the usual embarrassing stories that mothers like to tell."

"I'd love to hear them," Charlie chided. "But I have to get back to Taylor's reports. And then I want to try to catch Emma before she leaves for Wisconsin."

At the mention of Emma's name, Vicki rushed back towards Charlie with her eyes narrowed. "Emma! Do you think it could be her checking up on me?" Charlie sat forward in his chair. "Why the hell would Emma want to talk to your mother?"

"I don't know. Why does she look at old police files or do any of the things she does?"

"Oh, come on. Emma has absolutely no reason to be checking up on you. She's not a super-sleuth, you know."

After last night, Vicki knew not to push the issue. Instead she asked, "So you haven't set up your meeting with her yet?"

"No, I got tied up with Taylor. But as I said, she's next on my list." Then he added, "I'll let you know if she mentions your mother."

"Very funny," Vicki fired back at him on her way out the door.

33

Since talking with Danielle Schorr, Emma had spent the past hour packing for her night at the farm. She made a trip down to her car with her sketches for Athena and her portable drafting table, which she liked to use for presentations. On her way back up, she stopped in at the deli on the street level of her building. She already had a medium-priced bottle of Chardonnay chilling upstairs in the fridge, and she picked up some Baby Swiss cheese, sesame crackers, grapes, and two apples to serve along with it during her meeting with Athena. Keeping in mind Athena's affection for the struggling artist, she was careful not to get too fancy—not that her budget would have allowed it, anyway.

Back upstairs in her condo, she had thrown a few overnight things into her duffel and then turned to her outfit for the evening. Her favorite over-sized linen sweater was a definite. But it had taken her a few minutes to choose between an old favorite, her denim jumper, and a relatively new wardrobe addition, a paisley-print rayon skirt. She finally decided the jumper was too worn or too dated or too something and tossed it aside.

She had just climbed upstairs to her office to pack her brief-case when the phone rang. She grabbed the receiver and said hello.

A long distance operator asked, "Will you accept a collect call from Danielle Schorr?"

"Sure." She looked at her watch. It said 1:05. *All My Children* had just ended.

After a slight delay, Danielle came on the line. "Howdy, Barbara. Bet you're surprised to hear back from me?"

Actually, Emma wasn't surprised at all to be hearing back from the lonely woman. Nevertheless, she answered, "Well, a little."

"I'm sorry for havin' to rush off earlier."

"That's okay."

"Say, did you call me back during my soap?"

"No."

"Someone did, and I just let it ring. I thought for sure it was you with some more questions."

"No, it wasn't me," reiterated Emma, wondering how many more drinks Danielle had downed in the last hour.

"Well, no matter. I needed to call you anyway. I kept thinking over our conversation during my program, and I came up with something else that might be of interest to you."

Emma reached for the pad of paper she had been using earli-er for notes. "What's that?"

"Remember I told you about Vicki's real daddy?"

"The guy who died in Vietnam?"

"Yeah, him. Well, what I forgot to tell you is that he was actu-ally born in Minneapolis. Thought it was kind of an interesting coincidence with Vicki livin' up there now," Danielle commented. "His family moved back East here when he was just a little kid. Sometime in the late 'thirties. They bought a small market or something, but lost it after a few years. They were dead broke, just like me, when I met Greg in the late 'fifties—"

Emma wanted to make she was following the chronology. "Greg is Greg Stephens, your first husband?"

Danielle laughed. "No, no. Stephens was my second husband's name. John Stephens. He adopted Vicki after we got married." She paused a moment. "I told you he was a good man."

"Where does 'Schorr' come from then?"

"Third husband," answered Danielle. "And my current one as far as I know. Haven't seen much of him in the last few years."

How do you lose track of a husband? Emma thought, but decided not to raise the question with Danielle. "So Stephens is Vicki's adopted name?"

"Yeah, she used to be Vicki Lindgren."

Emma perked up. "What did you say?"

"Lindgren," Danielle repeated. "Greg Lindgren, that was her daddy's name."

"And you said he was born in Minneapolis?" As Emma asked the question, she turned the pad back and found the information she had jotted down at the library the day before. Her recollection was confirmed. Lindgren was the name of Matthew Kelly's driver.

"Yeah, but he moved out here when he was three."

Lindgren was a fairly common name in heavily Scandinavian Minnesota. Emma tried not to get too excited. "Do you remember when his family moved?"

"Oh, not for sure, but I think it was not too long before the war."

"Do you know his parents' names?"

"His mother's name was Kristin. She was dead by the time I hooked up with Greg, so I never knew much about her."

"And Greg's father?"

Danielle laughed. "The only thing Greg ever called him was 'son-of-a-bitch.' But his real name was Thomas."

Emma was stunned.

Danielle droned on. "And the old guy was mean. He was still around when Greg went to Vietnam. In fact, he died just shortly before Vicki cleared out. I remember that cuz they were actually kind of tight and saw each other from time to time."

Emma's heart was pounding, but she tried to stay calm. "Well, all that is very interesting. Do you know anything about Greg's family when they lived up here?"

"Not really. It wasn't a family that did a lot of talkin'."

Emma was now eager to get off the line. "Well, I may dig around up here a little bit. I'll let you know if I find anything."

"Be sure and do that."

"I want to thank you for calling me back, Mrs. Schorr."

"Heavens, make it Danielle," the woman said, sounding depressed that their conversation was coming to a close.

"Okay, Danielle. Thanks."

34

Overwhelmed by Danielle Schorr's information, Emma collapsed back in her desk chair. After a few minutes, she collected herself and attempted to sort through everything she had heard. Vicki's biological father was Greg Lindgren. His parents were Kristin and Thomas Lindgren, who had moved from Minneapolis sometime shortly before World War II when Greg was three years old.

That brought her to the big question. *Could Greg Lindgren's father be the same Thomas Lindgren who had been Matthew Kelly's driver?* Her mind continued racing. *Certainly not if Greg Lindgren's family was no longer living in Minnesota when Kelly vanished in April of 1937. But how to determine that?*

Emma thought for a moment, and it finally came to her. *Greg Lindgren was three when he moved.* So his birth date was the key. If he had been born before April 1933, he would have turned four before April 1937 and his family would have relocated to Ohio before Kelly disappeared.

From past research for reports on various historical sites,

Emma knew that the State Registrar of Vital Statistics was located in Southeast Minneapolis and had records dating back to the 1860s. Greg Lindgren's original certificate of birth should be there. She looked at her watch and determined that there was still plenty of time for research before Taylor showed up. She slapped together a peanut butter-and-banana sandwich to eat in the car, grabbed her backpack and raced out the door.

The registrar's office was very well organized. All birth and death certificates were entered into a computer, and it was possible to search by year and by alphabetized last names. Within fifteen minutes, Emma found the birth certificate for Gregory Lindgren. Just as Danielle had said, his parents were Kristin and Thomas Lindgren. Emma looked at the birth date. August 10, 1933. The dates fit.

In fact, they just fit, Emma thought to herself. Thomas Lindgren testified at Will's trial in Minneapolis in mid-May 1937. And he was living in Ohio less than three months later when his son, Greg, turned four. Emma just sat there and stared at the screen. *Not only were Kelly's driver and Vicki's grandfather most likely the same person, but also he and his entire family had apparently left the area immediately after Will's conviction.*

Emma dug a dime out of her pocket. She fed it into the printer attached to the computer. Ten seconds later she had a copy of Greg Lindgren's birth certificate and was out the door.

Another thought occurred to her as she got into her car. *Vicki Stephens, the granddaughter of Thomas Lindgren, had probably been involved in torching the Randolph mill on Friday night. Did that make it any more likely that the skeleton was Kelly? Maybe, but not necessarily.* None of this made much sense. She was way out of her league. She took a deep breath and started for home.

Emma crossed the Mississippi River over the Tenth Avenue Bridge. As she drove through the Seven Corners area and turned onto Washington Avenue, she decided that it was definitely time to turn her haphazard investigation over to Serg. All of it—the skeleton's possible identity, her arson suspicions, and Vicki's ancestry. She'd call him during her afternoon drive over to Wisconsin.

35

After leaving Charlie's conference room, Vicki had returned to her office and tried her mother once more, but still couldn't reach her. Vicki typically worked right through lunch, and today was no different. She sat down to draft several sales directives based on the meetings with the Company's distributors earlier in the week.

Forty minutes later, the buzz of her phone interrupted her work. Not wanting to be disturbed, she let the call roll over to her voice mail, but changed her mind when she heard the start of the message:

"Hey, this is Malone. Thought you should know our nosy little friend—"

Vicki quickly picked up the receiver. "Malone, you there?"

"Oh, glad to catch you in person. I hate leaving anything too personal on those damn machines. If you know what I mean."

"Yeah, good idea to be careful," Vicki agreed. "What's up?"

"Our buddy from the grain elevator called me this morning. She wanted to talk about the other day."

"What'd you say?"

He laughed. "I told her I had nothin' to say, and that she should take her questions to you."

"Well, I haven't heard from her."

"If you do, tell her to leave me alone." With that, Dave Malone ended their conversation.

Vicki rose from her desk and looked out the window. So Emma had called Dave Malone this morning. Who else had she called? Maybe she was the mysterious Barbara Michaels after all. Sitting back down, she redialed her mother's number. After only two rings, Danielle answered this time.

"Ma, this is Vicki."

"Who?"

"Vicki, your daughter."

"Why the hell you callin'?"

Vicki rolled her eyes as she caught the obvious slur in her mother's speech. "Is there some law against a daughter phoning her mother?"

"Guess not," the older woman conceded.

"I tried to reach you earlier today. Where were you?"

"Oh, so that was you."

"You were there?"

"Where else would I be?"

"Why didn't you pick up the phone?" Vicki asked, feeling her usual exasperation with her mother.

"I don't talk to anybody during *All My Children*. You would know that if you called more often."

"Christ, Ma, get a life. And an answering machine while you're at it—"

"Hey, where you calling from?"

Vicki shook her head. "Minneapolis, where do you think I'm calling from?"

"I thought you were in Europe."

"Well, I'm not." Vicki thought for a moment. "Who told you that?"

"This reporter from Minneapolis."

Shit, Vicki thought before asking her mother, "I thought you weren't taking calls today?"

Danielle had missed the sarcasm in Vicki's voice. "I already told you. That was just during my program. She called before it started."

"Was this reporter named Barbara Michaels by any chance?"

"Yeah, that was her name. And she told me all sorts of interesting things. Like how you're some sort of big shot up there and making all kinds of money—"

"Ma, I don't have time to get into all that right now."

"Well, what if I want to."

Vicki raised her voice. "I mean it, Ma. You'll never see any of that money if you don't shut up and listen to me."

There was silence on the other end of the line.

Then Vicki made an effort to speak more calmly. "Okay, now tell me everything you told her."

"It was just family stuff." Danielle was counting on the reporter's word that she wouldn't use the embezzlement story, and she didn't plan on telling Vicki that she had shared it.

"What kind of family stuff?"

"Just about your two daddies and being adopted and all that."

"Any questions about granddaddy?" Vicki inquired nervously.

"Not in the first call. But he came up when I called her back—"

Vicki exploded on the other end of the line. "You what? You called her back?"

"Well, yeah," Danielle answered sheepishly. "I had to go watch my show when we were talking earlier. So I called her back when it was over."

Vicki pushed her chair back from her desk and jumped up. "Ma, this time you've really done it."

"Done what? What have I done?"

"Forget it. Do you still have the reporter's number?"

"Yeah, it's right here." Danielle read the number to Vicki.

"I gotta go," Vicki announced impatiently.

But before she could hang up, Danielle asked, "Am I going to see any more money?"

Vicki slammed down the receiver. She opened her drawer and pulled out the phonebook to look for Emma's phone number. There it was, the exact same number as Danielle had just given her.

"God damn it," Vicki swore aloud as she pounded her desk. Thoughts flooded her brain. *Emma now knows all about my grand-daddy. Who will she call next? Could she possibly stumble into that mess in California?*

Vicki kicked herself whenever she thought back to that first year of business school. Not for what she ultimately did, but for being so stupid as to jeopardize her future over such a trivial amount of money in the first place.

Midway through her first semester at Stanford, she had landed an intern job with a sizable advertising company in Palo Alto. From time to time, when her bank balance was running low, she adjusted the books and redirected small sums to her account. She had made similar adjustments at a number of previous jobs and was good at it. So, even though the firm eventually realized the money was missing, they didn't know the "who" and "how" behind it.

At the start of her second semester, Vicki moved in with another business student, Jackie Young. Jackie was the roommate who intercepted Vicki's call from her mother after John Stephens died. She was also the daughter of the owner of the advertising agency where Vicki was interning.

After Jackie heard of Vicki's teenage embezzlement, she immediately suspected her of stealing the money that had been disappearing from her father's company, and she confronted her roommate when she arrived home that night. Vicki denied the accusations, but Jackie wouldn't let it drop. She threatened to talk to her father as soon as he returned from an overseas business trip.

Jackie Young never shared her suspicions with her father. She was dead before he returned from Europe. Vicki had worked too hard and risked too much to let Jackie destroy it all. Besides, she had resented her roommate's strong moral streak. In Vicki's opinion, it was just another luxury afforded by Jackie's privileged upbringing.

Laughter from the hall outside Vicki's office interrupted her memories.

Christ, I should go tell Charlie about Emma's calls with Ma, Vicki thought. She raced towards the door, but stopped halfway across the room and asked herself aloud, "What the hell is he going to do? What the hell is he going to do about any of this?" She returned to her desk and sat down to think.

Emma was threatening to expose her. Just like Jackie Young had threatened to expose her. Except this time, the stakes were even higher—prestigious career, wealth, social standing, and maybe even marriage to Charlie. She knew what had to be done and, after another ten minutes of thought, she knew exactly how to do it. *Time for that meddling little bitch to get hers.*

She walked down the hall back to Charlie's office and casually stuck her head into the open doorway. "Hey, can I use your car? I've got to go out and run an errand. I dropped the Rover at the ramp office for a detail-cleaning this morning, and it won't be ready for another hour or so."

"I'd like to help you out. But remember last night? My car's at the garage right now." Vicki, in fact, had not forgotten. On cue, Charlie offered, "Didn't Taylor say he had a lunch meeting here in the office? Maybe you could borrow his pickup, provided it doesn't ruin your image and you could have it back before he wants to leave at three."

"My image is not that fragile," Vicki quipped while looking at her watch. "This should take less than an hour. So I can be back long before three. Do you know where his staff meeting is?"

"No. You'll have to check out at the front desk. He probably has a room reserved."

"Will do." With that, she was out the door.

36

After arriving home from the Registrar's Office, Emma returned to her office to finish packing up her brief-case and saw the answering machine message light blinking. When she clicked on the tape, she was surprised to hear that four messages had come in during her short absence. The first two were respectively from a builder and an interior designer who were battling on one of her residential projects. She would call them back later.

The third call was from an old college chum with whom she was supposed to have dinner on Friday night. With everything that was going on, Emma had completely forgotten about it. She was relieved to hear that her friend wanted to cancel. A spring cold would spare Emma from another lengthy account of the woman's recently failed marriage. Not wanting to risk an actual real-time conversation just now, she made a note to e-mail her friend later to wish her a speedy recovery.

The last call was a shocker. It was from her cousin, Charlie, and had come in shortly after noon. He wanted to meet with her in the next couple of days and asked her to call him back.

I guess I better find out what he's up to. She dialed the number he had left on the machine.

"Thanks for calling back," he said after the call was put through to him. He meant it. Knowing his cousin's suspicions about the origins of the mill fire, he hadn't known if she would return his call.

"No problem. So you want to get together?" Emma was not interested in making small talk with her cousin.

"Well, yes. I thought it was time we talked."

"About what?"

"The mill. You and I have wasted eighteen months of our lives battling over those damn buildings, and I don't want to get into that again. Maybe we can figure out a way for both of us to get what we want."

Emma couldn't believe what she was hearing. She replied tentatively, "You won't get any argument from me so long as we talk restoration."

"Yes, of course," Charlie assured her. "We're confident we can accommodate the restoration of most of the buildings."

Emma laughed. "Could have fooled me with all your demolition talk the other day."

"Oh, that. We were just keeping our options open. Our engineers now assure us that demolition won't be necessary." Charlie appreciated his cousin's distrust of his intentions, but it annoyed him nevertheless. "So, when can we meet?"

Emma planned to be back from the farm early the following morning, but then she was to appear before the Planning Commission to obtain final approval of a zoning change for her Kenwood client. And most of Saturday was already tied up by a morning meeting with the Coalition engineers and the early afternoon dedication of the Stone Arch Bridge. "Well, it's probably going to have to wait until late Saturday. I'm busy until mid-afternoon, but I could probably get together after three."

"I bet I'm tied up with the same thing. The bridge ceremony, right?"

'Yes," answered Emma. She was initially surprised to hear that Charlie intended to attend the dedication, but then she realized it made sense. Whether either of them liked it or not, Charlie was part of the historical riverfront landscape. Besides, many city political leaders would be there, and the opportunity for glad-handing would be enormous. Emma planned to do a bit of that herself.

"So why don't we grab a cup of coffee after the ceremony?"

"Sure."

"I'll see you on Saturday then." With that, Charlie hung up.

"Can hardly wait," Emma mumbled to herself as she clicked off her phone.

As she finished stuffing things into her brief-case, she shook her head and moaned. *Saturday should be an interesting day. Joe and a heavy dose of other politicos at the bridge dedication followed by a meeting with Cousin Charlie. Dinner at the Suarez house will definitely be the day's bright spot.* She walked back downstairs to the kitchen to pack up the food and wine that she was taking out to the farm.

Shortly before three-thirty, her intercom rang. It was Taylor. She buzzed him in the front door of the building and went out into the hall to wait for him. As he got off the elevator and saw Emma, his bearded face broke into a big smile. He was dressed in wool army fatigues and his lucky fishing vest.

"So you're going to play Wisconsin farm woman tonight?" Taylor came in the door and gave her a hug.

"Should be rough, but I think I'll survive the twenty-hour ordeal," Emma joked. "Can you stay for a minute? I could make some coffee."

"I'd love to, but I have two eager fisherboys waiting to be

picked up." Taylor handed her the roll of plans. "Just drop these off at the front counter at Laducer's. They know they're coming."

"Consider it done."

"You still have your keys to the house, right?"

Emma nodded.

"Make yourself at home. The cupboards and fridge are a little bare, but you'll find a case of good Merlot in the basement. Help yourself."

"Thanks. But your dear wife informs me that Ms. Bergen is one of those uncultured drinkers of white wine."

Taylor laughed. "Horrors. Just one step up from a beer-swiller like me." He started back towards the door. "Oh, one more thing. They're predicting another chilly night down into the low forties, and the fireplace might not give you enough heat. The thermostat is set back, so you'll have to turn it up to snap the furnace on."

"And how about you? Could be a nippy weekend for camping."

"We'll survive. And, hey, it could be a blessing. Shouldn't be any bugs."

Emma smiled. "That's a good point."

She accompanied Taylor back to the elevator and wished him a good trip. She desperately wanted to ask him about Vicki's background and what Charlie might be up to, but knew that would be unfair to Taylor. Besides, she doubted he knew of some of the more interesting aspects of Vicki's past. It was also unlikely that Charlie would have discussed his most current scheme with anyone other than Vicki. Taylor's honesty and integrity had insulated him from such involvement over the years.

37

Emma left her condo shortly after Taylor departed and drove east on I–94. The weather was glorious, a nice change from the previous day of rain and overcast skies. East of St. Paul the traffic eased up, and she reached for her cell phone.

She tried Sam, wanting to fill him in on her review of the police file and her discovery concerning Vicki Stephens, but also wanting to tell him of her decision to turn everything over to Serg. She got Sam's answering machine. The message said he was out for the afternoon and evening until eleven. Sounded like fishing, followed by poker at Darryl Soderberg's. Emma hoped she would be fast asleep before eleven. So she left a message promising her father a call back sometime the following day.

Next she tried Serg Suarez. She was put through to him after a few seconds.

"Hi," Serg answered when he heard her voice. "Good timing.

I just walked in the door." Emma could hear him shuffling through a stack of messages. "What's up?"

"Listen, I know you're busy. But do you have a minute to talk?"

"Sure. For you, I'll always make a minute."

"Maybe not after I tell you what I've been up to," Emma admitted. "I've been out playing cop."

Serg groaned. "Em, I asked you not to get involved?"

"I know, I know," Emma conceded. "But I did anyway, and I've actually uncovered some stuff that'll interest you."

Serg chuckled. "Emma Randolph, you are impossible. Tell me what you've found, and then I'll decide if I'm interested."

"Okay, but I don't know where to begin because everything is kind of interconnected."

Serg made a suggestion. "Just begin where you first decided to completely ignore my request about playing detective?"

"Ouch," Emma said, accepting his scolding before tentatively opening her story. "It started with this wild idea I had about the skeleton in the grain elevator."

"Oh, him."

"Has the medical examiner given you anything more on the guy?"

"No, not since that initial report on Monday morning. I guess he hasn't been their highest priority with all the usual city mayhem to deal with. So what was this wild idea?"

Emma tried to sound as rational as possible. "I was talking to my dad on Sunday night. You know, about the fire and the skeleton and all that. Anyway, something he said triggered this crazy notion about who the guy might be."

She paused, waiting for a reaction from Serg. He just said, "Who?"

Emma took a deep breath. "Matthew Kelly. Know who he is?"

"Sure, I recognize the name." Emma then remembered that Serg was familiar with the old case. They had discussed it shortly after they met when Serg asked about her relation to the Randolphs of Randolph Foods. "The guy your grandfather supposedly killed."

"That's him," she confirmed. "He disappeared in 1937, around the time that shaft in the grain elevator was sealed, and his body never did show up." Emma took a breath before continuing. "And the cops never searched any of the mill property for Kelly's body—"

Serg interrupted. "Hold on. How do you know that?"

"I did some research."

"Where?"

"Police Records over in City Hall. I looked at the old case file just yesterday under the watchful guise of the Wicked Witch of the West."

Serg laughed. "Oh, you mean Ms. Kron. It does take her a while to warm up to people. Most of us in the Department are still waiting."

Emma smiled at Serg's comment before continuing. "Anyway, the search for Kelly's body was limited to Will's property on Hidden Lake. They never investigated anyone other than my grandfather, and they figured there hadn't been enough time for him to dump the body anywhere else."

"And there wasn't, as I recall."

"Right. But what if someone else knocked off Kelly? Then he could be anywhere. And that's what's so attractive about my hunch. If Kelly's remains show up some place other than Hidden Lake, like that grain elevator for example, my grandfather might be exonerated."

Serg was silent for a moment. "Possibly," he finally agreed. "But your wishful thinking doesn't necessarily make our guy Kelly."

"I realize that," admitted Emma. "I only bring this up because you mentioned something the other day about going through old missing-persons files."

"Someone's been assigned to go back through all the old missing-persons and unsolved homicide files from the late 'thirties through the mid-'forties, and that should include the Kelly case. But the review—and your skeleton for that matter—isn't a high priority." He paused a moment before offering, "I'll tell you what. I'll pull the Kelly file myself and take a look at it. Probably get a chance sometime tomorrow afternoon. How's that sound?"

"Fantastic! I really appreciate the favor."

Then Serg asked, "Any more interesting theories, Detective Randolph?"

Emma cleared her throat. She knew Serg would be less thrilled with this next part. "I'm afraid there's more. You remember my arson suspicions, don't you?"

"Yes," Serg answered slowly, as if he was afraid to hear where this was heading.

"Well, I was making some inquiries—"

"Inquiries? What kind of inquiries?"

"You know, regarding the fire," Emma answered and before Serg could interrupt again, she quickly added, "And I learned a few things about Vicki Stephens."

"Like what?"

Emma abandoned her chronological account and skipped right to her last, and biggest, discovery. "Vicki is connected to the old Kelly case."

"You mean if that skeleton was Kelly, right?"

"No, regardless of that."

Serg laughed. "Come on, Em. What could Vicki Stephens possibly have to do with a murder back in the 'thirties?"

"Plenty," Emma assured him before she explained. "Matthew Kelly had a driver, a guy named Thomas Lindgren. And his testimony was critical to Will's arrest and conviction. It's all in the file. Anyway, the chauffeur had a son, Greg, who was a little boy when Kelly disappeared. And it turns out, Greg Lindgren is Vicki's biological father." She paused before commenting, "Pretty unbelievable, huh?"

"That's one word for it," answered Serg truthfully. "How did you manage to discover that?"

Emma backed up and recounted the overheard conversation she had recalled between Dave Malone and Vicki Stephens in the grain elevator and her subsequent observation of Malone's house. She told Serg that both incidents had raised her suspicions of arson and piqued her curiosity about Vicki's background. Next she described her morning phone conversations as Barbara Michaels, the first with Vicki's assistant, which had led her to Danielle Schorr; and the subsequent two with Vicki's mother, which had revealed Vicki's juvenile embezzlement and her family history. Emma finished with an account of her trip to the registrar's office.

"You've been playing cop pretty well," said Serg, obviously impressed.

"Well, what do you think?"

After a minute, Serg answered, "Let me start with the arson. That exchange between Vicki and Mr. Malone is interesting. But as you said, you only heard bits of it over that Bobcat engine. I certainly wouldn't try to hang a case on it."

"Okay, but what do you think of Vicki's embezzlement?"

"That doesn't exactly make her an arsonist. We all do some pretty stupid things when we're young. That's why we expunge juvenile records when folks hit eighteen." Then he moved on to Vicki's family history. "And it's not a crime that her grandfather testified in a murder case up here."

"Lindgren and his family left Minneapolis right after the trial. Don't you think that's kind of suspicious?"

"Why wouldn't they? Lots of people want to start over after going through something like that."

Emma suddenly remembered something else Danielle Schorr had told her. "Vicki's mother claims that Lindgren bought a store when he got to Ohio. That was still in the middle of the Depression. Where did he get that kind of money?"

"Who knows, Em. But the fact that he had some spare change

in his pockets doesn't necessarily mean the guy did anything wrong."

Emma looked down at her speedometer. Her speed had increased along with her agitation. She lightened her foot on the accelerator and tried to calm her voice. "Well, what about Vicki returning to Minneapolis after her family left all those years ago?"

"Why wouldn't she? She has family roots in the area."

"But to end up at Randolph Foods? Don't you think that's a little odd given her grandfather's connection to the Company's history?"

"Why not Randolph Foods? It is a major regional employer."

"But—"

Serg cut her off. "Yes, it's all fascinating, Em. But as a cop, I'm telling you that none of it necessarily makes Vicki an arsonist or her family in any way responsible for Matthew Kelly's disappearance."

"You're probably right," Emma reluctantly conceded. "But it's still pretty damn amazing. Especially if our mystery man should turn out to be Kelly."

"I'll at least give you that," Serg admitted. "But going forward, leave the sleuthing to me. You understand?"

Emma laughed. "Most definitely. I don't have the time to do both your job and mine. I'm out of the police business."

"Is that a promise?"

"Yes, sir. But you have to promise to let me know if you find anything when you go through Kelly's case file."

"Will do," Serg agreed. "You haven't told anyone else about Vicki's past, have you?"

"No, just you."

"Good, keep it that way. God only knows what Vicki would do to you if she discovered your little investigation." He chuckled. "I doubt even I could protect you."

Cellular static interrupted their conversation. "I think we're breaking up, but I should go anyway," Emma said. "I'm on my way out to Gretch and Taylor's farm, and I just got to my freeway exit. Thanks for listening and not laughing too much."

"It's part of my job description."

"Well, thanks anyway. See you Saturday night if not before."

38

Emma turned onto the frontage road along the freeway and made her stop at Laducer Nursery to drop off the landscape plans. Then she spent another half-hour driving south on Highway 65 through the rolling hills and coulees of Wisconsin dairy country, including the sleepy towns of Beldenville and El Paso. Neither seemed more than a three-block reduced-speed zone past a couple of taverns, a well maintained church, and a small cheese cooperative.

It was just after five when she arrived at Gretchen and Taylor's entrance road. The drive was a quarter-mile long, and after Emma made its final curve, the handsome home came into view. The design was simple and followed the lines of a traditional western ranch house. A large front porch tucked under the low, overhanging roof gave the modestly sized structure a rambling appearance that blended in perfectly with the hilly topography surrounding it. Emma was very pleased with the house, but what was more important was that both Gretchen and Taylor were thrilled with it. Emma's many tedious months of design, redesign, and construction supervision had paid off.

Emma parked around back outside the garage, grabbed her duffel and the bag of groceries she had picked up at the deli, and carried them into the house. After unlocking the back door, she crossed the mudroom that served as a rear entryway into the kitchen. She flipped on the kitchen light and left the groceries on the counter.

Proceeding through the kitchen, she entered the large vaulted living/dining room. With its soaring field-stone fireplace, exposed cedar beams, and custom-built wooden furniture, this room was the focal point of the house. She dropped her duffel on the floor near the steps leading up to the sleeping loft and opened the blinds. Then she went back outside to finish unpacking the car.

As she was walking out the back door, she heard a vehicle approaching. There was no mistaking the identity of the driver. It was Jesse Clark, the retired farmer who had sold Gretchen and Taylor this wooded twenty acres. And he was still a neighbor. The turn off the highway onto Gretchen and Taylor's private entry road was only fifty feet from his driveway.

Jesse made regular visits during construction of the cabin, and Emma had gotten to know him and his truck well. His 1979 Ford pickup was on its last legs, and it backfired every ten seconds or so. He usually appeared if he heard someone driving in. He was a bit of a pest, but Gretchen and Taylor liked his keeping an eye on the place. And from time to time, they came up with a few odd jobs around the place for him to do.

"Hi, Jesse." Emma waved as she strolled around the side of the house to see him getting out of his truck. She went over to the Ford and shook his hand. She planned to be cordial, but she didn't want him staying for more than a few minutes.

"How ya doin', Miss Randolph?"

"Just fine. And, you know, it's Emma."

"Yeah, right. Out here for the night?" Jesse reached into his shirt pocket and lifted out a pack of off-brand cigarettes. He leaned back against his truck and slowly pulled one out of the package. He obviously planned to stay at least long enough to finish his smoke.

"Yes. I'll be heading back sometime tomorrow."

"Well, I was in there yesterday fillin' the wood box."

"I appreciate that. I was just going to build a fire."

After a long inhale on the cigarette, Jesse offered, "You okay making the fire? I'd be happy to come in and lay one in for ya."

Having learned long ago to pick her battles, Emma didn't think there was much point in recounting her numerous successes with campfires in the middle of both snow and rain storms. Instead, with just a hint of sarcasm in her voice, she politely answered, "No, thanks. I think I can manage."

Jesse was unfazed. "Say, were you out here earlier today?"

"No, I just got here ten minutes ago. Didn't you just hear me drive up the road?"

"Oh, right. Well, someone was out here earlier."

"Wasn't me," repeated Emma.

Jesse took a long drag on his cigarette. "Yeah, guess it couldn't have been you. Cuz I just saw you're still drivin' that foreign rice-eater."

"It's called a Subaru, and it's actually assembled in Indiana someplace," Emma corrected him, even though she knew it would-n't make any difference. "Now, what's this about an earlier visitor?"

"Well, it was at least a couple of hours ago, now. I was on the phone with my sister, Colleen. She lives over in Eau Claire. Colleen was telling me about her neighbor's parakeet that got stuck up on the roof." Jesse's detour continued. "And some poor guy who went up to rescue it fell off the ladder and—"

Emma knew Jesse's excruciatingly detailed story could go on forever. She interrupted as nicely as she could, "Sounds awful. But what about our driver?"

Jesse smiled. "Oh, yeah. Anyway, while I was on the phone, I heard someone drive up the road. It must have taken me at least fifteen minutes to get Colleen off the line, and by that time, this person had already left and was turning back onto the main road. Saw they were driving one of those fancy off-road rigs. This one was kind of a funny shade of green and in a real hurry."

Emma shrugged. "Doesn't ring any bells with me. Might have been one of the subcontractors finishing up some work."

"I don't know," Jesse said, as he took a final puff of his cigarette. "I could have sworn there was a lady driving it, and it looked like a mighty fancy vehicle for a working stiff. Besides, Taylor told me all the guys were done in there."

"Well, there's always something left to do. Trust me, I know." Emma had decided there was little to be gained by reminding Jesse that there had been several female subcontractors employed on the house. Besides, she knew this idle speculation regarding the identity of the afternoon visitor could go on forever. "Listen, Jesse, I have a client coming out later, and I have to finish up some work before she arrives. I really should get to it."

"Okay, I guess I'll head on out then." He ground out his cigarette on the side of his truck and threw the butt in the back. "Have a pleasant evening, and keep those doors locked. This isn't exactly the big city, but we have our share of weirdoes roaming around out here."

Emma smiled warmly and meant it. She appreciated his concern. "I will." Then she added, "My client is coming at seven. So if you hear a car, it'll be her. No need to check it out."

Jesse grinned and opened the door to his truck. "Okay, I can take a hint. I won't pester ya." He climbed up behind the steering wheel and waved as he drove off. His truck backfired twice before he turned the first curve in the road. Emma shook her head and returned to the rear of the house to finish moving in her things.

Back in the house, she first built and lit the fire and then turned to the groceries. She fixed a small fruit and cheese platter and put it, along with the wine, into the refrigerator. Next she unpacked her sketches and site plan and set up for her presentation on the four-season porch off the living room. The fireplace was two-sided, and the flames shone through on the east wall of the porch. The evening sun was streaming through the west-facing windows. At this time of day, the porch was definitely Emma's favorite part of the house.

She made a quick list of things she wanted to point out during her tour of the house with Athena and roughed out a few business points she wanted to go over after the presentation of her design ideas. Just before seven, she carried her duffel upstairs and changed out of her jeans and rugby shirt into the mid-calf-length paisley skirt and pale-blue linen sweater.

As Gretchen had forewarned, Athena Bergen was late. She pulled up in her Lexus just after seven-thirty, offering no excuses for her tardiness. *Glad I decided against my denim ensemble*, Emma thought as she followed the trim fifty-eight-year-old woman into the house. Athena was dressed in a stunning leather-trimmed denim dress and was adorned with tasteful turquoise and silver jewelry.

"Love your earrings," Emma said.

"Oh, thanks," Athena responded coolly. "An artist friend in Taos made them for me."

"Do you spend a lot of time in New Mexico?"

"I used to, right after Erik died." She paused. "I call it my Santa Fe period."

Images of Athena mushing sled dogs and sporting the very best in extreme weather gear flashed into Emma's mind. "And now it's on to the Ely period?" she joked. Athena smiled only slightly.

Emma kicked herself for being overly familiar with her not-yet client. In an effort to recover, she turned immediately to business. "Well, shall we get right down to work? I thought we'd start with a short tour of the house and then take a look at some of my ideas for your place."

"Fine with me," Athena agreed, sounding friendly for the first time since she had arrived.

Athena loved the farmhouse and was equally impressed by Emma's concept sketches for her Lake Vermillion property. The design job was hers, and she and Athena closed the deal out on the porch with firelight and Chardonnay.

By the time Athena got up to leave, it was already well past dark. Emma had stoked the fire several times during Athena's visit and didn't realize how chilly the rest of the house had become until she walked Athena out to the front door. As they said their good-byes, she turned up the thermostat and wasn't surprised to immediately hear the furnace snap on.

"I'll send you over a contract early next week," Emma said. "Then I'll rough out a design schedule with some possible meeting dates. You should have that by Wednesday."

"I like your style. No nonsense. You get right on things."

"I do my best." Emma accompanied Athena outside and waited on the front porch until Athena's car disappeared from view.

When she turned to go back into the house, a ragged calico cat brushed up against her leg. She recognized the cat from past visits. "Hi, Puss," she said in greeting. The animal belonged to someone in the area, but was willing to befriend anyone with a handout. He was used to Gretchen's generosity and appeared to expect the same from Emma.

She picked up the cat and carried him into the house. In the kitchen, she poured some milk into a bowl and then set both Puss and the bowl down on the floor. "Go at it. It's a night for celebration."

Emma hadn't eaten a thing during her meeting with Athena, and she, too, was hungry. She retrieved the fruit and cheese plate from the porch and made herself an omelet with some eggs she found in the refrigerator. She poured the last of the wine into her glass and carried her belated dinner into the living room. Slipping an Ella Fitzgerald disc into the CD player, she sat down to savor her evening's work. When the music ended, she returned to the porch to jot down a few points Athena had made during their meeting.

After just fifteen minutes, Emma had to quit working. Her head was pounding, and she was having trouble concentrating. *Maybe I should have skipped that last glass of wine*, she told herself. Deciding to make herself some tea, she wandered back through the living room towards the kitchen.

At the kitchen entrance, she tripped over Puss who was stretched out in the doorway. "Hey, move it," she snarled at the cat, as she caught herself from falling. When the cat didn't move, Emma gave it another gentle shrug. There was still no movement. She picked up the animal and realized it was barely breathing. *What the hell?*

Standing in the middle of the kitchen, she suddenly felt extremely dizzy. While still holding Puss, she grabbed the counter with her right hand to steady herself. "I'm not feeling so good either, little buddy," Emma said to the limp animal cradled in her left arm. "We gotta get out of here."

As Emma stumbled out the back door, she gulped in a huge breath of the cool evening air. It tasted almost sweet. She staggered another fifteen yards away from the house and gently dropped Puss down onto the dirt drive. Shivering in just her skirt and light sweater, Emma ran to her car and grabbed the two blankets she kept in the back. By the time she got back to Puss, he was already breathing more easily. She wrapped the cat in the smaller of the blankets and pulled the second one around her shoulders. She realized she was feeling better, too. Her headache was clearing and the dizziness was gone.

Something in the house was making them sick. She knew the most likely candidate was carbon monoxide, because she had felt fine all during Athena's visit and right up until an hour or so after she had turned up the thermostat. But the house was less than a year old, with a state of the art heat exchange-and-ventilation system that had been installed by professionals and checked by umpteen county housing inspectors.

She considered going back inside to open some windows, but decided against it. It was better to stay put, call the fire department, and let them deal with whatever was causing the problem. She walked back to her car and grabbed her cell phone to dial 911.

Emma was very relieved when she heard the siren that signaled the approach of the volunteer fire department vehicle. She left Puss, who was now lazing comfortably in the blanket, and went around to the front of the house to meet it.

40

The St. Croix Volunteer Fire Department staff was extremely professional. The driver, Kevin, a friendly, good-looking guy in his mid-thirties, appeared to be in charge. He took Emma's name and a brief statement, while the other two crewmembers, Becca and Dan, donned oxygen masks and entered the house with several gauges and monitors.

They came out just a few minutes later and reported carbon monoxide levels of approximately four hundred and twenty parts-per-million. They then returned inside to shut off the natural-gas main to the house and to open windows. Kevin turned to Emma after his associates went back into the house. "You're a lucky woman, Ms. Randolph. Those concentrations can be life-threatening after just three hours. That stray cat might have saved your life."

Emma smiled and looked over at Puss. "I'll bring cream and caviar on my next visit." Then she asked Kevin, "Think it could be the furnace? I turned the heat on earlier."

"Most likely. Although sometimes the water heater can cause the problem."

Emma shook her head. "Whatever the problem is, it's really strange. The house is brand new."

"And you said the owners used the house all winter without any problems?"

Emma thought for a moment. "Not even the slightest headache, as far as I know."

"Well, Becca and Dan will see if they can find the problem once they shut off that gas main."

"Think I'll be able to go back in tonight?"

"Just to collect your things. I'm afraid we don't want anyone staying here until we're certain this won't happen again. There's a motel over in Ellsworth if you don't feel like driving all the way back to the Cities tonight."

"That might be a good idea. It's nearly eleven and it's been a long day."

Then Emma heard the backfire of Jesse's truck. Both she and Kevin turned to see the old Ford coming to a stop behind the parked fire truck. Emma waited for Jesse to approach within ear range. "You're here just in time for all the excitement," she said. "The house is filled with carbon monoxide."

She introduced Kevin to Jesse. Kevin brought him up to speed on the situation, which Emma greatly appreciated. Kevin was much more patient with Jesse's endless questions and theories than Emma ever would have been. After ten minutes or so, Jesse seemed satisfied with the whole explanation.

While Becca and Dan continued their work inside the house, Emma gave Kevin more detailed information concerning the owners of the house and the reason for her visit. Jesse nodded and confirmed everything she said, even though no one was doubting her in any way.

"Any carbon monoxide detectors in the house?" Kevin inquired.

"Not yet. I know they've been on Taylor's list. He'll kick himself for not having gotten to it. He's kind of a detail guy."

"They really should have one on each level."

"Believe me, Taylor will have a hundred of these things in here after this."

Kevin laughed. "More the better."

A few minutes later, Becca and Dan came out of the house and rejoined the group. "How we doing?" asked Kevin.

Becca pulled off her mask. "Levels are already down below a hundred PPM. And we found our problem."

"What is it?" Kevin asked.

"The furnace."

"What's wrong with it?"

"An obstructed vent," answered Becca, before launching into a more detailed explanation. "The sheet metal duct from the furnace to the chimney is disconnected, and the furnace end is hanging down close to the floor so the exhaust can't clear properly. The exhaust is probably just backing up and causing the furnace to burn inefficiently. That inefficient burn produces the CO."

Emma jumped in. "How could that have happened?"

"Looks like it was never screwed down during installation. The holes were drilled, but the rivets are missing. Without those, just a bump could have knocked that vent free." Becca looked over to the cat. "Maybe even by Mr. Puss climbing around down there."

"I don't think so," Emma responded. "I just let him in late this evening, and I don't think he could have gotten down into the basement."

"If that joint wasn't fastened down, the vibration from the furnace cycling off and on all winter might have worked the duct free," Kevin offered.

"Possibly," Becca agreed. "But hard to tell for sure."

Jesse jumped in. "I was in there just yesterday, and I didn't get sick or nothin'." But then he added, "Of course, I was only in and out long enough to haul in a few loads of wood."

"And the heat probably wasn't on," Emma pointed out.

"Oh, yeah, that's right," Jesse conceded.

"Did you go downstairs?" Becca asked him.

Jesse was taken aback by the question. "No, ma'am! I wasn't anywhere near the furnace."

Becca laughed. "I wasn't implying that you were."

The man remained defensive. "Well, someone could have monkeyed with that vent. And I wanted it understood that I—"

With a skeptical frown, Emma interrupted. "Oh, come on, Jesse. You think somebody intentionally removed those screws? Why would anyone want to do that? You've been watching too many reruns of *Murder, She Wrote*." The firefighters laughed and nodded in agreement with Emma. Tweaking Jesse a little more, she suggested, "Hey, maybe it was our mystery visitor in the green vehicle?"

"Maybe," he said defiantly. Jesse was obviously not amused by Emma's kidding.

Kevin interrupted their banter. "Listen, we're not going to solve this here. Let's do a final reading and see if we can let Ms. Randolph back in to pack up her things."

Becca returned and reported that the carbon monoxide levels had dropped to below fifty parts-per-million. With that news, Kevin gave Emma the green light to return to the house, and he walked with her back inside while Becca and Dan packed up their equipment. Along the way, Emma scooped up Puss and handed him to Jesse who was trailing close behind them. "This little fella has earned a sleep indoors," she said. "Can you put him up for the night, Jesse?"

"My pleasure. Got room for you, too." He had obviously forgiven her for the earlier teasing.

Emma responded quickly. "Thanks, but I think I'll just head

on back to the city." She looked over at Kevin hoping he wouldn't mention her actual plans to stay at the local motel. He just smiled, and Emma was grateful for his silence.

Once inside, they first went downstairs to the utility room to survey the disconnected duct. They could see the holes in the dangling sheet metal where the rivets should have been. Kevin pointed to a red tag hanging from an overhead pipe. "Tell your cousin and Mr. Alexander that the furnace has been tagged. That means that the main gas line into the house has to stay off until the county inspector gets back here to verify that their heating contractor has properly reconnected and fastened that vent. And hopefully, both the contractor and the inspector will do their jobs right this time. It's not exactly brain surgery."

Back upstairs, Jesse, still clutching Puss, wandered back outside to pester Becca and Dan. Kevin closed up the windows while Emma packed up her sketches, clothes, and the little bit of perishable food she had left in the refrigerator.

On the way out the back door, Kevin reached into his wallet. "Here's my card. I'll be writing up an incident report, which should go in the mail to your cousin and her husband sometime tomorrow. But tell them to give me a call if they have any questions before then."

"Thanks, I'll pass that along." Emma stuffed his card in her pocket. "You guys accept tokens of gratitude? Gretch and Taylor will want to send something."

"None expected. But always appreciated. We are volunteer, after all."

Before walking over to her car, Emma said, "Thanks for not spilling my actual plans to my buddy Jesse out there."

Kevin laughed. "No problem. No one deserves a night around him after what you've been through."

Emma reached out to shake his hand. "You guys have been great. I really appreciate it."

"Our pleasure, Ms. Randolph." Emma got into her car, and

Kevin started around the front of the house. Then he turned back to Emma and motioned for her to roll down her window. "By the way, I love the house. I'll be in touch when I win the lottery."

Emma laughed. "I'll expect your call." She waved and pulled around to the front and waited for the fire truck and Jesse's pickup to pull out before she left.

FRIDAY

41

After leaving the farmhouse, Emma had driven several miles back to the west to the Tip-Top Motel in Ellsworth. Just two other cars and a semi-trailer rig were parked in the brightly lit parking lot, but the neon "no vacancy" sign was lit. She had rung the night buzzer until a sleepy clerk appeared and checked her into Room Nineteen. There had been no reference to the no-vacancy sign.

The room was exactly as she expected—clean, but still dingy and depressing. It had a bed, though, and that's what Emma was looking for most. She considered trying to reach Gretchen to tell her about the furnace, but then remembered she was probably still at the hospital. When Emma had finally hit the bed, it was well past midnight and she slept soundly until the early morning sun peeked through the thin curtains a few minutes before seven.

Emma opened her eyes and took a moment to remember where she was. Pulling the covers up around her, she lazed for another fifteen minutes or so and then crawled out of bed to face the instant coffee provided with the room's hotpot. After washing up, she phoned Gretchen.

Gretchen greeted her brightly. "Good morning."

"You're sounding way too chipper for someone who worked late last night."

"It's always like this. The exhaustion never sets in until mid-day. So how'd it go with Athena last night?"

"Well, as they say, some good news and some bad news."

Gretchen laughed, "Hit me with the good news first."

"Okay. I got the job."

"Fantastic! Now what's the bad news?" Gretchen didn't wait for an answer. "Wait! Don't tell me. Athena expects to break ground next week?" Before Emma could say anything, the diesel semi roared to life out in the parking lot. "What is that?" Gretchen asked.

"Actually that's part of the bad news," Emma said. "I'm at the Tip-Top."

"The Tip-Top? Why aren't you at the farm? Is everything okay out there?"

"Yes, calm down. Everything is fine, now. But I had quite the scare last night." She described the previous evening's events to Gretchen.

"Em!" Gretchen exclaimed, after Emma finished. "You could have died. I guess Athena could have too."

"Yes, if I had turned on the heat any earlier. I'm so glad she was gone. I don't think a near-death experience would have been the best deal-clincher."

Gretchen didn't laugh. "How could this have happened? Taylor and I were out there last weekend and didn't have any problems."

"Was the furnace running?"

Gretchen thought for a moment. "Yes, it was. I remember it dropped close to freezing on Saturday night."

Emma recounted Kevin's theory that the furnace operation could have gradually worked the loose joint free. Then she added, "Of course, it's also possible that someone was down there since you were out here last weekend and bumped it."

"I don't think so. As far as I know, no one's been in there this past week."

"Jesse was in there on Wednesday loading wood," Emma reminded her.

"Oh, that's right. Taylor asked him to do that in case you got out there after dark."

"And you also had a mystery visitor yesterday." Emma told her about the woman in the green vehicle that Jesse had seen leaving the entry road earlier in the afternoon. She concluded by wryly observing, "I think time weighs a little heavy for Jesse."

Gretchen chuckled. "You got that right." She then returned to the green truck. "As far as I know, we weren't expecting anyone to be out there yesterday except for you. And the vehicle description doesn't ring any bells with me. I'll ask Taylor about it, though. It's probably something he set up and just forgot to tell me. So you think either Jesse or our mystery subcontractor could have knocked that vent when they were working in there?"

"Not Jesse," clarified Emma. "He didn't go down into the basement. He made that very clear to the fire crew."

"Why, did they accuse him of anything?"

Emma laughed. "Oh, no, not in any way. Jesse was the one suggesting foul play."

Gretchen laughed too. "Well, I hate to disappoint him, but I can't really think of anyone who might want to kill Taylor or me. How about you? Anyone want you dead?"

"Maybe Charlie and his gal-pal, Vicki," Emma answered in jest.

Gretchen feigned indignation. "Hey, that's my brother you're accusing."

"Well, you asked."

"Enough nonsense. What's the deal with the furnace?"

"The gas is off right now. You have to get the duct fixed and then have it reinspected by the County before you can turn it back on."

"Okay, I'll give the contractor a call right away. They're going to get an earful about those missing screws, first from me and then, I'm sure, from Taylor. He's not going to be happy when I tell him your story."

Knowing that Taylor was not a cat lover, Emma added, "Tell him that he's going to have to be nice to Puss from now on."

Gretchen chuckled and then said in a more serious tone, "You're lucky that crazy cat passed out in the kitchen doorway."

"Very lucky, is more like it."

Before saying goodbye, Gretchen asked, "Hey, you free tonight?"

"Matter of fact I am. Why?"

"Let's get together for dinner. I want to see you in the flesh. Make certain you're okay and hear more about Athena's house. "And," she joked, "I'd love to hear more about your new fireman friend."

Gretchen wasn't a big Joe Buchanan fan, and she never missed an opportunity to promote a substitute for him. Emma never took her suggestions too seriously. "There's nothing more to tell about my new fireman friend," Emma protested mildly. "Other than that I told him you'd be forwarding a nice contribution to the volunteer fire department. But I'd love to get together anyway."

"Great! Let's plan on seven. Call me later in the afternoon. We can make final plans then."

"Will do. See you tonight."

Emma packed up and checked out of the motel. Then she walked two blocks over from the motel to a local café, where she ordered real coffee and blueberry pancakes. She started back to the city a short while later. When she hit the freeway, she reached for her cell phone to call Sam, but the battery was dead. In all the excitement last night after she had called 911, she had forgotten to turn it off.

She simply shrugged, popped in a reggae tape, and drove west listening to Bob Marley.

42

On her way back from a late lunch meeting, Vicki passed by Charlie's office and overheard his assistant, who was seated at her desk in an alcove outside Charlie's door and was talking on the phone, tell Charlie that she had reached his father and was going to put the call through to the inner office.

Vicki had been curious about Charlie and Peter's private chat on Wednesday night. She backtracked down the hallway and slipped through the outside door leading into the conference room adjoining Charlie's office. She closed the door behind her. Across the room, the door leading into the office was standing ajar a few inches.

Through the crack, Vicki could see Charlie sitting at his desk with his back to her. His feet, shod in expensive tasseled loafers, were propped up on the credenza behind his desk. He was holding the receiver to his ear. Staying out of the line of sight from Charlie's desk, in case he turned around, Vicki crept across the conference room closer to the open door. From there, she could eavesdrop on Charlie's side of the conversation with Peter.

"Dad, I just had an idea. Why don't we have a little family cocktail party up at your place tonight? You, me, Gretch, and dear Cousin Emma."

Vicki winced at the mention of Emma's name. She continued listening.

"Yes, I talked to her yesterday about our decision to restore the mill.

"Well, she wasn't totally convinced I meant it.

"No, I don't want to get into that tonight. She and I have a meeting already set up for tomorrow afternoon to go over those details. Tonight, we're going to give her the second dose of our generosity. Tell her the Company is willing to sell Lake Salish to Sam.

"Yes, Gretch should be there. It'll add sincerity to our gesture.

"No, he can't make it. He's up north fishing with his nephews.

"No, of course I haven't said anything about all this Kelly stuff to either of them. And I never will. But I plan to fill Gretch in on the Lake Salish situation before tonight.

"I know she'll think we're up to something. She doesn't trust me, or you for that matter. But that's exactly why she'll be here. To protect her dear friend Emma from the likes of us.

"Of course, we're using her. But what should she care as long as Emma walks out of here tonight with Lake Salish. Besides, it's time my dear sister does her part in trying to save this family.

"So I'll try to arrange it for seven-thirty.

"Did Mom leave for Chicago?

"Good. I think she'd only confuse things.

"No, she won't be there either. This is a family matter. And despite what she knows and expects, it's time for Ms. Stephens to bow out of our affairs.

"See you at seven-thirty, then. Try to go easy on the booze until we get there. I don't want any slip-ups tonight."

Vicki seethed as she listened to Charlie conclude his conversation with Peter. *So now he's suddenly the expert on family survival. Little late to the game, lover boy.*

She heard Charlie's chair squeak and guessed he was turning back to his desk. Next, she recognized the pushing of buttons on his phone. She held her breath and stood perfectly still until she again caught the creaking swivel of the chair and the scrape of Charlie's loafers back on the top of the credenza. As she quietly exhaled, she heard Charlie say, "Hi, Gretch."

Vicki considered picking up the extension phone on the conference room table, but decided not to risk it. She listened again to Charlie's part of the conversation.

"Glad I caught you. Can you stop up at Dad's at seven-thirty this evening?

"Actually, that works out well. I was planning on inviting her, too. There's some family business Dad wants to discuss with her.

"No, this isn't regarding the mill. Besides, you've made it very clear that you don't want to be dragged into the middle of that controversy. This is old family stuff, some ancient history that Dad wants to clear up."

Charlie explained the Lake Salish situation to his sister and concluded with, "That's it. Dad thought it would be nice if you were there. You know, good news from a friendly face as well as from the two of us.

"Honestly, nothing else is going on here. This is Dad's idea.

"How would I know why he wants to do it? But it seems to matter to him. So I'm going along with it.

"I know, you think me incapable of any compassion for that old drunk. But he is my father, and I'm not totally heartless.

"Apology accepted. Hey, do you know where I can reach Emma? Is she still out at the farm?

"What? Carbon monoxide at your place?"

There was a long pause in Charlie's end of the conversation before he finally said, "God, she's lucky to be alive. We have something else to drink to tonight. See you later at half past seven."

In the adjoining room, Vicki swore under her breath when she learned that Emma was okay. She stayed in her hiding place while Charlie left a message with the cocktail party details on Emma's answering machine. Then she heard footsteps and the rattle of ice being scooped into a glass. Vicki knew Charlie was now standing at the wet bar on the other side of the adjoining room. It was out of the line of sight of the conference room door, and she used the opportunity to sneak out through the hallway door and return to her own office.

Trembling with anger, she slammed the door behind her. *Charlie's an idiot. It's going to take a lot more than his generosity to get rid of Emma. And he'll never have the balls to do it.*

Vicki paced back and forth across her office, mulling over Charlie's revelation about Lake Salish and about his plans for the evening. After twenty minutes had gone by, she laughed and announced to the empty room, "We'll see who's going to bow out of family affairs." She marched over to her desk and reached for the phone.

43

Serg Suarez returned to his cramped office at three after an endless policy review meeting with his staff. Waiting for him was the Kelly file. He had requested it from Police Records after talking to Emma earlier this morning. He poured himself a cup of coffee from the pot sitting on the corner of his desk and sat down. Loosening his tie, he began paging through the file.

He shook his head in disbelief when he confirmed that the search for Kelly was limited to the several acres surrounding Will Randolph's property. *Guess police work was pretty political even back then.* His secretary came into his office carrying a stack of phone messages. One of the messages was from Laura Finney at the medical examiner's office. He returned the call and was put through to the doctor.

"Hi, Serg. Just wanted to let you know we've finished up with Lefty."

Serg was confused. "Who?"

"Oh, sorry. The old skeleton found after the mill fire. We nicknamed him Lefty because his right arm had been amputated just above the elbow. It—" Laura suddenly stopped in mid-sentence.

Serg guessed she had just remembered that he was also missing an arm. "Go on," he encouraged.

"Oh, Serg, I'm sorry about the nickname."

"Hey, don't worry about it," Serg assured her and meant it. He was well aware of the dark humor bantered around the medical examiner's office. His office was the same way. It was one way of coping with the pressures of the job. "Please continue."

"Okay," the relieved examiner said. "After we couldn't find the right radius, ulna, or metacarpals in that debris, we took a closer look at the right humerus. And sure enough, the lower end of the bone was severed. Must have happened at least several years before he died, because the stub end was completely scarred over."

Serg let Laura talk on as he scrambled back through the Kelly file. When he found the reference to Kelly's industrial accident that he remembered having read a few minutes before, the enormity of the medical examiner's findings sunk in. He uttered, "It actually could be him."

"What did you say?" Laura inquired.

"I may know who that guy is. And if I'm right, his name isn't Lefty. It's Matthew Kelly."

"Who?"

"One of our long-unsolved homicides from back in the 'thirties." Serg filled in the examiner on the generalities of the old case. He concluded with a warning. "We'll have to tread lightly on this one. Lots of prominent people still might have a stake in this one."

"You know we never talk to anyone unless you guys give us the green light."

"I know," Serg acknowledged. "Now, what else can you tell me about Lefty?"

"Well, that old amputation was the only sign of torso trauma that we found."

"So the crushed parietal area was the only trauma coterminous with death?"

"As far as we can tell."

"No sign of any gunshot wound?" Serg pressed.

"Again, not as far as we can tell," Laura answered. "Why are you asking? Was this Kelly guy supposedly shot?"

"Supposedly. Listen, how long before I can get a full written report?"

"Well, as you know, this one hasn't been a top priority. But I could put a hustle on it if you give me the say-so."

"Consider the say-so given. See what you can do to speed it up."

"You'll probably have something later today; tomorrow, at the latest."

Serg rubbed the shoulder joint of his missing arm as he mulled over the murder of sixty years ago. *Was the entombed skeleton actually Matthew Kelly?*

It looked likely. The amputated arm certainly matched Kelly's description. The dental work and the boots did date back to the 1930s. And the warehouse had been completed at the same time as Kelly's disappearance. After receiving the medical examiner's report, he'd start looking for Kelly's still-living relatives, if any, for possible DNA matching.

He topped off his coffee and continued musing over the file. *What if the skeleton is Kelly? Then how does that affect the case against Will Randolph?* There was the issue of his insufficient time to dispose of the body away from Hidden Lake, as Emma had pointed out the previous day, but also the skeleton revealed no sign of having been shot.

Serg paged back through the file. Three witnesses, Thomas Lindgren, Mrs. Terry, and Will Randolph, had all heard shots that night at half past nine. But only Lindgren had testified that the shots came from inside the house. *Why would Thomas Lindgren lie about the night's events?*

And now, what to make of the connection of Vicki's family to the case? If the skeleton did turn out to be that of Matthew Kelly, what was the likelihood that granddaughters of both Will Randolph and Thomas Lindgren would be present when he was unearthed sixty years after his death? Coincidence always made Serg suspicious.

All hell will break loose if we open this thing back up after all these years!

Serg knew he couldn't call Emma, even though he had promised her an update after reviewing the Kelly file. As he had told Laura Finney just moments before, this old case involved a lot of high-profile people, both living and dead. And Emma was certainly one of them. He now regretted even his preliminary reports to her earlier in the week.

44

Emma's drive back from Wisconsin was uneventful, but pleasant. The day was one of the first truly warm ones of this late spring, and Emma was excited to finally see farmers planting in the fields and the leaves opening on most of the trees.

Once back in the city, she stopped at home just long enough to drop off her things before walking over to City Hall for the planning commission meeting. She was fifth on the agenda, but it still took over four hours to wade through the first four items. So, even though the zoning change had won approval, she was tired and grouchy when she arrived back at her condo just before five.

Waiting for her were three phone messages. She played them back as she unpacked her briefcase and portfolio at her desk.

The first call had come in at two-thirty-five:

"Hi, Emma, it's Charlie. Say, I was telling Dad about our meeting tomorrow afternoon to discuss the mill. He was so pleased to hear that you and I were finally working together, that he suggested we all come up to his place at seven-thirty tonight for a celebratory drink. I can make it. And I already talked to Gretch. She said you two were getting together tonight anyway, and she didn't think you'd mind too terribly much if you kicked your evening off up there. So I'll assume you can make it. If not, give me a call."

Emma stiffened as she replayed his message. Because she was much more comfortable with Charlie as an enemy, his new tone made her nervous. *I can't handle this Mr. Nice routine. He's got to be up to something. Hopefully, Gretch will clue me in so I'll know if it's safe to enter the lions' den up there tonight.*

She clicked on the second message and chuckled when she heard it was from Gretchen. It was another of her usual rambling monologues:

"Hi! Hey, I haven't heard from you. Hope you're still alive. I know, that's not very funny. About tonight. You got Charlie's message, no doubt. I know you're probably very hesitant to accept the invite. But trust me, his intentions are friendly. Besides, I'll be there to keep both Charlie and Dad in line.

"I've got to stop by the hospital before going over to Dad's, so I'll just meet you there. We'll make our escape after one drink and then go down to my place for dinner, probably courtesy of that new Tuscan deli up the street. And I'm heading downstairs to raid the cellar as soon as I hang up. The wine here will definitely be better than what we're likely to get up at Dad's. He's big on serving those sweet German monstrosities.

"Oh, I told Charlie we're coming casual. So no need to pull out your estate wear. See you there."

The third call was from someone identifying herself as Charlie's assistant:

"Hello, Ms. Randolph. This is Jeannine, calling from Charlie Randolph's office. Mr. Randolph apologizes for not calling you himself, but he's tied up in a late-afternoon meeting outside of the office. There is a slight change of plans for cocktails tonight. Mr. Randolph's father is feeling a bit under the weather and requested an earlier time for the gathering. If possible, please arrive an hour earlier than planned, at six-thirty. I will also be calling Mr. Randolph's sister to apprise her of the earlier time. There is no need to call me back unless you are unable to make the earlier time. Thank you."

"Shoot," muttered Emma after hearing the third message. "Only an hour before I have to leave." She decided to devote part of it to some yoga, in an effort to shake her ugly mood.

After switching into sweat pants and a T-shirt, Emma picked up the receiver from the kitchen phone and carried it into the living room. She wanted to confirm that Gretchen was also planning to arrive up at Peter's at the earlier time. She punched in Gretchen's home number and sat down on the floor to start her stretches. The phone rang several times and then rolled over to Gretchen's answering service.

Damn, she's already left for the hospital. Emma disconnected the line. She thought about trying to reach Gretchen in her car, but decided not to bother her. *She'll show there eventually. I can survive for an hour without her if I have to.*

45

Gretchen had left her Southwestern Minneapolis home for University Hospital at half past four. As she pulled her Volvo wagon onto I–35W, her cell phone rang. It was Taylor calling from a campsite up on Lake Agnes in the western reaches of the Boundary Waters Canoe Area Wilderness.

"Hi," she greeted him. "The hunter-gatherers are checking in on wireless?"

"Just wanted to see if this thing works up here," Taylor explained. "Where you headed?"

"Over to the hospital for a couple of hours. How was the fishing today?"

"Couldn't have been better! All three of us limited out. Right now, the kids are out gathering wood for our fried-walleye feast. Much to their surprise, they actually found the whole fishing thing pretty exciting. They're anxious to get at it again tomorrow."

"I'm glad they're having fun. But you know your real challenge will come when the fish stop biting. See how exciting the teenagers find that."

"It'll never happen. I can smell the fish."

Gretchen laughed. "I've heard that before. Usually right before five or six long hours in the boat without even a nibble."

"Hey, but that's five or six hours with me. That has to be a thrill, huh?"

"Right."

"So what's happening down there?"

"Lots, actually. The biggest excitement was out at the farm last night." She told Taylor about Emma's carbon monoxide scare.

"God, I'm so relieved Em's all right," he said. "Sounds like she had quite the night."

"And she's in for another one." Gretchen then filled him in on the impromptu cocktail party called up at Peter's, including the Lake Salish proposal planned for Emma.

As the chief financial officer for the Company, Taylor was surprised that he had never been told of the actual ownership of the Lake Salish property. "We've probably missed out on all sorts of deductions over the years."

"Oh, you are such an accountant. But don't feel left out. Apparently, it's been Dad's secret for years. He just told Charlie about it."

"Wow, why was that?"

"Don't know. I haven't actually talked to Dad. I got the story from Charlie. You'll probably get all the details on Monday."

"I'm sure I will." Then Taylor returned to the problems out at the farmhouse. "Quite the couple of days for Emma. I still can't believe that near miss out at the farm. Those damn CO monitors have been on my list for months. Just didn't seem that urgent with a new house and all."

"You wouldn't think so," Gretchen agreed. "Anyway, I called the mechanical contractor and talked to Paul. You know, the foreman of their crew. He's going to stop out first thing Monday morning."

"Not until Monday, huh? We better have Jesse drain the water lines tonight in case it drops below freezing again this weekend."

"Good idea. I'll give him a call as soon as we're through." Taylor chuckled. "He'll be more than willing to help."

"You know," Gretchen said, "Paul claims those rivets were there when they finished the job. Claims there's no way the inspector would have approved their work without them."

"Oh, come on. Why can't he just admit everybody messed up?"

"He swears they were there. He remembers putting them in himself."

"Well, they were missing last night, right?"

"Yeah. But as Paul pointed out, something held that duct together all winter."

"There's that vibration theory you mentioned. That probably takes a while. Besides, either Paul forgot to fasten down that joint, or some mystery person broke in and sabotaged it. Which sounds more plausible to you?"

"You're right, but I still don't think Paul intentionally lied to me. He's just mistaken."

"Whatever. As long as he does it right this time."

"He promised he will. And it's interesting you mentioned a mystery visitor. That was something else Emma told me. According to Jesse, someone—a woman he thinks—was out at the farm earlier on Thursday before Emma arrived. Were you expecting any of the subcontractors to stop back out?"

"No. The only thing left to do is the landscaping, and there's no reason for them to be out there until the weather warms up."

"Jesse saw the vehicle as it was leaving. He said it was a fancy off-road rig. I presume he meant a sport utility vehicle. And he described it as a funny shade of green."

"Still doesn't sound like any of the subs." Taylor paused before commenting, "Actually, the only person I know with a fancy green truck is a woman. Vicki Stephens got a new Range Rover a month ago. She describes it as sage, but I'd call it pale-green."

Gretchen chuckled, somewhat nervously.

"What's so amusing?"

"Oh, nothing, really. It's just that earlier today Emma and I were joking around about Vicki Stephens wanting her dead. Apparently, there's still no love lost between the two of them?"

"Tell me about it. It's only gotten worse since the fire. Then they were both there the other morning when that damn body showed up. But Vicki—" Taylor stopped in the middle of his sentence. "Oh God, I just remembered something."

"What?"

Christ, I can't believe I'm even thinking this, Taylor thought to himself before explaining to Gretchen. "Yesterday morning, I was meeting with Charlie to go over last month's numbers. As we were wrapping up, I said something to Charlie about having to leave the office early. So I could drop off those landscape plans at Emma's."

Gretchen interrupted and asked incredulously, "Are you implying that Charlie had anything to do with this?"

"No! But Vicki came in near the end of our meeting. She was standing there when I explained that Emma was heading out to the farm last night." Before Gretchen could interrupt again, he continued. "And then, forty-five minutes later, Vicki stuck her head into my staff meeting and asked to borrow my pickup for some kind of personal errand. She said her vehicle was getting washed downstairs. She only had my keys for an hour or so, but it would have given her plenty of time to have a copy made of the farm key. There's a locksmith near the office."

"Oh, stop it," Gretchen insisted. "This is a vice president of Randolph Foods we're suspecting."

Taylor was undeterred by her comment. "You said Paul was absolutely sure about those screws?"

"Yes. But earlier you thought I was crazy to believe him." Gretchen turned onto the freeway entrance ramp. "Come on, Tay. How and why would it ever occur to Vicki Stephens to poison

Emma? And what would she know about furnace venting?"

"Listen, Vicki's a woman of many hidden talents. We've always said she's capable of anything." Taylor paused before asking, "Listen, what time is it?"

"Going on five. Why?"

"Hold tight. I'll call you right back."

"What are—" Before she could finish her question, the line went dead.

Gretchen accelerated and merged into the I–94 traffic heading east across the river. A few minutes later, Taylor called her back. "Me, again. Sorry I cut you off, but I wanted to catch a couple of people before they left for the weekend."

"Who? And why?"

"Maureen, the parking garage attendant, for one." Taylor was very excited. "She remembers Vicki leaving in my truck yesterday."

"Is that something she'd necessarily notice?"

"Absolutely," Taylor assured her. "Maureen keeps pretty close tabs on everyone's comings and goings. She said Vicki returned about forty-five minutes later. But now here's the interesting part. Apparently Vicki left again, this time in her own vehicle, shortly after that. Must've been right after she returned my keys. And she got back at five-fifteen, just as Maureen was pulling out of the garage to go home for the day. That's plenty of time for Vicki to get out to the farm and back."

"Taylor, get a grip."

"Listen. There's more. Maureen said they washed Vicki's Rover on Wednesday, not yesterday. So Vicki lied about needing to borrow my truck. And I also called Vicki's assistant and asked her to check Vicki's calendar. She had a three o'clock meeting scheduled yesterday afternoon with several of her account managers, but apparently she canceled it at the last minute. The woman also confirmed Maureen's story about Vicki being out of the office the latter part of the day. The assistant is only a temp, though, and she didn't have any idea where Vicki might have been."

"You're not kidding about this, are you?" Gretchen asked seriously.

"I don't think so," Taylor responded tentatively. "Listen, I'm not saying that Vicki necessarily tried to kill Emma. I'm just saying that it's possible."

"You're giving me the creeps."

"Listen, maybe we should talk to Serg Suarez."

Gretchen was confused. "Why Serg? The farm is a long way out of his jurisdiction."

"But we know him. And he knows both Vicki and Emma. We'll just run it by him. He can decide if it's worth bothering the Wisconsin authorities."

"He'll think we're crazy, you know?"

"He probably will," Taylor admitted. "But he's a homicide cop. He deals with crazy people all the time. Besides, what if my hunch is right? What if Vicki really is trying to hurt Emma?"

Gretchen finally relented. "Okay, okay. Are you going to call him from up there?"

Taylor hesitated for a minute. "I was hoping you could talk to him."

"What? It's your hare-brained idea."

"I know. But I can't really call him from up here and discuss this with the kids around."

Gretchen wasn't convinced. "Call him on your way back to the privy or something."

"Listen, I just have this one battery. I should really save it in case we have an emergency or something." He heard Gretchen groan. "Come on, Gretch, please. I work with Vicki. It will be less awkward if Serg hears all this for the first time from you."

Taking a deep breath, Gretchen hesitated a moment. "Oh, why do I let you talk me into these things? Okay, I'll do it. But only because it's Emma."

Worried Gretchen would change her mind, Taylor moved on. "You probably shouldn't say anything to Em until after you talk to Serg."

"Good idea," Gretchen agreed. "Emma can get a little crazy sometimes."

"Give me a call back later tonight if you get a chance. I want to hear what Serg had to say. And how your little family reunion went."

"What, not worried about your precious battery?"

"Okay, I admit I was stretching with that one. Anyway, we'll probably be up past midnight. Tonight's poker night around the campfire."

"Don't lose too much money to those card sharks."

"I'll try not to. Good luck with Serg."

"Thanks a lot," Gretchen drawled, and then closed with, "Love you. Say hi to the kids."

46

After clicking off from Taylor, Gretchen called Jesse. As usual, he was at home and answered on the second ring. Trying to keep the conversation short, she still had to listen to his lengthy version of the previous night's events. It wasn't until she pulled into the staff parking lot at the hospital that Jesse finally let her go, after assuring her repeatedly that he would drain the water in the farmhouse immediately.

Gretchen parked the car and rallied her nerve for the next call. She reluctantly phoned the downtown police station. And, after a minute or so, Serg came on the line.

"Gretchen Randolph. What a pleasant surprise. It's been ages."

"Yes. New Year's Eve at Emma's."

"So what's up?"

Gretchen answered truthfully. "Hopefully nothing." Then she told Serg of Emma's near-miss out at the farm.

"I'm glad she's okay," Serg said, before asking, "Got any ideas on how this happened?"

"Well, the most likely explanation is that the contractor forgot to put in the sheet metal screws. But he swears he did. So Taylor and I have been kicking around other possibilities."

"And?" Serg prompted.

Hesitating for a moment, Gretchen said, "And at least one of them is pretty horrible."

"I take it that's why you called me."

"Right. We know Western Wisconsin isn't exactly your jurisdiction. But you know all the people involved, and we thought this might make more sense to you than to anyone else."

"I'm all ears," Serg encouraged.

Gretchen detailed Taylor's theory of Vicki's possible involvement in the carbon monoxide incident, concluding with a description of his calls to the parking garage operator and to Vicki's temporary assistant. When she finished, she waited for his reaction.

Much to her surprise, she didn't hear hysterical laughter from the other end of the line. Instead, Serg remarked, "All of a sudden, everyone's a detective."

Gretchen was confused by his comment. "What was that?"

"Oh, nothing. Just thinking out loud." He cleared his throat. "I know Emma and Vicki aren't exactly bosom buddies. But that's hardly enough reason for Vicki to do something like this."

"I know. It really doesn't make much sense, does it? I probably shouldn't have called, huh?"

"No, I didn't say that. Your hunch is pretty far-fetched, but that doesn't mean you're wrong to call. Emma did come close to dying last night, and that's a very serious matter. If there's even the slightest possibility that the poisoning wasn't accidental, the matter needs to be fully investigated."

"That's kind of where Taylor and I came out earlier."

"But as you've mentioned, this did occur outside my jurisdiction. I know Kurt Anderson, the sheriff over in Hudson County. I'll give him a call and pass along your information."

"What do you think he'll do with it?"

"Don't know for sure. He's a good guy, but not overly aggressive."

"So he might decide to do nothing?"

"Good chance. But if that's the case, I'll offer our help and see if he's willing to let us run with it. He shouldn't have too big a problem with that. But you should know, Gretchen, this could get very messy. I don't think I'd be able to keep your names out of it if we decide to talk to Vicki."

"We realize that. But don't worry about us. We'll deal with it somehow." She looked at her watch. "Listen Serg, I have to run. I'm parked outside the hospital and patients are waiting. Let me know what Sheriff Anderson has to say. And thanks for all this."

"No problem, that's why they pay me the big bucks. Go save some lives. I'll be in touch."

47

Serg shook his head as he hung up the phone after his conversation with Gretchen. *What was it about Vicki Stephens?* He remembered his earlier uneasiness with the incredible coincidence of both Vicki and Emma finding Matthew Kelly after all these years. Even he was suspicious of her.

Serg's secretary stuck her head into his office. "You want anything more before I leave for the weekend?"

Serg looked at his watch and saw that it was already after five. "One little thing. Can you get me the direct phone number for Sheriff Kurt Anderson over in Hudson County?"

She buzzed him less than thirty seconds later and gave him the number. He bid her good night and then put in the call to Sheriff Anderson. The call rolled over to an after-hours receptionist, who told Serg that the Sheriff was just wrapping up a meeting with several county supervisors and would get back to him shortly.

While awaiting the man's return call, Serg picked up another file on his desk and started dictating a few case notes. However, the image of Vicki Stephens in her green Range Rover roaring down a rural Wisconsin road kept flashing through his mind.

Oh, this is crazy, he thought and finally gave up on the dictation. He grabbed a note pad and jotted down everything he knew about Vicki Stephens, including all the information Emma had given him yesterday afternoon. "Well, there's something interesting," he remarked aloud to himself as he finished the last notation concerning Vicki's alleged teenage embezzlement from the Ohio heating contractor. *I wonder if Vicki managed to pick up a little knowledge about furnace venting while she was also doctoring the books.*

Several minutes later, Serg's thoughts were interrupted by the buzz of his phone. It was Sheriff Anderson.

The two men took a moment to exchange pleasantries before the Sheriff asked, "What can I do for you, Serg?"

"Well, I'm not exactly sure, Kurt. I just wanted to alert you to a possible situation out your way." Serg described Emma's experience out at the farm the previous evening.

"I saw a report on that earlier today. Looked pretty routine, as I recall."

"And it probably is. But I also happen to know that Emma Randolph recently uncovered some potentially embarrassing details about a business adversary."

"What kind of embarrassing details?"

"Well, that's a long and very complicated story. You got a minute?"

"Yeah. I don't need to be back out on patrol until nine."

Serg laughed. "I think I can get it all out by then." He first relayed the whole story about Kelly's disappearance, the mill fire, and the likely identity of the discovered skeleton. Next, he shared the profile of Vicki Stephens that he had jotted down earlier. He concluded by describing Gretchen and Taylor's suspicions of Vicki's possible visit to the farm the preceding afternoon.

"That is one hell of a story!" the sheriff exclaimed when Serg had finished his account ten minutes later. "Are you planning on talking to Ms. Stephens about the CO scare out at the farm?"

"I'm not planning on doing anything without your okay."

"Oh, you mean because the farm is out here in Hudson County?"

"Yes."

"Don't get hung up on that. If anything fishy happened out here yesterday, it's most likely related to that other stuff you're working on. The old Kelly case and the fire. I think it makes sense for you to run with the whole works."

"We can certainly do that."

"All I ask is that you keep me informed."

"No problem," promised Serg. "The first order of business will be to try to pin down Vicki's whereabouts yesterday afternoon. I'd like to do that without having to question her, but I don't know if that's possible. There'll be hell to pay if I drag her into this thing, and it turns out she was nowhere near Hudson County. Which is likely, of course."

"You'll probably find out she was off with a friend sneaking in some late afternoon shopping or something."

Serg laughed. "That's not really her style, Kurt, but it would be nice. I'd be delighted to hear that she spent her afternoon browsing in the Oval Room at Dayton's."

48

After his talk with Sheriff Anderson, Serg was satisfied that interjurisdictional protocols had been observed. He then turned his concentration back to his note pad. Below his written profile of Vicki Stephens, he began listing all the things he didn't know—hobbies, interests, close friends, school chums, college and business school employment, ex-lovers, and current lovers. Serg grinned at this last point as he remembered something else Emma had told him the previous afternoon. *Other than Charlie Randolph, that is.* He made a note to talk to Gretchen and Taylor for possible help on the hobbies, interests, and close friends.

Then he looked at his watch. It was approaching six o'clock. *But only four in California.* He dialed directory assistance for the Palo Alto area and asked for the number of the Stanford Alumni Association. There was a separate listing for the Stanford Business School Alumni Association, and he dialed that number. Within fifteen minutes, a very helpful young woman had e-mailed him a complete list of graduates from the master's program since 1960 that were presently living in the Twin Cities metropolitan area. Current business or home addresses were also available for most of the names.

He first studied the list for the years 1983 through 1985 and found nine names, including Vicki's. None other than hers was familiar to him. So he started from the top and finally found a name he recognized in the class of 1973. It was Cal Petrola, the city finance director. Although both men worked in City Hall, their professional paths seldom crossed. But their eight-year-old daughters were on the same soccer team, and Serg and Cal had gotten friendly the previous summer while sharing assistant-coaching responsibilities.

Serg put in a call to Cal and caught him just as he was walking out the door of his office. "Knocking off early?" Serg kidded, remembering that it was now after six.

The man laughed. "Thought I'd take the rest of the day off."

"Do you have a minute before you go?"

"Yes, what can I do for you?"

"You might be able to help me with a case I'm working on."

Cal laughed again. "Ah, my chance to play Watson along-side the great Holmes. What's up?"

"You got your MBA from Stanford, right?"

"Eons ago. In '73."

"Is there a local alumni organization?"

"Yes. There's a fairly active group of us here in the Twin Cities. We get together a few times a year. We're supposed to be networking with each other—whatever the hell that means. But it's really more of a social club. We've even gone back to Northern California for a couple of football games." Cal paused and then asked, "Why do you want to know?"

"I'm trying to get some background information on another business school grad. Vicki Stephens. You know her?"

"You mean Vicki Stephens out at Randolph Foods?"

"Right."

"I worked with her on the city investment in their riverfront deal. Smart lady. Never knew she went to Stanford though."

"Graduated in 1984."

"Well, I'll be."

"So I take it she's not active in your alumni group?"

"No, she's not."

"Apparently, there are eight other Stanford business alums living in this area who graduated around the same time she did. Let me run them by you."

Cal listened to the eight names. "Four of those people are pretty active in the alumni group."

"Think any one of them would be more willing to talk to me without running to Vicki Stephens and making a big fuss?"

"I guess it depends on what you want to know. What's this about anyway?"

"Nothing really," Serg answered, but he knew he had to offer Cal some sort of explanation. "Did you hear about that skeleton we found after the Randolph fire?"

"Yes."

"Well, Ms. Stephens was there in the grain elevator when it showed up. So policy says we have to run a background on her. Just a routine check."

"Then Sean Desmond's probably your man. He's a real talker—bit of a bore actually. But if he knew her at Stanford, you'll hear all the details. You have his number?"

"Just his office number over at Norwest."

"That's all I have, too. But he's likely to still be there. Strikes me as a workaholic."

Serg laughed. "Just like the rest of us, huh?"

"Hey, we're not hopeless. We'll be out there cheering in two weeks when the kids start playing again."

"And thankfully as fans only. I'm glad two new fools stepped up as assistant coaches this year. That was incredibly time-consuming."

"I'll second that. Will I see you at the parents' meeting next week?"

"Most likely. Paloma will be there for sure. Thanks for your help, Cal. I'm going to try Sean Desmond right now."

Serg punched in Sean Desmond's number. The man answered on the third ring. Serg introduced himself and gave the same reason for calling as he had given Cal earlier.

"Yeah, I remember Vicki Stephens back in business school. We didn't spend a lot of time together. But the class wasn't that large, and you kind of got to know a little something about everybody before the two years were up. Haven't seen much of her since then though, other than in the papers and stuff. I suggested getting together when we both ended up here in Minnesota. But she wasn't much interested."

Cal was right. This guy is a talker, Serg thought. "So what was she like back then?"

"She kind of kept to herself," Sean recalled. "Especially after what happened to her roommate."

"Why? What happened to her roommate?"

"There was a terrible accident involving her roommate during the spring near the end of our first year. Another business student named Jackie Young. Vicki was down in New York for the weekend and came home to find Jackie dead."

"What happened?"

"Carbon monoxide, apparently. They lived in an old house, and the darn furnace malfunctioned." As Sean rambled on about the tragic accident, including funeral details, Serg shuddered. *Jesus, Emma could have ended up the same way.*

Sean continued. "But Vicki didn't let the whole mess sidetrack her too badly. Managed to finish out the semester and graduate near the top of our class the following year." Sean stopped, but not for long. "Let's see, what else can I tell you?"

"That's plenty for now. As I said, this is just a routine check."

Then Serg quickly ended the conversation.

Serg sat at his desk planning out what to do next. *Okay, hell to pay or not, I have to talk to Vicki Stephens.* Serg first tried to reach her at Randolph Foods, but was told that she had left for the evening. When she didn't answer at home either, Serg ordered a squad car to watch her house in Kenwood and contact him when she had returned.

After making those arrangements, he dialed Emma's number and got her answering machine. He left a message and then tried her cell phone. He was greeted with a recorded announcement:

"The cellular number you are trying to reach is not in service in this dialing area."

He hung up the phone thinking, *Either Emma's not paying her bills or her damn battery ran down.*

Next he tried to reach Gretchen, but was connected to her answering service after just one ring. "Dr. Randolph will have to get back to you. She's unavailable at this time."

"I'm a policeman," Serg implored. "This is an emergency."

In a flat voice, the receptionist responded, "Dr. Randolph is unavailable. If this is an emergency, you need to dial 911."

"It's not that kind of emergency. It's more of a personal nature. It's urgent that I talk to Dr. Randolph as soon as possible. Can't you page her or something?"

"No, not when she's seeing patients. Please leave your name, and we'll ask Dr. Randolph to get back to you just as soon as she checks in for her messages."

"Okay, but tell her to call me right away." He left his name and number.

49

Emma pulled into Peter's driveway at Hidden Lake a few minutes after six-thirty. She grimaced as she looked at the huge neo-gothic house. Even in the soft evening sunshine, it was pretentious and oppressive, much like the reputation of its original occupant, Marcus Randolph. She could never figure out why Peter had lived here all these years.

She was distressed to see that she was the first to arrive. She had hoped that Gretchen wouldn't be too late and would at least arrive before Charlie did. Emma parked the Subaru and approached the massive front portico. She felt very underdressed in her corduroys, cowboy boots, and leather jacket. But Gretchen had said casual.

She reached the front door and rang the bell. While she waited for an answer to her ring, she turned around and smiled at the image before her. Her well-traveled Subaru looked a little ridiculous parked in the sweeping circular driveway. While she was still chuckling, the door opened.

Peter was standing in the doorway. He was obviously fresh out of the shower and was wearing only a bathrobe and slippers.

"Emma, you're early."

"Oh, I thought Charlie's office said six-thirty."

"Well, there's been some sort of mix-up. The time was half past seven."

"Initially, I know. But then someone from Charlie's office called and left a phone message with this earlier time. Her name was Jeannine. She said you weren't feeling well."

"Jeannine? She must be new. And confused, because I feel fine."

Not knowing what else to say, Emma offered, "Listen, I can go run some errands or something and come back later."

"Don't be ridiculous. Come on in. I just mixed myself a drink, and it's so much more pleasant not to drink alone."

Emma accepted, even though the situation was awkward because she and Peter had spent very little time together over the years. But he seemed relatively sober, and this might be an opportunity to talk to him about the ownership of Lake Salish. "Berta isn't here?" inquired Emma, stepping inside.

"No, she's out of town for the week visiting some old friends. Our maid is gone too. So just throw your coat and bag on the bench here, and come on into the library. I'll get you some wine, and then I'll go up to finish dressing. When I come back down, we'll catch up while we wait for the others to arrive."

Peter and Emma walked into the library. Peter showed Emma across the room to one of the chairs near the fireplace and brought her a glass of Liebfraumilch from the bar. Then he retrieved his martini from the desk and left the room to go upstairs.

Just a moment later, Emma heard Peter shouting at someone out in the hall. "What do you think you're doing? You can't just walk in here like that." Emma stood up and made her way over to the doorway. She was shocked to see Vicki Stephens, wearing sunglasses and an oversized designer trench coat, striding towards her from the kitchen across the hall. Peter, still in his robe, was following the woman and screaming, "Get out of here right now."

Vicki ignored him and kept walking. She brushed past Emma and entered the room, pausing for a moment to flip her sunglasses up onto the top of her head. Then she proceeded over to the bar and poured herself a Scotch.

Peter stopped just inside the library doors where Emma was still standing. "Maybe you'd better leave, and come back later. Apparently, Ms. Stephens has something she would like to discuss with me. I apologize for her incredible rudeness."

Emma was stunned by Vicki's sudden appearance and was unsure of what to do. "Are you certain you want me to leave? Will you be okay?"

"Yes, I'll be fine. I'll see you back here in an hour."

"Okay," Emma agreed somewhat hesitantly and started out of the room.

"Did I say you could leave?" Vicki said from the bar across the room. "That old drunk doesn't give the orders around here."

Emma stopped in the doorway and turned back towards Vicki. "Listen, I don't know what's going on here. But I do know this is Peter's house, and if he wants me to leave, I'll leave." Emma looked over to Peter and offered, "But I think it might be best if I stayed."

Peter rushed over to Emma. "No, leave. This woman is nothing but trouble, and you don't need to get involved in it."

"She stays," repeated Vicki, removing her sunglasses from the top of her head and putting them on the bar. After taking a long drink from her glass and putting it down on the bar as well, she smiled coyly over at Emma. "Jeannine doesn't want you to go."

Peter looked confused, but Emma wasn't. "You knew I was coming up here tonight. You were the one who called and moved up the time. What's this all about? Tell me right now, or I am leaving."

"You're not going anywhere." With her right hand, Vicki pulled a small .22 caliber pistol out of her coat pocket and pointed it at Emma and Peter. "Get back over there, and sit down."

"What are you planning to do with that?" Emma demanded,

as she and Peter stepped slowly over towards the fireplace. Vicki kept the gun pointed at them the whole way.

When they stopped between the walnut table in front of the couch and the fireplace mantle, Vicki finally answered, "Let me put it simply. I'm going to kill you."

Peter took a sip of his martini and then fell into the leather chair closer to the fireplace. Emma stayed focused on Vicki still standing at the bar pointing the weapon at her. "Did I hear you correctly? Did you just say you were going to kill me?"

Vicki glared at her. "That's exactly what I said."

"Why would you want to kill me?" Emma was amazed at how calm she felt. Maybe this wasn't really happening.

"You know why, Miss Snoop. I won't let you destroy everything I've worked for."

"Come on, Vicki, I know we've had our differences. But nothing worth killing me over," Emma responded truthfully. She couldn't think of anything she had unearthed about Vicki that would even remotely warrant murder. "This makes no sense. Besides, you'll never get away with it."

"I won't have to. I'll be long gone by the time the cops get here. They'll think dear Peter did you in."

"Why would they think that?"

"Because that's the story he's going to tell them," answered Vicki very matter-of-factly. She moved around to the back of the couch as she explained, "You barged in here threatening him about that swamp your family's been squatting on all these years. He asked you to leave. And when you refused, he pulled this gun out of his desk drawer." She nodded towards the pistol. "You rushed him and, fearing for his life, he shot you."

Emma wasn't surprised that Vicki had stumbled onto the truth about the ownership of Lake Salish. She looked over at Peter who still sat slumped in his chair. "Would you go along with this?"

Peter didn't respond. Vicki laughed and answered for him. "Of course he will. He'll do whatever I tell him to do."

Emma crouched beside the old man. "Is that true, Peter?" He just looked straight ahead past Emma and said nothing. As she stood up, Emma felt her earlier calm melt away. Nevertheless, she managed to look Vicki directly in the eye and say, "No one is going to believe that story."

"It's amazing what people will believe. You've been known to get pretty riled up from time to time."

Emma lost it. She turned and knocked the martini out of Peter's grip into his lap. "How can you let her do this?" Peter still said nothing, but Emma noticed his now-empty hands were shaking.

Vicki continued answering for him. "He really doesn't have much choice. Either he claims he killed you in self-defense and takes those lumps, or the fraud he calls his life comes to a grinding halt."

Emma continued looking at Peter. "What is going on here?"

Finally, Peter spoke. "She has a right to know."

Vicki looked at the clock on the mantle. "Okay, tell her, old man. This could actually be fun. But make it quick."

Emma took a deep breath to collect herself. "Talk to me, Peter," she said encouragingly to the trembling man before her.

Peter rose slowly out of his chair. He wiped his martini-dampened robe with a napkin, crept over to the bar and poured himself another drink.

"Oh, right, have another," sneered Vicki, continuing to point the gun at Emma. "That's the only thing you've ever been good at."

Peter, holding his glass up in the air, turned back towards Emma. "You know, this has been my only true friend over the years. I wish it were different, but it all went wrong so long ago."

"I'm listening," Emma said. Peter returned to the chairs in front of the fireplace. He and Emma both sat down. Vicki stood several feet behind the sofa facing the two of them. She was still pointing the gun at Emma.

50

Charlie stopped working at seven. He changed into the casual slacks and sweater he kept at the office and walked out towards the elevators. He liked working into the evening on Fridays because the office was usually quiet after four-thirty. Most Fridays, Vicki would come back to the office after a late afternoon workout and massage at her club, and then they'd go through the agenda for the following week. They usually knocked off around eight, grabbed some dinner, and spent the night together at his townhouse.

But earlier in the day, he decided not to inform Vicki of his alternative plans for the evening. Formally breaking their Friday night date would only acknowledge its existence. Besides, he wasn't in the mood for more of her wrath.

As Charlie passed by the security desk on the ground floor of the building, he stopped to leave a message with Herb, the elderly night guard.

"Evening, Herb."

"Evening, Mr. Randolph."

"Say, I'm leaving for the evening and—"

"Early for you!" interrupted Herb.

"Can't work all the time." Charlie strained to make small talk with the guard. "Could you do me a favor?"

"Sure thing. What'd you need?"

"If Ms. Stephens comes back this evening, would you tell her I've left for the night?"

"Yes, sir. I know how you two usually have your business meeting on Friday nights." Herb winked at Charlie. Charlie cringed at the familiarity. His management style generally precluded such exchanges. Charlie started to walk away from the desk when the old man added, "But your message won't be necessary tonight. Miss Stephens left an hour ago and said she wouldn't be back."

"An hour ago. That's odd," mumbled Charlie.

"What's that?" asked the guard.

"Oh, nothing. It's just that Ms. Stephens usually leaves a little earlier than six on Fridays."

"Oh, you mean for her fitness class. That woman does take care of herself, and it shows, huh?" Herb gave Charlie another wink.

"She'll be glad you noticed," quipped Charlie, trying to end the uncomfortable male repartee.

Charlie was only partially successful. The old man continued. "I get paid to notice, remember. But some things I'd do for free. Anyway, about her leaving later than usual. I don't think she was doing any muscle toning today. She didn't have that leather satchel with her. You know the one?"

"Yes, I know the one." Anxious to be on his way, Charlie turned towards the door. "Well, then I guess I won't need your favor after all."

"Maybe some other time. Just let me know."

"Right, will do. Keep up the good work." As he left the building, Charlie thought to himself, *Good work, my ass.* He doubted that the old man noticed much of anything that wasn't female and under thirty-five.

While he was relieved at not having to stand up Vicki, he was a bit surprised that she had waltzed out of the office without a word to him about her evening plans. She was either really upset with him for his behavior earlier in the week, or she was up to something. Either way, Charlie figured it meant trouble for someone, and that someone was probably him.

Well, he'd deal with that later. He was anxious to get up to Peter's before Gretchen and Emma arrived. He knew his father. Peter was probably well on his way to being drunk by now and could prove to be a liability if left alone with his other guests.

51

Peter stared into his drink and explained, "That body, the one you found in the elevator. It's Matthew Kelly."

Emma flinched. *God, Sam was right.*

Vicki looked at Peter. "She probably already knows that. Get on with it. Remember, I told you to make it quick. I want to be long gone when the others get here."

Emma stole a quick look at her watch. It was just past seven. Maybe she could stall Vicki in hope that either Charlie or Gretchen would arrive early. "I don't know anything," she announced to Vicki and Peter.

Vicki exploded. "Then why did you call my mother? Who else have you talked to? Anyone in California?"

"California? What are you talking about?" asked Emma, genuinely perplexed.

Vicki took a deep breath and calmed down a bit. "It doesn't matter. We don't have time to get into all that. You see, I respect how smart you are. That's what these clowns don't understand."

She pointed the pistol over towards Peter. "This idiot here and his smooth-talking son, Charlie."

Damn, thought Emma. *Charlie is tied up in all this too. So much for him coming to my rescue. I guess that leaves Gretch.*

"They were planning to distract you by throwing you a couple of bones." Vicki took a few steps towards Emma and Peter until she was standing directly behind the couch. She again aimed her weapon at Emma. "As if restoration of the mill and ownership of that god-forsaken lake would have been enough. I know what you're really after."

"Vicki, I honestly have no idea what you're talking about." Turning away from Vicki, Emma bent over towards Peter and begged him to continue. "Tell me what is going on."

Peter sat up in the chair and looked at Emma. He cleared his throat. Without any of his previous hesitation, he then told her, "Your grandfather Will didn't kill Matthew Kelly. My father, Marcus, did it."

It took a moment for Peter's admission to sink in. Even then Emma could hardly believe it. "What?" she said, as she stared back at Peter. "How do you know that?"

"I know because I was there." Peter looked at Vicki and added, "Along with Kelly's driver, Thomas Lindgren."

"Your grandfather," Emma blurted at Vicki before she realized it.

Vicki sneered. "And you said you didn't know anything."

Peter ignored their exchange and continued. "I put Kelly in the grain elevator and watched Will take the fall. He lost everything that Marcus should have lost. His family, the Company, and ultimately his life."

"Now," said Vicki, looking at Emma, "you know the whole touching story. Get over by the desk. It's time to get this over with."

52

It was well after seven when Gretchen left the hospital, and she still had a long drive from the University up to her father's house. She'd be late, but she knew Emma could more than fend for herself until she arrived. Five minutes into the drive, she checked with her answering service and picked up Serg's message. She immediately returned the call and was surprised when he answered his office phone on its first buzz.

"Serg," Gretchen said, "I didn't expect to hear back from you so soon. Have you talked to Sheriff Anderson already?"

"Yes, I caught him earlier. He's fine with having me help on this Vicki Stephens thing, so now I'm looking for Emma." Serg kept his voice calm, not wanting to alarm Gretchen. "I know you talked to her earlier today. Any ideas on where she might be?"

Gretchen laughed, "Actually I do. I'm meeting her in twenty minutes. She's probably in her car too. Do you need that number?"

"I tried it earlier, but it's not working. Where are you two going to meet?"

"At my father's house on Hidden Lake. We're having drinks with Dad and Charlie."

"Not that it's really any of my business," Serg commented. "But I didn't think Charlie and Emma saw much of each other socially."

"Well, they don't. But tonight's an exception. We've got some old family business to discuss." Gretchen then asked Serg, "Why the sudden interest in Emma's whereabouts?"

"I need to talk to her right away," explained Serg. "Would you mind if I stopped by your father's?"

Gretchen felt a pit opening in the bottom of her stomach. "Serg, what is going on?"

"I'll explain everything when I get there."

"Okay," Gretchen responded tentatively and gave Serg directions to her father's house on Hidden Lake.

"I'll round up Don Lovich, my partner, and we'll leave in ten minutes. That should get us to the house at a quarter to eight. Will that work?"

"Sure. I'll be there shortly before that, and I'll let the others know you're coming."

"Okay, see you then."

Gretchen turned off her phone and picked up her speed.

53

Emma now knew help wasn't going to arrive in time. *I have to somehow get close enough to Vicki to make a grab for the gun.* She ignored Vicki's request that she leave the fireplace and move over to Peter's desk. Instead, she stood up, stared at Vicki over the back of the couch, and laughed.

Vicki was confused. "You find this amusing?"

"A little. Here we are more than a half of a century later, and the same thing is happening all over again. Kelly was no threat then, and I'm no threat now. So what if I know you're Lindgren's granddaughter? Even Serg Suarez knows that."

"What? How does he know that?"

"I told him," Emma explained, trying to sound calm, as she took a few steps away from the fireplace mantel and around the coffee table. "Just like I told him the body might be Kelly."

"Shit!" Vicki's voice quavered.

"Don't panic, Vicki," Emma offered. She wanted to keep Vicki talking until she could get closer. "Serg isn't much interested in your family history or the identity of the skeleton. Killing me will just open up trouble. Cops take a lot more interest in fresh corpses than they do in sixty-year-old ones."

Peter jumped in. "She's right. With a new body, Suarez will put two and two together."

"Shut up," Vicki screamed, cutting Peter off without diverting her eyes from Emma. "She's probably bluffing about the cop. Besides, she knows the whole story now. She can bring down the whole Company."

Emma slowly advanced several more feet and stopped this time at the end of the couch. "I don't give a damn about the Company. I'd settle for having my grandfather's name cleared. Besides, the cops would probably go easy on Peter if he told them the whole story. He's a sick man, and there's not much to be gained by prosecuting him at this point."

Vicki glared back at Emma. "I don't buy it."

Emma edged around the couch and started slowly towards Vicki. "Why do you care so much about the Company? Why is it so important to you?"

"Stop! Stop right there," Vicki insisted.

Emma stopped six feet from her. "Okay, I've stopped. Now tell me why all this is so important to you."

"I only want what's mine," Vicki answered angrily. "Marcus Randolph bought my grandfather's silence for two thousand dollars. A measly two grand. That silence helped make Randolph Foods and this whole family what it is today. I deserve a piece of that."

"Maybe," Emma agreed, trying to keep Vicki talking and distracted. "But how are you going to get it?" She took another step towards Vicki. "What's your plan?"

Vicki smiled confidently. "Charlie can't live without me. I've seen to that. Someday, he'll walk out on that worthless wife of his and marry me. Then I'll be co-owner of a controlling block of Company shares."

Emma laughed. "And I thought your idea to kill me was crazy.

Do you really think that Charlie Randolph would ever marry you? He's been using you, just like old Marcus used your grandfather."

Vicki's smile was gone. "Shut up. You don't know anything about it." The gun was shaking in her right hand. Emma, who had resumed her careful advance forward, was now directly in front of Vicki. "And when he's done using you," Emma pressed further, "he'll get rid of you. Although I doubt your price will be a meager two thousand bucks. This one will cost poor Cousin Charlie. But you won't get the Company."

"Stop it," raged Vicki, as she brought up her left hand to steady the gun.

It's now or never, thought Emma. She lunged forward and knocked Vicki's right arm, trying to divert the muzzle of the pistol before grabbing it.

But Vicki was too fast. The .22 went off, and Emma slumped to the floor. Vicki glared down at her. "I told you to shut up."

Unnoticed during the exchange between Vicki and Emma, Peter had worked his way over to his desk. By the time Vicki realized he was no longer sitting near the fireplace, he was pointing a .357 magnum at her.

With the .22 hanging down at her side, Vicki sneered at Peter as she backed up against the couch. "Am I supposed to believe you'd actually shoot me?"

"Someone should have done it a long time ago," stammered Peter.

"You don't have the guts," taunted Vicki.

"Maybe I do."

Vicki laughed. "Calm down, old man. Enough of this nonsense—"

Peter closed his eyes and pulled the trigger. For a split second, a surprised look appeared on Vicki's face. Then she toppled backwards over the couch and fell onto the floor next to one of the ornamental feet of the Queen Anne coffee table.

54

Charlie arrived at his father's house shortly before seven-thirty. He was surprised to see Emma's car already parked in the driveway. *God, I hope Dad is sticking to small talk in there,* he thought as he walked towards the front door.

Charlie let himself in. "Dad, it's Charlie," he announced, as he closed the heavy door behind him.

Peter yelled from the library. "Hurry! Come quickly!"

"Now what?" grumbled Charlie, rushing down the hall towards the library. He stormed through the doors. Peter was kneeling with his back to the entry in the middle of the room behind the couch. He was still dressed in only his bathrobe and slippers, and the .357 magnum was on the wood floor beside him.

"What the hell?" Charlie said, as he rushed into the room and stepped around his father. Emma was unconscious on the floor in front of Peter. Blood from a wound in her chest was pooling at Peter's knees. "What the hell?" Charlie repeated.

Peter looked up at his son. "Call an ambulance."

Charlie rushed for the phone on the desk, but stopped half way across the room. "Hold on a minute. I don't want this place swarming with cops before I know what happened here." He walked back over to Peter and, after picking up the nearby handgun, handed his father a handkerchief. "Hold it firmly against the wound. That should help. And then for God's sake, tell me what happened."

Peter pressed the cloth against Emma's chest. She winced and mumbled incoherently. "Vicki Stephens shot her with a .22 pistol."

The couch was blocking Charlie's view of Vicki. "What? I didn't see her Rover out front."

"She came in through the kitchen, so she must be parked in the side service drive."

"Where is she now?" Charlie asked.

Peter nodded over towards the fireplace. "Over there. And in a lot worse shape than Emma I'm not sorry to say. She got it with the .357."

Charlie peered over the back of the couch and saw Vicki sprawled on the floor. A good portion of her head was blown away and splattered across the leather cushions below him. "Oh, shit," he mumbled, as he gagged. "Did Emma do this?"

"No, I did."

"You!" Charlie exclaimed, turning back to his father. "Why?" Peter trembled and then began to cry. "Everything was going to be okay again. We were finally going to do right by Emma and her family, and you can't know how much I wanted that to happen. And then Vicki barged in here and ruined everything."

Charlie pointed back over the couch at Vicki. "And this made it all better again?" Not waiting for an answer, he came back over to his father and looked down at Emma. "How much does she know?"

"Everything," Peter answered between sobs.

"Christ," Charlie staggered over to the bar and poured himself a drink.

"This isn't working," Peter said. He stopped crying and held up the blood soaked handkerchief. "She's still bleeding. We really need to call an ambulance."

Charlie ignored his father and finished his drink before returning to the middle of the room. "Let me see her." Charlie crouched down next to Emma and inspected the wound. "You're right. It looks pretty bad. If she doesn't get help soon, she'll probably bleed to death."

"So I'll go call the ambulance." Peter tried to get up.

Charlie grabbed him. "Not so fast, Dad. We have an opportunity here, and I think we should take it."

"What do you mean?"

Charlie loosened his grip on Peter's arm. "You know, it might not be the worst thing if Emma and all our dirty little family secrets expired here on this carpet."

"What are you saying? Not call an ambulance?"

"No," Charlie calmly said. "Just delay for a while longer. Then I'll call and tell the police I just got here and found you in shock. And your story won't be far from the truth. Vicki came in here and shot Emma. Fearing for your life, you grabbed your gun and shot Vicki."

Peter stared at his son. "What? Do nothing, and just watch Emma die?"

Charlie smiled sardonically. "You did it once before. Just pretend she's Matthew Kelly."

Peter's stare hardened as he fought back more tears. Then he shrugged off Charlie's hand and staggered over to his desk. As he picked up the receiver, he turned to Charlie. "You're a monster, just like your grandfather. I should have stopped him sixty years ago, but I didn't. But I'm not going to let this happen again. I'm going to make this call. And when the police arrive, I'm telling them the whole story. You'll have to shoot me to stop me."

Charlie looked down at the .357 magnum in his hand, slowly raised it, and pointed it at his father.

55

"Charlie, don't!" a voice pleaded from the doorway of the library. Charlie looked over his shoulder and saw Gretchen standing there. Their eyes met, and he hesitated for only a moment before lowering the weapon.

"Make the call, Dad," instructed Gretchen, as she approached Charlie carefully. He didn't resist when she grabbed the gun out of his hand and threw it out into the hallway. She then immediately crouched down to attend to Emma. "God, Charlie, did you do this?"

"No, Vicki Stephens did."

"How long ago?" Gretchen demanded, as she initiated her assessment of Emma.

"I don't know for sure," Charlie stammered.

Over at the desk, Peter started talking to the 911 dispatcher.

Charlie pointed over towards his father, but continued staring down at Gretchen. "We can't let him call the cops. You have no idea what's at stake here."

Gretchen ignored him. When Peter hung up the phone, she asked, "Are they on their way?"

"Yes. One ambulance should be here any minute because someone else on the lake had already called when they heard the gunshots. I told them not to bother hurrying with the second."

"The second?" asked Gretchen.

"For Vicki," Peter answered. He pointed beyond the couch. "She's on the floor in front of the fireplace."

Gretchen flinched. "God, I just assumed she had fled. What kind of shape is she in?"

"She's dead," Peter answered again.

Gretchen looked up at Charlie. "And did you do that?"

Before Charlie could say anything, Peter spoke up. "No, I did."

Charlie grabbed Gretchen's shoulder. "I told you this was complicated. You have to listen to me. If the ambulance is on its way, so are the cops. What are we going to tell them when they get here?"

Gretchen pulled away from him. "Say whatever you want. Right now, my only concern is for Emma."

Frantic, Charlie turned to Peter. "What's our story? The cops will be here any minute."

There was a loud rap on the front door, followed by footsteps and shouts coming from the hall. "Gretchen? Emma? Anybody here?"

"In here," Gretchen yelled, before turning to Charlie. "Hey, big brother, I got news for you. The cops are already here."

Serg and Don Lovich, guns drawn, appeared at the library door just a second later. "Jesus," Serg uttered, seeing Gretchen applying pressure to the wound in Emma's chest. "We heard the call reporting the shots on the police scanner on our way out. Apparently, one of your neighbors called."

"Ambulance is right behind us," Don assured the group.

Gretchen looked up at the two men. "There's another victim

over there behind the couch. It's Vicki Stephens. I haven't gotten to her yet, but Dad thinks she's dead." Don crossed the room and spotted Vicki's body in front of the fireplace. One glance confirmed Peter's diagnosis.

Serg shook his head. "God, what the hell happened here?"

Peter was the first to speak. "I wonder if it was the Kohns."

"What are you babbling about?" roared Charlie at his father.

Peter continued, seemingly oblivious to everyone else in the room. "The neighbors. The ones who heard the shots. It could have been the Kohns. They live down the lake in Will's old house." Then a strange smile came over his face. "Ah, don't things have that way of coming full circle."

Peter's odd discourse was interrupted by the wail of sirens. The ambulance arrived just moments later. Gretchen let the emergency crew take over with Emma, but insisted on accompanying her to the hospital in the back of the ambulance.

After the ambulance left, Serg returned to the house to begin sorting out the night's events. Peter had changed out of his robe into slacks and a sweater, and he and Charlie were waiting in the dining room with Don. Vicki's body remained in the library awaiting the medical examiner, the fingerprinters, the forensic photographers, and all the other police crime-scene specialists now making their way to the property.

SATURDAY

56

"Emma, are you awake?"

Emma heard Gretchen's voice, as if from a distance, and she struggled to open her eyes. The room was blurry, but after a moment, she was able to make out Gretchen standing on the right side of her bed. Gretchen was wearing clean powder-blue surgical scrubs, and her hair was wet.

"Where am I?" Emma cringed with pain as she tried to turn towards Gretchen.

"Take it easy," Gretchen advised. "You're at Fairview South-dale Hospital. We brought you here last night."

"Oh, I remember. I was at your dad's, and Vicki was there."

"Yes, we know. You were shot."

Emma shut her eyes. "How bad is it?"

Gretchen looked down at her friend and thought, *Fortunately, not as bad as you look.* Emma's face was pale, and her hair hung limply against the pillow. Her midsection was heavily bandaged, and an intravenous line fed into her right hand. The left side of the bed was lined with machines monitoring her heart rate, respirations, and temperature.

Gretchen, herself, had just returned from a short nap, a shower, and a change of clothes in the doctor's lounge. She hadn't looked much better than Emma before that—tired, having been up all night, and still wearing her clothes stained with Emma's blood.

Gretchen stroked Emma's right arm and gave her the prognosis for her recovery. "You've lost a lot of blood, but you're going to be fine. Good as new before you know it. The bullet missed your ribs, but punctured your left lung and nicked the pulmonary artery on that side. That's where all the blood came from. They did surgery last night. Repaired the damage and drained the hemothorax."

"The what?"

"That's just the blood that pooled inside your thorax. No big deal. Then they reinflated your lung. With that." She pointed to a tube attached to Emma's chest. "They'll keep it in for a couple of days in case you develop another leak."

Emma looked over at the line leading into the back of her right hand. "What's the rest of this stuff?"

"Don't be alarmed. They've been giving you some fluids and antibiotics. And a morphine drip to help with the pain."

Emma tried for a smile. "You mean I could actually feel worse?"

Gretchen grinned at her. "You'll find out soon enough. They won't let you enjoy that morphine for long. It's pretty addictive."

"And I can't opt for the addiction?"

"Afraid not."

"How long am I going to be in here?"

"Not long. Just a few days until you get your strength back. And to watch for pneumonia."

Emma winced, as she tried to sit up a bit. "Does Dad know?"

"I called him right after you came out of surgery. Then I heard back from Ginny at four this morning. She and Sam were just leaving Lake Salish to come down here." Gretchen looked at her watch. "They should be here soon."

Emma heard someone come into the room behind Gretchen. "Is she awake?" It was Joe Buchanan. Gretchen stepped up to the head of the bed as Joe approached Emma.

"You look like hell," Emma said. His clothes were wrinkled, and he had huge bags under his eyes.

"He's been here all night. Serg called him," said Gretchen, before turning to Joe. "She's still with us. And, as you just heard, difficult as ever."

Joe reached the bed and lightly clasped Emma's right hand. "God, it's wonderful to hear your voice."

Emma grinned at Joe. His hand felt comfortable in hers. Then she looked back at Gretchen. "What happened after I got shot?"

"Dad killed Vicki."

"What?" Emma asked excitedly, setting off a surge of pain through her midsection.

Gretchen stroked Emma's forehead with one hand and pushed the morphine pump with the other. "I know it's hard to believe, but apparently there was a lot of history there." Then she recounted the whole Kelly saga just as Peter had confessed it to Serg the previous evening. Gretchen's voice was controlled, as if she was telling the story of strangers.

Even through the haze of the pain medication, Emma managed to catch most of the account. "God, my poor grandfather."

Gretchen then gave Emma the details of the prior night's events after Emma had been shot, leaving out only Peter and Charlie's confrontation over calling an ambulance, as she had also done earlier with Serg. She concluded with Charlie's admission about the arson of the old mill.

"I can't believe that! Charlie told Serg about setting the fire?" Emma asked incredulously.

"Well, he didn't really. Dad found out somehow, and he told Serg."

"And what did Charlie say?"

"Not much. He didn't have the energy to deny it. He fell apart after the cops got there. Dad, surprisingly, was the most clear-headed and composed I've seen him in years."

"Confession will do that for people," Joe commented.

"So what's happened to your father and Charlie?" Emma asked.

Gretchen's eyes finally filled with tears, and she looked away from Emma. "Right now, both Dad and Charlie are in jail. But they have bail hearings later today, and we expect both of them to be released." She sighed before adding, "What an unbelievable twenty-four hours."

Gretchen wiped her eyes and reached over to grab her coat from the chair. She came back to the bed and gave Emma a kiss on the cheek. "I leave you in Joe's capable hands. I have to go out to the airport and meet Mother's plane. As you can imagine, she is beside herself."

"This must be a nightmare for her. For you too, huh?"

"Yes, it is," Gretchen wearily admitted. "But we'll all get through it. Right now, I just want to survive the hearing this after-noon and get Dad and Charlie home by this evening."

"Have you talked to Taylor yet?" Joe asked.

"I reached him last night. He was going to break camp first thing this morning and should be in sometime later this afternoon. He's already got meetings set up for first thing Monday morning to start sorting through all the ramifications for the Company. It should be a real mess."

Gretchen put on her coat and turned to Emma. "But don't you worry about that for now. Your only job for the next several weeks is to rest and get back on your feet. Those are doctor's orders."

"Yes, Doctor." As Gretchen started to leave, Emma offered, "Hey, good luck at the hearing this afternoon."

Gretchen turned in the doorway. "You mean that?"

Emma looked seriously at her friend. "Yes, I do. We can't let our family's past ruin our lives, like it has so many others'."

"I couldn't agree with you more. Thanks for the support."

"Let us know how things turn out."

"Will do. See you," Gretchen said, as she walked out the door and down the hall.

"'A mess is right," Emma observed to Joe. "Life just isn't going to be the same for that side of the family."

"You reap what you sow," Joe said. He looked at Emma. An uncomfortable silence hung in the air for a few moments. Emma saw tears now well up in his eyes.

"Hey, why the long face?" she asked, trying to lighten the mood.

"I never really believed we were over. I was still imagining you campaigning around the state with me. God, then last night, I almost lost you for good." He was openly crying now. "Em, I've missed you so much."

After a few moments, he straightened up and shook his head. "Listen to me. They just took a bullet out of your lung, and I'm blubbering on about my miserable life."

Emma laughed as much as her bandaged left side would allow her. "You are being a bit melodramatic. But your blubbering is a nice distraction from this tube in my chest." Then Emma looked seriously at him. "Joe, you have to know I've missed you, too. But nothing's changed. I can't go back to the way it was."

"But don't you still love me?"

"It's not that simple, and you know it. If we're going to be together, I need to be the center of your world. And that's not possible right now with all your energy going into winning the Senate seat."

"I can't give that up," admitted Joe.

"And I'm not asking you to. You want it too badly." Stiffly, Emma reached across her body with her left hand and brushed Joe's arm. "So, go win. And then be the best U.S. Senator this state has ever seen. I'll be your friend and supporter through all of it. I just can't be your lover. It hurts too much."

Joe leaned over and kissed her. Now both of them were crying.

A few minutes later, Emma looked up and saw Sam standing in the doorway. Ginny followed him into the room. Joe stepped away from the bed as Sam approached his daughter. "Look at you. I couldn't believe it when Gretchen called last night. This is all so crazy."

The significance of Peter's confession the night before swept over Emma when she saw her father. "You heard the whole story, I take it."

"Well, the highlights at least. You can give us the details when you feel up to it. Right now, all that's important is your recovery."

Ginny sidled up to the bed and gave Emma a gentle hug. "You and Dad and your wild hunches." Emma smiled, as Ginny added, "Getting shot at. Now that's a new one even for you, Em."

Joe spoke up. "She really does look a lot better than last night. She was in pretty bad shape when they brought her in."

Sam turned to Joe as if he just realized he was in the room. "And what are you doing here? Haven't you got a city to run or something, Mr. Mayor?"

Emma frowned at Sam before answering for Joe. "He's been here all night, Dad."

Joe sensed the room was a bit small for both Sam and him. At least, if he wanted to keep Emma calm. He smiled at Emma. "Now that reinforcements have arrived, I think I'll take my leave. I'm going to still try to make the bridge dedication. I'll stop back later tonight, Em. Serg and Paloma said they'd drop in too."

"What about their dinner party?"

"You mean the one I wasn't invited to."

"Yeah," Emma responded sheepishly.

"Postponed until you get out of here." He walked over to the door.

"Hey, Joe," Emma called after him. "Thanks for being here."

He turned around and blew her a kiss before walking out.

After he left, Sam apologized to Emma, "I'm sorry. He didn't have that coming after being here all night."

"He certainly didn't, but don't worry about it. He's a politician. His skin is pretty thick."

"So you guys back on again?" Ginny inquired.

"No, we're not 'back on' again," Emma responded with a bite. "But he still cares about me. I did get shot last night, you know."

"Okay, okay, no more third degree. We didn't drive all the way down here to upset you." Ginny grabbed Emma's hand. Emma relaxed and settled back against her pillows "So are you up for talking about last night, or do you want to get some rest?"

Emma laughed. "Rest? I just woke up after twelve hours of sleep."

Ginny and Sam pulled up chairs. "We're all ears," Sam said. "Talk as long as you're up to it."

AUGUST

Epilogue

On a hot, humid August day, Emma emerged from the fifty-story IDS building to face a small group of reporters. She had spent the morning in her lawyers' offices, signing the final settlement documents concerning Randolph Foods.

During the past three months, while Emma had been getting back on her feet and regaining her strength, a team of lawyers had worked with Taylor to sort through the various claims to ownership of the Company. Taylor's legal experts advised him that Sam Randolph and his descendants might very well have at least a fifty-percent claim to the Company and arguably a one hundred-percent claim. And, against Charlie's wishes, Taylor shared their conclusions with Emma.

But Emma had informed Taylor that she, Sam, and Ginny had no interest in ownership of Randolph Foods, nor in the protracted litigation that Charlie, as still the largest shareholder, would wage in opposition to them. Instead they made a settlement offer which was very modest, given the millions probably owed to their family. It had been quickly accepted.

Sam was now the owner of Lake Salish, and he had a comfortable nest egg to supplement his teaching pension. College trust accounts had been funded for Emma's niece and nephew; and a new house, to be designed by Emma, was in the works for Ginny and Jack on the east bay of Lake Salish. A small non-profit organization, the Ellen Randolph Fund, had also been set up to help promote arts education in the Ely area.

The bulk of the settlement had gone to establish the William Randolph Preservation Foundation with Emma as its director. Its first project was a joint effort with Randolph Foods and the Riverfront Coalition to restore the Randolph riverfront milling complex.

The reporters approached Emma. "Ms. Randolph, would you care to comment on your settlement with Randolph Foods?"

"Sorry, folks. No comment at this time. The Company president, Taylor Alexander, will have a brief press release in an hour or so. You'll have to wait for that."

"Have you spoken with your cousin since his jail term commenced?"

"Again, no comment."

Making the dead Vicki Stephens the heavy, Charlie had negotiated a second-degree arson plea with the District Attorney. He was currently serving a fifteen-month jail term in Stillwater Prison. Emma kept track of his prison trials and tribulations through Gretchen. Charlie was surviving and counting the days until his release.

Peter had also plea-bargained a third-degree murder charge for his involvement with Kelly's death. Because of his young age at the time of the murder and his current ill health, he had been placed on parole, which no one was monitoring closely.

"So, what are your plans for the rest of the summer?" another reporter asked.

Emma was willing to answer this question. "Well, my car is packed. And for the next four weeks, I've got a date with a canoe. Call me in mid-September. I'll let you know how the fish are biting."

Ms. Funk grew up in LaCrosse, Wisconsin, but has made her home in the Twin Cities for over twenty years. She is a former bartender, lawyer, and real estate developer. She currently resides in Southwest Minneapolis with her husband and spends her days writing, trying to learn Spanish, and chasing squirrels away from her garden and bird feeders.

To purchase additional copies of *Bone Flour*
for yourself or to send as gifts, please contact
Midwest Bookhouse at

www.midwestbookhouse.com

or call

1-877-430-0044.

Quantity discounts available.